Haven's End

BY
JOHN P. MARQUAND

HAVEN'S END

THE LATE GEORGE APLEY

WICKFORD POINT

H. M. PULHAM, ESQUIRE

SO LITTLE TIME

REPENT IN HASTE

B. F.'S DAUGHTER

POINT OF NO RETURN

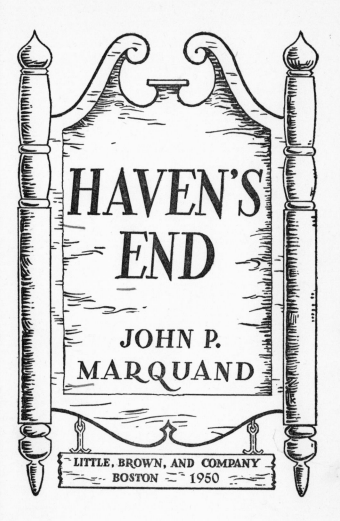

HAVEN'S END

JOHN P. MARQUAND

LITTLE, BROWN, AND COMPANY
BOSTON — 1950

HR

Contents

THE ILLUSTRATIONS WERE MADE BY

ROBERT LAWSON

1

Going – –

The Swales have lived in Haven's End since the days of the founders. Their sharp features and high-held heads were as familiar on the town streets as Hapsburg noses in European courts. The Swales have never been popular, have never courted popularity, but for generations the town has been proud of them, proud even of their disdain. No conversation in Haven's End ever wandered far without bringing up with a Swale. Their family history offered food for conversation, much of it to be told in hushed tones with an eye over one shoulder.

Here is the chronicle of the Swales, which is at the same time the chronicle of Haven's End, that mellow New England town of mild aspect and gentle people, which first knew prosperity when rum could be traded for blacks in Guinea, and again when privateers reaped a harvest in the West Indies. Here is the story of the boy who pulled the lion's tail, of the pirate who made his daughter an honest woman, of the privateer who married hastily and of others as odd and varied.

The Swales are gone but Haven's End still stands. You will not find it on the map, but most New Englanders will easily identify it.

≈ 1 ≈

Going – –

WHEN SAM WHISTLE WAS NOT THE undertaker, he was the auctioneer at Haven's End. He was not inspiring, standing on the granite steps in front of the arched doorway of the Swale house. He was a thin man in a baggy store suit, with a high forehead and a pinched, perspiring face. He kept fidgeting with a key-wind silver watch, holding it almost on the tips of his fingers, and screwing up his face to see the dial.

"If the ladies can hear better settin' down," he said in a flat, metallic voice, "there's chairs. Joe, you go inside and kind of keep pushin' 'em out, will you? No need for 'em to keep millin' around inside."

The crowd on the lawn had begun to bunch together about the steps. The individuals in the crowd moved half consciously, as though a current pulled them, but the crowd moved all together. It moved beneath a hum of conversation until some one called:

"What's the matter, Sam — waitin' for the hearse?"

Ignoring the subdued, appreciative titter, the auctioneer bent his long neck over his watch again and squinted up his eyes.

"Gather 'round," he called. "Please to step this way, everybody. I guess you won't see any more if you try. I guess you all of you seen all there is to see."

And then the same voice called out again, "Don't everybody git your chances, Sam."

The front door opened behind him to let out a few of the stragglers who hurried down the steps like late-comers at a show. There was a glimpse of a dusky wide hall behind them, which ran from front to back, an impression of twisted posts, of a flying staircase, and of sunlight striking on peeling wall paper before the door slammed shut. With the slam of the door, Sam Whistle was left entirely alone on the steps, the center of attention, with the house behind him like a curtain.

The house had the dead flatness of any deserted house, and Sam was like an undertaker until he began to speak.

"Ladies and gentlemen, I guess I don't need tell anybody here whose property this is. A lot of you maybe've never seen it inside before. That's why we've given everybody this opportunity to go all through the house and outbuildings. Maybe we won't have such an opportunity again."

He straightened his back and waved a skinny arm toward the brick wall, and the crowd followed his gesture dully. They were listening, and the house and the elms on the lawn had joined in that attention. The flat twang of his words struck against a sheet of silence which made them as distinct as print.

"I guess you've all of you seen the description. The parcel comprises four acres and of course all buildings on the plot. An' if there's a better location or a better home in Haven's End, you tell me. There's been a lot of experts come here, who know about such things, and architects from New York City have been up here to measure it. I guess some of you know more than me about cornices, but I know a handsome, old-time house when I see it. And I know—and you know—you couldn't duplicate this home, if you was to build it to-day, for inside a hundred thousand dollars.

"This home is what is known as genuine Federalist architecture. She was built when builders knew what was what. She was framed by local carpenters, and I'd like to see any of 'em better it now. Friends, she's plumb. There ain't an inch of settlement, not one speck of dry rot. This home is as trim as when Captain Daniel Swale, Esquire, moved into it, back in Seventeen-ninety and riveted that spread-eagle knocker on the door behind me. There's been bigger houses, but this has always been *the* house in these parts. And if I wanted to take your time—Joe, fetch out the kitchen table and the mallet."

He paused and coughed before his high flat voice went on:

"I'm here to run an auction, and some one's here to buy this home from the estate of the late Mr. Dennis Swale. It's all strict business, but if I wanted I could keep here trainin' with you about the Swale house. I could stay here telling stories. This house is a landmark. I'm aware there's those who want to buy it for its insides, but no matter what, you can't stop it being a landmark. I could tell you—"

He stopped. The church bells were ringing twelve o'clock.

"But I won't," Sam Whistle said. "There's noon, and the sale is called for noon. . . ."

2

The Powaw's Head

They generally acknowledg'd and worship'd many Gods; therefore greatly esteem'd and reverenc'd their priests, powaws, or wizards, who were esteemed as having immediate converse with the Gods.

—MAGNALIA CHRISTI AMERICANA

2

The Powaw's Head

THE FINEST HOUSES IN HAVEN'S END
were built a century ago, but they still are very
fine. They stand on a ridge above the Main
Street, where they may overlook the river and the sea.
They are the square New England type, of wood or
brick, each with a cupola and railing on its roof. The
elms rise about them, and the brick walk of the street
before them is checked and crossed by the shadows of
elms. Of all that row the Swale mansion is the finest,
for it epitomizes the spirit of all the rest — the grace and
cool superiority and supercilious perfection. It rises
from a lawn and garden which are somewhat unkempt
to-day. The ivy on its walls is ragged, but its bricks are
rich from years of sun and weather. The arch of its
doorway and the arch of the great window above it
are exquisitely proportioned and meticulously carved
by shipwrights accustomed to work in pine. There is a
richness to the detail of its cornice which has grown
more splendid with the years. Sometimes in the gath-

ering dusk, when the street lights strike it through the moving branches of the trees, it has a ghostly loneliness, and when the church bells ring you can imagine that a voice is saying:

"I am the Swale mansion. Before there ever was a house or town, a Swale was magistrate of this township. Whether my paint is old or new, I stand for something indefinable, not to be attained by gold, though gold may make it fair. I stand for something which bears a dozen names — and none of them is right — which many hate, but which only the greatest do not envy."

Down the ridge at the foot of crooked streets another building stands, gaunt as a prison, surrounded by high wire fencings. It stands by the very edge of the river, close to the abandoned customhouse, in the midst of the ruins of warehouses and rotting wharves. It is the only building which is new and solid. Above a door a name is written, facing toward the Swale house on the ridge, though the ridge is far away. "John Scarlet," it reads, "Shoes—Office", and it contains a brevity and crudeness, a harsh reality, that make the memory of the Swale house dim. That building, as any one can tell you, is the Scarlet shoe shop, the last large factory in the town, and there is the whole story from the beginning to the end.

Those are the forces which have struggled always in Haven's End, while other names have come and gone — the Swales and the Scarlets — until, at last, time and a changing world have left them face to face. For there has always been a Scarlet and a Swale.

II

They landed together on the Lower Green, two miles away by the salt marshes, with the freemen and their wives and their bond servants and cattle, to build a new plantation. The first Swale, though a cadet of his house, was a gentleman with a coat of arms. The first Scarlet was a weaver's son with dye stain on his fingers. It was Captain Swale who commanded the train bands when the Indians first came down the great river in fifteen boats of bark, just short of three hundred years ago. Even then the Scarlets could see through make-believe; and even when they knelt by the river bank, side by side, to listen to their minister's prayer of thanks, Goodman Scarlet exchanged a cool and worldly glance with Captain Richard Swale.

A boy, shivering with cold and with an excitement which he had never known, saw that look and told of it. The boy was Enoch Porter, whose descendants still live on the Porter farm, close by the Lower Green. His story lies in a trunk among old Porter letters — all that is left to single out that day from a sea of lost ones which whisper through the trees.

Enoch Porter could not have been more than ten when the Indians came down. When he told the story to his great-grandchildren in the kitchen of the Porter house, he must have been close to ninety years, and all the time of which he told must have grown blurred and kindly, filled with the mendacity which any old man gives to the days of his youth. The freemen who had landed at the Lower Green with their families, their neat cattle and indentured servants, were nothing but the shadows in an old man's mind by then. And yet, despite the lapse of seventy years and more, the tale was very harsh. The weals of shivering days were white upon his soul.

Though it was May, a chill northwest wind was blowing hard beneath a leaden sky. Looking from the Lower Green, the drab death of the marshes was already changing. The trees were bare of foliage by the marshes' edge; but though the sky was dark and the sea beyond the marshes leaden and very rough, there was life in the air.

There was activity among the hovels clustered about the lower green. Though the day was harsh and stormy, those among the settlers who had windows in their walls of squared oak and wattle had opened them to let in the air. Where there were no windows, the doors were open wide, giving glimpses of trampled earthen floors and of scanty household goods among the shadows. The vapor was rising from the roofs of sod and thatch. The log stockades and shelters were open, for the cattle were at last upon the common. The women were pouring kettles of steaming water into troughs hewn out of logs, for the spring washing. By the edge of a small salt creek Goodman Scarlet, his heavy arms bared was calking his shallop. Almost any day it would be ready to take him up the coast for his trade in beaver at the Indian towns.

Two bond servants, in the soiled red knit caps and worn green vests edged with red tape which they had worn from England, were hewing at beams for the great house belonging to Captain Swale. Even in later days it seemed to Enoch that the house was very large. It stood out from the other straggling huts, square and solid, covered by neatly cut oak clapboards. In the front were two casement windows with diamond panes of actual glass from home, instead of parchment; and its chimney was of English brick. It was larger even than the meetinghouse, which faced it across the green.

As Enoch neared the green that morning, his footsteps faltered, for his conscience was heavy inside him. He had left his corn planting in the Porter field deliberately, despite the ordinance which laid down the hours for children's labor. The selectmen had ordained in meeting that from the age of six upward, all children should be set to tasks of carding wool, tending cattle or working at the corn hills. It was specified as well that each child be lightly clad and thinly shod, to accustom its body early to the rigors of the climate. Delinquency at tasks and noisy play were punished by lashings of a birch rod upon the bare back, followed by a prayer.

Though the knowledge of his sin and the consequence of sin lay on Enoch, a fascination stronger than conscience impelled him to hover near the house of worship. Goodman Snead was seated in the stocks, but Goodman Snead in the stocks was a familiar sight. Once a week, not infrequently on the night before the Lord's Day, Goodman Snead would exceed himself in secret with berry wine or ale. The initial D sewn upon his leather doublet had proved as useless to stay him as was prayer. Seated in the stocks, the desires of the flesh seemed strong upon him, and malice was bright upon his broad pale face. Even when the goodman in his degradation winked at Enoch, after looking sharp in all directions, and stuck out his tongue, it was not the Goodman Snead whom Enoch saw. The whipping post by the meetinghouse was vacant. It had been used last when Mr. Whistle's indentured man had been brought from the forest by two strange Indians, for a trade already was plied in escaping servants. Although these savages had already seized upon the man's leather doublet and green vest, they had asked ten lengths of calico in payment for their hunting. A darkening stain of blood upon the post showed where its last victim, in wincing from the lash, had torn his wrists against the thongs.

The new addition to the plantation's monuments of justice was a pole made of a straight young pine, denuded of its branches, dripping still with pitch. Upon the top of the pole was impaled an Indian's head, shaved at the skull save for a single lock that hung pendulous from the very top of the cranium. The distortion of the face was horrible enough to draw the eye by the sheer attraction of a revolting object. The mouth was gaping. The sightless eyes were staring upward at the clouds. Two days before, a servant of the Salem court had brought the head in a bag across his saddlebow.

"Ay," said Goodman Snead, "look on him whilst you may, young master. See the fine lovelock of him waving. There'll be naught of him, come another week. The rooks will spoil his face. There will be no face to a good clean skull."

"Be silent," said Enoch. "Please not say any more."

It shamed him that his voice shook and that he was close to tears.

"Squeamish in the belly, are you?" said Goodman Snead. "Yet you hear how on lecture days. . . . Pray that I may see light on lecture days. Keep you, young master, from the path of evil which I have trod to my undoing and so sit here in atonement. Ah, whilst the twig is supple yet to the bending, turn — ah, turn."

A sudden nasal, singsong note had entered Goodman Snead's speech. All at once he stared straight before him, looking beyond Enoch with frozen intensity. Enoch turned and, as he did so, his knees smote sharp together. Striding toward him was Captain Richard Swale, a gentleman and a magistrate of the plantation.

"Boy," said Captain Swale, "who are you?"

"Please, sir," said Enoch, "I am Jack Porter's son."

Captain Swale was six feet tall, but in his high military boots — the only ones in all the settlement — in his cloak and high-crowned beaver, he seemed far taller. His face was thin and hard, set by prayer and discipline into lines of spurious calm. His eyes were dark and moody, yet very deep and clear.

"Please, sir," said Enoch, "I came to see the Pow-aw's head."

"Very well," said Captain Swale. "Look on the Pow-aw's head then before I lead you home, and tell me how it came there."

"Please, sir," said Enoch, "they brought it in a bag."

"Yes," said Captain Swale, "but how came it in a bag?"

"They hanged him, sir," said Enoch.

The captain did not answer, and finally Enoch dared to look at him; first at his great jack boots, then up at his face.

"Listen, boy," the captain said. "He is not placed there for children to glut their fancy on. I have seen better heads than his by the town gates at home—of godly men and even county gentlemen. Is it not so, Goodman Snead?"

"Amen!" said Goodman Snead. "Amen! An eye for an eye and a tooth for a tooth; it is the justice of the Lord. . . . And now, sure, Your Honor, my time must be nigh up. Order me unloosed, so please Your Honor. The head there is hurting my poor wits. Twice I've seen it roll its eyes, sure as my soul knows light."

A look of amusement changed the lines in the face of Captain Swale. He had seen too much of suffering to let it stir him, for he knew that agony of mind and body were a more common part of life than pleasure. There was a grim humor in the thought that a man who came before him week by week for debauchery and blasphemy should dread the sight of a head upon a pole. But though the captain permitted himself to smile, he spoke with piety.

"It may be a greater power," Captain Swale remarked, "that makes a head mock you in your sight in payment for your sins. Think upon it, Goodman Snead. And surely you know devils, for I have heard you screech of devils often. And now—"

Still smiling, he turned away and perceived that Enoch was standing listening with all the rapt attention that one might listen to a play.

"Now get you home," said Captain Swale. "I will not report your delinquency. There is punishment enough here, but mind you this: A new land is born of blood and misery. If it so happen that you live to see a town born here, remember that we stood alone — with only our hands and our faith to protect us from savages who would do far worse than set our heads on poles. He never told us what he did with Goodman Dowel's gold."

Nailed upon the pole was a rustling square of paper where the sin was printed clear:

Here stands ye Hedde of ye Powaw of Nimnuck. Ye all may regard his juste Deserts for Ye Bloody Murder and Robbery of John Dowel bachelor.

Enoch could remember when the men had brought the Powaw down from the hill, strong in life. His arms had been trussed behind and a halter was about his neck. They had seized him in drunken slumber on the floor of John Dowel's hut, which stood near the common pasture. A bloody stone maul which had smashed John Dowel's skull was in the Powaw's open hand. Enoch could remember the clamor of the voices, as women and children left their work and men ran from the fields. His limbs were bare and scarred, and you might have thought he did not hear, though every one was saying, "Kill him! Kill him!"

All priests, or powaws, as one called them, were magicians among the Indian folk. Many a man had crossed his fingers when the Powaw had stalked silently across the green or had stood to watch the women beating out the flax. Enoch was about to get him gone, as Captain Swale had ordered, when Goodman Scarlet walked upon the green, still holding a fistful of oakum.

"Good morning to you, Captain Swale," said Goodman Scarlet, and raised an awkward finger to his forehead.

Without pleasure, without malice, Captain Swale looked upon Goodman Scarlet. The goodman was a side of life disturbing and despicable, which the captain could not understand. It had to do with weights and measures and quarts of ale, for Goodman Scarlet kept an ordinary in the first room of his dwelling, and his back room was high with pelts.

"Friend," said Captain Swale, "what do you want of me?"

"'Tis this, sir," said Goodman Scarlet, and he shifted his square toes nervously. "I spied you watching the Powaw's head. I was hoping, sir, that you might be commanding it took down."

"Well?" said Captain Swale. "Why do you want it down?"

"I ask your pardon, sir," said Goodman Scarlet. "It's bad for trade, putting one of yon heads on a stick. It won't do no good, sir — putting up heads. It only heats their blood and they think we mean a war. The natives up the river will be passing bundles of their arrows, mark you. They'll be on us some fine night. Nay, last night John Indian from the falls told me their young men are murmuring."

Captain Swale's lips were thin. It was not the habit in those days to cross or question Captain Swale, when the social barrier was as strong as the barrier of faith. Not what Goodman Scarlet said but the insolence of his saying it aroused the captain's wrath.

"Man!" said Captain Swale. "Do you dare stand before me and criticize the justice of our court?"

"No," said Goodman Scarlet. "Lord forbid. I only say it is a Powaw's head, not a common man's. The Powaw was a priest, sir, among his people — a man of rank, the same as you — and the Powaw was not bad, though he loved liquor like others I could name."

Captain Swale smiled without kindliness or mirth and drew his long black cloak more closely across his shoulders.

"I'll say this to you," he answered, "for, with our Lord's help, I have controlled my anger and have given ear like an humble man while you have given tongue. Goodman Scarlet, you and I are different men, and when our day comes we'll be judged. Though the woods be filled with ravening savages, Goodman Scarlet, the head stays on the pole."

"Sir," said Goodman Scarlet, "I only meant it for our good. I know their ways and speech."

Enoch thought that no man in the world could be so fine as Captain Swale. Although Enoch still stood upon the green, his mouth half open, Captain Swale did not appear to notice. The captain stood with his head down, deep in thought. It was Goodman Snead, shouting in the stocks, who roused him.

"May it please you, sir," said Goodman Snead, "is my time not up?"

"What?" said Captain Swale.

"Is my time not up?" said Goodman Snead. "I was to be here for but an hour."

"Your time is up," said Captain Swale, "when the constable comes to set you loose."

"Please, sir," said Goodman Snead. "It is looking at the head. It drives me fair crazy, sir. Its eyes have turned right at me, and he was a black magician, sir. Please, sir, I can give you information if you let me loose. Listen, sir. Goodman Scarlet sells spirits against the law. He'll give up a gallon for a gold pistole. I know it, for I've bought."

Captain Swale walked slowly toward him, his hands behind his back.

"Ah," said Captain Swale, "for a gold pistole?"

"Yes, if it please you, sir," said Goodman Snead, "for a gold pistole."

"And how"—all at once the voice of Captain Swale was loud and terrible—"and how did you come on a gold pistole, you drunken dog?"

All at once the face of Goodman Snead had gone as blotched and white as sour milk. He did not answer; he opened his mouth, but he did not answer.

"Speak!" said Captain Swale. "Or I'll make you speak! Dowel had gold. Where were you the night John Dowel died?"

But Goodman Snead did not answer. A ray of sunlight, dull and leaden, had come through the gray clouds and had struck clear against the pole, so that the shadow of it fell across the stocks and over the goodman's face.

"Please, sir, if you believe in mercy," shrieked Goodman Snead, "let me loose or take that head away."

"There'll be time enough for that," said Captain Swale. "Who's shouting out my name?" Enoch had already heard.

"Captain Swale!" some one was shouting. A boy was running toward the green; he was one of the Matthews boys, ragged and torn by briers and splashed with mud, who had been sent to watch the cattle on the hill. One of his shoes had been lost in his haste; his breath was strangled from his running.

"The great river, Captain Swale!" he gasped. "The great river is full of Indians in boats of bark."

"Hold," said Captain Swale. "Stay where you are!" And his eyes fell on Enoch, who stood rooted, staring. "Boy," said Captain Swale, "run yonder to the meetinghouse and beat on the great drum!"

There was no bell in those days upon the house of worship; instead, beneath the porch, to keep it from the rain, was a great drum of bull's hide, stretched taut over a hollow stump, like the war drums of the Indians. A stick lay beside it, weighted in the head.

"Did you hear me?" shouted Captain Swale. "Beat upon that drum!"

And Enoch smote with the stick and the sound was like thunder. "Boom!" went the drum — "Boom!" — so loudly that it seemed to tear at the voice of Captain Swale, as he shouted to his servants by his house.

"Thomas! Will! Bring out my breast piece and the pistols, and your pikes!"

"Boom!" went the drum. "Boom!" It swung and creaked against the ropes that held it to the porch rafters. It was like a living thing, trembling in its fury, calling in a voice that all could understand. It was conjuring up such a scene as no one would live to see again. The pitiful starkness of the town stood out against the booming of that drum. The sonorous phrases of the Scriptures seemed to vanish with the pulsing beat. All that gave a dignity to suffering and squalor was beaten to the distance.

"Boom!" went the drum. "Boom!" Women with drawn white faces, their drab dresses and their hoods plain and slatternly from toil, called out to their children. Men were running from the oak woods by the marsh, their broadaxes in their hands. Men were hastening from the hill, driving in their cattle; stumbling in their haste until they reached the green — bareheaded men and men in soiled red caps, freemen and bondsmen. The four or five who might be termed gentlemen, and those who were selectmen, gathered in a group apart. The Reverend Wayne was there, older than the rest and very thin; and Timothy Parlin, short and broad of shoulder, with narrow squinting eyes; and Mr. Thomas Whistle, in an old doublet with slashed sleeves. A broad silver buckle, newly polished, flashed on Mr. Whistle's belt. His cuffs were resplendent with lace, although the General Court was already legislating against such finery, and of all the men in the plantation Mr. Whistle alone wore shoes with long and pointed toes.

"Boy!" shouted Thomas Whistle, buckling on his sword. "Stop that accursed drum!"

"Mr. Whistle," said the Reverend Wayne, "that drum was placed there for a godly purpose."

"Sir," answered Mr. Whistle, "with all reverence to your cloth, this is not the time for admonition — when savages are on the river."

In its majesty and in its meanness, all truth came out with the beating of that drum. The small men were washed away like sand before its sound, leaving the greater standing, and the Reverend Wayne was great. Fanaticism burned in him like a fever; it had long ago burned away all thought of self, until it left him only a shell of a man, seared by energy and devoid of fear.

"Thomas Whistle," said the Reverend Wayne, "were we in the very shadow of the valley, I'll admonish whom I please, according as I am given light!"

He would have continued as he had started if a new interruption had not turned his words. A woman had burst through the crowd; it was plain to see that she belonged to that vagrant sect which continually disturbed the tranquillity of the land. Her dress was in horrid disorder, her hair fell in lank strands upon her shoulders, and her eyes burned with insane triumph.

"Repent ye!" she shrieked. "Repent ye, for the day of judgment is at hand."

"Seize her!" cried the Reverend Wayne.

Some one had already seized her, and the interruption seemed neither strange nor fanciful, but simply a part of that life.

Captain Swale and Mr. Parlin and the rest had scarcely noticed. The men whom Captain Swale had drilled in training days had taken up their arms and were forming a ragged line. They had pikes and long harquebuses for the most part. The charges for their weapons were attached to baldrics on small metal cylinders which seemed like ornamental bells. Some wore burnished steel caps; some carried long, thrusting swords, but it must have been a sad sight for Captain Swale, who had served in a good regiment of pikes in other days. Of them all, Captain Swale alone looked like a soldier, in his shining breast piece with his long sword in his hand.

"Put the women and children in my house!" he shouted. "And close up the cattle! Set the water heating! And you, Mr. Parlin, make the defense here! Who will follow me? I want twenty men!"

It was not a time for talk or argument beneath the beating of the drum. The men came fast enough — Goodman Scarlet and Goodman Hughes, and Mr. Whistle and John Porter, and Will and Thomas, the two bondsmen, and Goodman Hewett, the farmer, and Shadrach Symmes, who had been taking fish.

"What are you planning, sir?" asked the Reverend Wayne.

Captain Swale turned holding his bare sword in his hand. "I am going toward the river to meet them," said Captain Swale.

"And may the Lord of Hosts go with us, for I am going too!" the old minister said. "And now, brothers, make clean your hearts and raise your voice in psalm."

"This is no time for psalms!" said Mr. Whistle.

"Thomas Whistle," said Captain Swale, "hold thy tongue. Move forward and strike out a psalm!"

"Captain Swale!" It was Goodman Snead who was shouting from the stocks. "Will you not loose me, sir? Will you leave me here alone?"

"Leave him," said Captain Swale. "No, constable, leave him, let him keep a watch upon the Powaw's head."

"Deliver me from mine enemies." Above the tumult of voices there rose the nasal chant of the Reverend Wayne. "Defend me from them that rise up against me. Deliver me from the workers of iniquity and save me from bloody men."

Toward the great river, along the sodden track, Captain Swale and the men were marching. And Enoch Porter followed them unheeded, filled by a curiosity and wonder that was greater than fear.

Before you reach the river from our lower green, the road runs a mile or more along a ridge above the marshes. The track which existed then twisted and turned more than the road does now, to avoid bowlders and clumps of trees.

The men, with their muskets and their pikes, splashed through the sodden turf in silence, when the minister had stopped his psalm. There was no sound but the splashing of boots and now and then the faint ring of steel. The musketeers had lighted their fuses and held their hands cupped over the smoldering wicks. Now and then a puff of the smoke would blow into their nostrils, acrid and different from the fresh smells of wood and water.

Goodman Scarlet carried one of the muskets, shouldering it as he had been taught in the train band at home. A few paces ahead Captain Swale was walking, looking sharply to right and left. Like other cadets from county houses, he had served in the Low Countries and knew battle. The blood of fighting men was hot in Captain Swale; the noise of battle was already in his ears.

"May it please you, sir," the Matthews boy was whispering, "we shall sight them over the next slope. 'Tis where I saw them drawing their bark boats to shore."

They had reached the ridge, as it is called in our town to-day; a desolate rise of ground then, with a few scrub oaks and cedars growing among charred stumps where the Indians had burned for planting long before. The land was nothing but a stretch of uneven ground and bushes, sloping gently to a swamp beside the river, as desolate as wilderness; and loneliness and vacancy were all about. The river flowed past marshy banks, broad and leaden beneath the sullen sun. In its vastness and its loneliness, the river was telling of infinite distances and of forces which God, but never man, could hold in check. It flowed in solitude, but whence it flowed no one knew. It might have been from the western sea; it might have been from a land of dwarfs and devils. Its current was flowing outward into the sea, and where its waters met the sea there was a fringe of waves upon the sand bars, and even from the distance where they stood, there was the melancholy sound of waves, carried on the rising wind.

"Keep close, men!" said Captain Swale. The Matthews boy was pointing toward the river bank. His voice was quivering in a sharp infectious excitement which sent a blaze of color into the captain's face.

"Yonder, by the river," he said, "there they be, sir. Do you spy their boats of bark?"

From where they stood, the boats seemed very small, a dozen or more drawn bottom upward on the brown marsh reeds. They had landed on a bit of shelving open beach where white fishermen sometimes dried their catch in summer. Beside the boats was a group of strange, dark men, nearly naked despite the sharp wind, and in the distance one could plainly hear the beating of a drum.

"Move on," said Captain Swale. "The Lord has delivered them into our hands."

Silently and cautiously, like figures in a dream, they started down the slope. The wideness of that river and the grayness of the sky made them silent — all except the Reverend Wayne.

"And though I walk," said the Reverend Wayne, "through the valley of the shadow of death, I will fear no evil."

The boats were growing larger to their sight; the dark men could be clearly seen, like strange animals, moving to the beating of the drum.

"Move on," said Captain Swale, and then he added in a lower tone, almost to himself: "They see us and they do not move."

He might have known that the dark men first had seen him long ago. He should have known that their senses were sharper far than his. When they were a hundred paces off the beating of the drum ceased. Captain Swale's face was like a mask, except for the glitter in his eyes.

"Halt!" said Captain Swale. "Musketeers two paces forward. Steady and take aim."

A man was moving from the Indians — a solitary figure, tall and straight, with his hand raised above his head.

"What's this?" said Captain Swale.

Goodman Scarlet stepped forward, for of all that group of men only he knew the Indians' speech.

"Easily, please you, sir," he said. "Go easily. They intend no war."

"Stand aside, you fool!" said Captain Swale.

"I tell you," said Goodman Scarlet, "they intend no war. The sachem is coming toward us, making a sign of peace."

"The more fool, he!" said Captain Swale. "They have their weapons in their hands."

"But wait," said Goodman Scarlet; "it's better to speak them fair."

"Get back to your place!" roared Captain Swale.

But Goodman Scarlet walked forward as though he did not hear, with his hand above his head. The Indian man had drawn very near; one could see that he was old. Except for a breechclout of deerskin, there was no covering on his shrunken limbs, and now that he was nearer, he was a dirty old man, with three oily feathers tied to his single lock of hair, and with pock-marks on his face.

Three paces away from Goodman Scarlet, halting, he began to speak in a rusty, quavering voice, filled with strange coughs and gutturals.

"Move off!" shouted Captain Swale. "I'll give the word to fire."

"Don't, sir," said Goodman Scarlet; "you'd be doing a bitter wrong. He is a sachem of the Pennacook men. He says he comes in peace."

"Do you hear my order?" shouted Captain Swale.

"No," said Goodman Scarlet. "I'll not move. I say they come in peace."

For an instant every one was quiet while the good-man stood his ground. It was the first time that many had seen a commoner speak his mind, staring a gentle-man in the face.

"You pretty scoundrel!" shouted Captain Swale. "Get back or I'll pass my sword through you!"

It was the Reverend Wayne who stopped them, who flung himself between them with his psalm book in his hand, while the old sachem stood watching.

"You're wrong, sir," said the Reverend Wayne. "What right have we to kill if these people come in peace? Speak the wild man fair, Goodman Scarlet. Ask what he desires. And you, sir" — he stared hard at Captain Swale — "enough! I tell you speak him fair."

And even Captain Swale forbore to cross a minister.

"Do you wish us killed?" cried Captain Swale. "Look! They're moving forward." Sure enough, the Indians were moving nearer — close to forty strange, dark men, coated with dirt, gazing with glassy, curious eyes. The old sachem was speaking again, moving his hands in gestures.

"What is it that he says?" said the Reverend Wayne.

"He says they come in peace," said Goodman Scarlet, "to make a prayer to the great water."

"A prayer?" said the Reverend Wayne. "Ask him how he makes his prayer."

"He speaks of the ocean," said Goodman Scarlet. "He says it has been their custom, long before white men came, to journey to the ocean. He says that they will fight if we bar the way."

"Does he?" said Captain Swale. "Then let us fight."

"But if we do not," said Goodman Scarlet, speaking to the Reverend Wayne, "he will give us fifty pelts of beaver."

"That's what you want — those fifty pelts!" said Captain Swale.

"Peace!" said the Reverend Wayne. "You will not cross a minister, Captain Swale. Ask him, Friend Scarlet, how they make that prayer."

"They go in their boats," said Goodman Scarlet, "across the bar and pray."

"The vanity of it!" said Reverend Wayne. "You say they will take to their wretched boats of bark on such a sea as this to worship heathen gods? Speak him fairly, friend. Tell him there is a greater God, who has made His heaven and hell before man was ever on the earth."

"He says he has heard," said Goodman Scarlet, "and he asks why was there a hell before there were men to punish."

The Reverend Wayne sighed and looked not unkindly at that group of naked men.

"Peace," he said. "Let them go in peace."

"Mark you, sir, you do wrong!" shouted Captain Swale. "Better kill vermin while we have them."

"Peace!" said Reverend Wayne. "Let them go in peace. What is it you say now?"

And the thing that Goodman Scarlet said was what any Scarlet would have said in any generation.

"I told him," said Goodman Scarlet, "that for another hundred pelts, I'll bring my shallop here and take them safe to sea."

"And what says he?" asked the Reverend Wayne, looking at the sea.

"He says," said Goodman Scarlet, "that they'll go in their own boats and pray to their own god."

Enoch Porter saw it all, standing behind the ranks; he saw with the eyes and heard with the ears of a child, though children in those days reached precociously to man's estate.

This may have been the reason, when he wrote of it, that all which he had seen so long ago assumed the fabric of a vision. The Lower Green and the Powaw's hand and Captain Swale and all the rest were sinking into shadow; and those Indians beside the gray, sad river were symbols and not shapes. Exactly what it was they wanted of the sea no one will ever know, for all one can get is a glimpse of them beside the river bank — naked, ugly men, examples of the degradation to which Satan led his children.

The old sachem with the pock-marked face had turned, and the rest of them turned to their pitched birch boats. Those boats seemed as light as baskets when they were carried to the water, as fragile as shells when they floated by the bank, dancing with each small wave.

They moved one by one toward the center of the stream, their occupants crouched low. As the river waves struck the boats, they scarcely seemed to cleave the water, but the paddles of the wild men rose and fell like pendulums.

"Look!" said Mr. Whistle. "Here's sport! I'll wager a silver pound —"

"Hold thy tongue, Thomas Whistle," said Captain Swale, and his cheeks were a dull, dark red. "They've gone when we had them in our hands. They'll be on us before night."

"And I say they'll not," answered Mr. Whistle.

"See them by the river bar! They'll not cross it in this water."

Out by the river mouth the boats were plain to see, tossing wildly in the cross chop of the waves. Then the tossing of one and then another seemed to lessen.

"They're shipping sea." It was Will, the bond servant, who spoke, and this his voice grew louder: "Look you! Two of 'em are sinking and one of 'em has tipped!"

It almost seemed as though a hand had struck those frail canoes, which were meant for silent, inland waters and not for the open sea. It almost seemed as though an invisible hand had passed over them, and nearly all were gone, leaving nothing but black specks of heads, struggling in the waves.

Goodman Scarlet, standing with his matchlock musket, looked away from the river bar at Captain Swale, for Captain Swale at last had roused the goodman's wrath.

"No, Captain Swale," said Goodman Scarlet, "they'll not be on us to-night — those of them that get to shore. There's other ways to kill a cat besides boiling it in butter."

Captain Swale may have known that he had been in the wrong, but he also must have known that he had been made foolish by a common man.

And then the Reverend Wayne spoke — his thought had been on higher things as he stood staring at the sea.

"It is the hand of God," he said. "Let us kneel and pray."

And Captain Swale and Goodman Scarlet knelt slowly side by side.

Whether it was heavenly justice or the red men's lack of judgment or a sudden gust of wind, one cannot tell, any more than why the Indians came.

"The last great band of Indians," the Reverend Wayne has written, "that came down our great river in boats of bark, or canoes, was said by their Powaw, or their sachem, to have come to make a prayer. By the mercy of heaven, half of them were drowned and the rest returned to their place."

And that was all, or nearly all, before the veil of obscurity covers that lean and distant time.

The news from the river had been sent ahead, so that, when they reached the Lower Green, the drum was beating. Hard-bitten men and stern, plain women, old before their time, stood waiting for the detachment to return. Although the drum was beating out a pæan of rejoicing; it made a hollow, mournful sound. As the armed band reached the village green, some one raised a feeble cheer.

"Huzzah!" an old man shouted. "Huzzah for Captain Swale!"

Goodman Scarlet smiled; he may have known that they would always cheer for Captain Swale. He may have known that men would never shout for such as he. He may have understood that they were not acclaiming the captain's prowess, that they may have seen the captain as a hard and narrow man. They were cheering for what the captain stood for, and not for Captain Swale, for something that was nearly lost in that hard land—for laces and ribbons and music, for the fine gesture, for prancing horses upon a dusty road.

"Ah me," some one was murmuring, "but he's the pretty gentleman!"

Mr. Parlin hurried forward to shake the captain's hand.

"There's been grave doings here since you've been gone," said Mr. Parlin, "and we've done a grievous wrong. What think you has happened? Goodman Snead has confessed to the murder of John Dowel. His conscience made him speak."

Captain Swale looked upon the empty stocks, then up at the Powaw's head upon its pole.

"And where is Goodman Snead?" he asked.

"He's in the meetinghouse in chains," said Mr. Parlin, "waiting on your pleasure."

"It's well," said Captain Swale. "And now take down the Powaw's head!"

Then a strange thing happened — indecorous and startling.

A slow anger which had been burning in Goodman Scarlet made him forget time and place.

"Ay," he said, in a voice loud enough for every one to hear, "take it down and cover up the folly. Huzzah for Captain Swale!"

Captain Swale stepped forward; whatever he might have thought, he did not show it.

He moved forward slowly, a shining man in steel and leather, as lithe and straight and clean as Goodman Scarlet was bent and grimy.

"Seize that man!" he said. "Tear off his doublet and bind him to the post. All of you have heard him speak treason against our law and raise his voice in raillery at a magistrate. Constable, give him a dozen lashes. Whilst I live and am given strength, there'll be justice in our town!"

3

The Best Ones Go

3

The Best Ones Go

UP TO A YEAR OR SO AGO THE BEST man to see was Harry Dow, if you wanted the ancient gossip of Haven's End. Harry made his living buying books and letters from the local attics and selling the best of them to city dealers. In his shop, one flight up above the main street, he had two rooms filled with rubbish, which should have been thrown away two generations back. Old newspapers kept cascading to the floor, and boxes of letters, which their owners had better have burned when they were still fresh from the post, kept getting underfoot.

The shop itself was old, two upper rooms of one of those square Federalist dwellings, whose ground floor had been turned into a grocery. You could still see the molding and wainscot behind the books.

"Yes, sir," Harry Dow would tell you, "I buy 'em all and lug 'em here in baskets. Trash and all, I buy 'em, when that Jew junkman don't come first. I can set right here and piece together facts that would surprise you. I don't believe there's any past. It's all somewhere, if you follow me — somewheres."

But you could not follow him all the way, for his mind had become a pudding of names and facts, as unreliable as a broken watch. The era of the China trade was recent when Harry Dow got started, and he could ramble back to the first "New England Primer" and the Freeman's Oath without a change of tense.

"Yes, sir," said Mr. Dow. "Here's Colonel Richard Swale's own writing now — the one that was magistrate of the first settlement. Listen to what I know about him — heh, heh — would you like to hear?"

Yes, Harry was the one who could dig up the Haven's End scandals. They might be imagination, but nothing seemed impossible when his voice droned on.

He snatched at a loose piece of paper and began to read. He had a knack of getting through old writing.

"This morning I called my grandson Micah Swale into my Great Chamber and asked him did he fear the Lord. On his telling me he did so fear Him I did tell him that I had small comfort in my two sons, to wit his father and his uncle; that they were better in the warehouses than keeping a fitting place as Gents.; that it was my desire he should have my Great House when I was gone to my reward and the Meadow land about it and two of my ships and the Goods within my House and my five tankards of silver; and my three slaves to wit the Negurs from the Guinea coast brought thence by Captain Haight I bade him hold his Head high as I have done. Then I bade him be humble for the meek are blessed having a care not to consort with Commoners; that he was a Gent.; with a coat of arms. Then I gave him ten pistoles and bade him dress him like a man of substance; that lace is not allowed to Gents."

The great house of Colonel Richard Swale has been torn down, but it was up as late as 1890, and a street by the river where the house stood is still called Swale's Lane. The Colonel built his house there in 1685, on a forty-acre rectangle, close by his own wharf.

In August, 1690, when Colonel Swale sat in his parlor, he could look through his window across the marshes to the sea, with no house to mar his view. A snatch of breeze through the window brought in the scent of grass and the smell of salt water. Distant sounds of hammering were carried on that breeze and the rumbling of a heavy wain and the tolling of a bell. Colonel Swale reached for his gold-headed cane and rapped on the floor three times, and Peter, his bond servant, opened the door before the rapping had ended.

"Is Master Micah not come yet?" asked Richard Swale.

"No, your Honor," Peter said.

"He's late," said Richard Swale. "He's late and drinking. The young men at Harvard College are always at strong liquor."

"Ay, your Honor," said Peter, speaking through his nose, as was still the fashion then. "It do be shocking, so please you, how the young bloods do carry on these days. What with wine and wenching—"

"Wenching?" said Richard Swale.

"Ay, your Honor," said Peter. "It's not the young master's fault. He's with the crew down to Scarlet's, drinking before they go on board. They've trussed up a tithing man, your Honor, and are a-going at the rum."

"They'll be drinking salt water at Quebec," said Richard Swale. "Where are the other tithing men?"

"They do be afeared, sir," said Peter. "The men with Captain Haight are lusty, your Honor. They'd stick a tithing man in the belly, the way I might stick a pig. They flung knives at Goodman Scarlet, and he's a powerful man."

Richard Swale's bent shoulders still bore the traces of his former strength, as he rose slowly from his chair.

He walked toward the chimney and seized his riding whip, which hung upon a nail.

"Go saddle up my horse," he said.

"Your pardon, sir," said Peter. "You ain't going to the tavern?"

"Saddle up my horse!" said Richard Swale. "I'll fetch Micah out of there."

Once in his saddle, he was still a pretty sight; old as he was, none in all the town could sit a horse as well. His jack boots were shining from fresh tallow; his dark coat had silver buttons and frogs of silver braid; his wristbands and his falling band were starched and spotless white.

"You'll want help, sir," said Peter. "Shall I sound the horn?"

"No," said Richard Swale, "why should I need help?" And he walked his horse slowly down the lane.

Upon his right hand was a field of Indian corn, upon his left were grazing grounds for cattle. The pumpkins by the corn hills were already growing golden on the rocky soil.

"It's too late for sailing to the northward," Richard Swale said. And then it came to him that soon he would be sailing on a longer voyage and that he would never see his town again. He could recall when there had never been a house by the great river, nothing but marsh and rocky, rising ground. Within the limits of the township now were close to twelve hundred souls and three houses of worship; and a fine, broad street, named King Street, sloped down to the river, where there once had been an Indian track, with solid houses of wood and brick on either side, most of them still uncolored by the weather. At the head of that street was a ropewalk and by the river he saw his own long wharf of oak and chestnut piles with new puncheon planking, fresh and shining from the broadax. Upon the wharf were stacks of good oak lumber, barrels of dried cod and pickled sturgeon, casks of rum and hogsheads of molasses.

Farther down the river, beside a rut lane, was a drying place for cod and herring. There was a distillery already in the town, where black molasses of the Indies was turned to rum, and there was a shipyard, run by one of Scarlet's sons who knew the shipwright's trade. There were two good mills and a tannery already in the town; workers in iron and wood had come across the sea.

Yet he could remember when it all was nothing, when the river was broad and bare, save for the flash and smack of sturgeon and the splashing of wild fowl rising in new flight.

A high-sterned, clumsy vessel was weaving in the tide. Colonel Swale glanced at her sharply; it was his ship, the *Prudence*, which was sailing that same evening to join the expedition for Quebec.

As he rode down the street, the wives curtsied and the men pulled off their hats, for they all knew him as the last, or almost the last, of the men of the old plantation.

"Good day, your Honor," he heard them say, as though he were a figure and not a man. And he heard some one whisper above the hoofbeats of his horse, "It's Colonel Swale. He was with the regiments when they took King Philip's head. Twenty years upon the Council of the Bay. It's the Colonel's ship that's sailing for Quebec."

Down toward the end of the street, close where the stores stand thick to-day, Scarlet's ordinary stood. It was run by the son of the first Scarlet he had known. Its roof was low and sloping. Its door stood open from dawn to dark. The sounds coming out that door were startling enough, for all merriment was startling then, when Haven's End was not yet inured to the noise of men from ships.

As he reined up his horse by the door, he saw that the noise had gathered a crowd of loafers.

"Hold the bridle," said Colonel Swale and dismounted. The men made way quickly as he walked by and once again he heard low voices.

"Look, it's Colonel Richard Swale."

"Go, fetch the constable!" said Richard Swale. "And call the tithing men."

Within the ordinary, some one was singing. It came over Richard Swale with something of a shock that it was his grandson's voice, and the song he sang rang upon the street in a peculiar way, like a desecration that flaunted decency and modesty.

> "When she danced upon the green,
>   She wore the sweetest garters,
>   That ever I have seen."

And after that came a chorus.

> "Sure the sweetest garters that ever
>   I have seen — "

Colonel Swale walked into Scarlet's ordinary with his whip dangling in his hand. It was a great, low-studded room in rough pine with heavy rafters, thick with tobacco smoke and reeking with that new beverage called "kill devil" or rum. About a long trestle table in the center of that room, twenty or thirty men were seated on pine benches, banging on the board with pewter tankards — in ragged clothes like Joseph's coat — with tanned faces and hair done up in pigtails. Their breeches were cut short off at their bare knees; the feet of most of them were bare and knives were thrust in sashes, bound tight about their waists.

But no one appeared to notice the Colonel until he spoke.

"Silence!" he roared.

There was a shuffling of feet and a rumbling of voices and then he heard a voice above the rest.

"Damn my eyes, it's Grandsire!"

Colonel Swale blinked and glanced toward the head of the table. His grandson was standing with a flagon in his hand, slender, hardly more than a boy, with the long, thin face of all the Swales. His coat was of deep purple silk and there were lace ruffles at his neck and wrist. He wore a rich brown periwig that fell in curls about his shoulders.

"Micah," called Richard Swale. "Set down that bowl."

"Boys," said Micah. "Don't mind him. It's only Grandsire's way."

Then Richard Swale felt a hand upon his arm. It was Captain Haight, the master of his vessel, a short, squat man in a greasy red coat.

"Out to the street, sir," said Captain Haight. "This ain't no place for you!"

A hand fell on his other arm; it was Goodman Scarlet in his dirty apron.

"Best get gone," said Goodman Scarlet. "There'll be trouble in the house."

The filthy place, the dirty, sandy floor, the greasy, spattered table seemed to rise and smite him like a blow. With a wrench, he sent Scarlet reeling a step backwards.

"Mind you how you hand me, sir, for I'm as good as you," Goodman Scarlet said.

"Are you so?" roared Richard Swale.

"Ay, I am," said Goodman Scarlet. "Your sons do business with me and your grandson's here."

Richard Swale stepped backward and thrust Captain Haight away. The men were laughing at the table; they were getting to their feet.

"Throw him out!" some one shouted.

"Laugh, will you?" Richard Swale shouted. "Well, take this in your teeth."

Then a man was stumbling backwards. Richard Swale had struck him clear across the face with his long, thonged whip.

"Draw back, sir," called Captain Haight.

Even then, he felt a faint distaste, in spite of his anger, at being caught up in a tavern brawl. There were faces everywhere like faces in a fever. A man was coming at him with a knife. He struck out with his whip, and the man drew back, half-blinded, and raised his knife to throw.

Captain Haight snatched out his cutlass, but he was not in time. Micah was the one who struck the man, clean on the head, with a three-legged stool.

"Ay," roared Micah, "that for you!"

The constable and the tithing men had come and were pushing the sailors out the door, leaving Colonel Swale standing swaying slightly upon the sandy floor. His eyes were on Micah, and Micah, too, was reeling. As he looked, a door opened, and a girl with yellow hair, that straggled beneath her cap, ran toward Micah Swale.

"Micah!" she cried. "Did they hurt thee, Micah?"

"No," said Micah, "no, my love."

"Throw cold water on that boy's head," said Colonel Swale, "and send him home."

Then the girl's eyes were on him. He saw her bosom rise and fall beneath her gray homespun dress.

"Sure," she said, "I'll send him, sir. He'll be right as rain, sir, when he's had a dash of water."

"And who are you?" said Richard Swale.

"Please, sir," she said. "I'm Submit Scarlet, if it please you, sir."

As she looked at him, he saw that she was afraid, but that did not surprise him. Then Goodman Scarlet spoke, staring straight at Richard Swale.

"Look at her, if you like," he said. "I mind you had my father triced up once and whipped. But you'll see a Swale and Scarlet walking up to the church."

"Keep your tongue," answered Richard Swale, still staring at the girl. Goodman Scarlet was grinning at him and rubbing his hands upon his apron.

"Ay," he said, "ask Micah, if you don't believe it. Ask him when he's sober."

With an effort, the Colonel moved his lips into a smile.

"Man," he said, "put your own head in water. Captain Haight, see your fellows are put aboard and follow me to my house."

Then he was on the street again; the hot August sun smote him and his knees were weak. There was a larger crowd upon the street,—of laborers and mechanics.

"Huzzah!" they shouted. "Huzzah for Colonel Swale."

"Mind me!" he still heard the Goodman's voice.

"You'll see a Swale and Scarlet walking to the church."

He raised his eyes toward the deep sky and, though he knew it could not be, he prayed in silence that a Swale might not wed a common wench, whose father kept an inn.

He dismounted at his door without a word. His black slave took his horse's head. His shadow fell before him, for the sun was growing low, monstrous and grotesque.

"Is all well with your Honor?" Peter asked.

"Yes," said Richard Swale. "Leave me in my room. Send me Captain Haight, when he arrives. Tell me when Master Micah comes."

Then he was standing in his own room, staring at its fine-hewn paneling. His Bible lay upon the table, his inkhorn and his papers. His breast and back piece and his iron cap hung upon the wall. A ray from the setting sun was reflected in them dimly, for they were covered with fine dust. Above the chimneypiece, his sword was resting on two stout pegs; it was a long, thrusting weapon, with an elegantly wrought hilt. The blade was of Spanish steel, whetted and sharp, with his coat of arms cut on it — a lion's head above water. He was holding the sword, balancing it between his fingers, when Captain Haight arrived.

Captain Haight was out of breath; his face was wet from his exertions. In those days the sea left its stamp on men, so that any one could read their calling. The Captain's shore clothes chafed him and made him look like a parody of a man. A great red handkerchief was tied about his throat; his boots were covered with dust and, as he walked, two small braids of black hair danced up his cheeks.

"Damme, sir!" said Captain Haight. "If you ain't looking white!"

"Look to yourself," said Richard Swale. "Have you got the men aboard?"

"Ay, my master," said the Captain hastily, "and I'll be blithe to go. We'll be out inside two hours."

Colonel Swale looked down at him; he was a head taller than Captain Haight.

"You'll be blithe to go," he said, "but I doubt if you'll come back alive. It's no time for fighting in the north, when the weather's getting late."

"Damme!" said Captain Haight. "'Tis better clawing off the rocks than rotting on this shore. Now I know you and you know me. Don't you come at me with any talk about that tavern fight. The men has got to drink."

"Mind your manners," said Richard Swale.

"Manners!" said the Captain. "I know you and you know me. You had your luck not to have a knife inside you, beating men from drink."

"Save your voice to pray that you'll come home alive," the old man said.

"Me?" said Captain Haight. "I'll take my chance on that, my master. Only don't go giving me your voice because the men were drinking."

Richard Swale looked down at Captain Haight and held out his hand.

"Take that purse off the table and put it in your pocket."

"Thanks," said Captain Haight; "I've liked you

better than others in these psalm-singing roads. I've
tossed an anchor in all the colonies. There's jolly boys
in Virginny and smiling maidens in New York and,
as for all the Indies, I swear you'd dance to see 'em,
but there's a pox on all the Bay colonies. Here's the
first land where a man can't rinse his gullet when he
comes off the water."

And then there was a knocking at the door.

"Your Honor," said Peter, "Master Micah's come."

"Tell him to come in," said Richard Swale. "And
Haight, are you the man to take my orders and no
questions asked?"

"Ay," said the Captain, "I'm your man."

"Go to the kitchen," said Richard Swale, "and wait
till I call again."

A change came over Captain Haight. He took a
quick glance at the half-open door.

"You ain't aiming to push him off, be you, Master?"
he inquired.

"How? Push him off?" said Richard Swale.

"Spike him with that dirk of yours." Captain Haight
jerked his thumb toward the sword.

Richard Swale threw back his head; his face was
deathly pale.

"No," he said.

"No offense," said Captain Haight. "No offense,
my master. It's not my custom to push 'em off, unless
they give a push at me."

A half minute later, Micah entered.

"Close the door and draw the bolt," said Richard
Swale. And he and his grandson were standing face
to face.

They made the contrast of the old that was leaving and the new which had come to seize all that the old had gathered — Richard Swale in his dark coat, with its silver frogs and buttons, and his long white hair; Micah Swale in velvet, with ribbons at his knees. They had the same long faces, the same hard mouths and the same glitter in their eyes.

"So here you are, you drunkard!" said Colonel Swale.

"Grandsire," said Micah, and he laughed. "You're still a hard old case."

"It's the liquor that speaks within you," said Richard Swale, "you drunken lout."

Micah Swale laughed again. "No, sir," he said. "You like it better when I speak to you like a man."

All at once Richard Swale smiled. "Micah," he said, "Micah, are you not afraid?"

"Of you?" said Micah. "No, sir. I'm not afraid of you."

"Micah," said Richard Swale, "you heard what Scarlet said. Tell me it's a lie. And then go to your bed."

"What did he say?" asked Micah Swale.

Richard Swale strode toward him and lowered his voice. "He spoke a libel. He said that you would marry that wench of his. I'm an old man, Micah; I've seen too many changes. Tell me that's not true."

There was a pause and Micah answered, "It's as true as the eye is in your face."

When Richard Swale drew in his breath, it made a choking rattling sound.

"Micah," he said, "there's no cause to lead her to the church."

All the while that Richard Swale was speaking, he seemed to be struggling with something stronger than himself, a force which bore him down and bent him to his knees.

"Now, sir," said Micah, "there are worse people than the Scarlets. Wait till you see her again, sir. Wait till you hear her speak."

Suddenly Richard Swale felt dizzy. He gripped at the table to keep himself from falling.

"Now!" he shouted. "Think who you are, fool. You came of the Swales of Norwich."

Even as he spoke, his own voice sounded hollow.

"Yes," said Micah, "and what are the Swales of Norwich here? Every freeman here has rights as good as yours."

"Be silent," shouted Richard Swale.

"No," said Micah, "I'll not be silent and I'll tell you this. The Scarlets have their money."

Richard Swale was composed again. He betrayed none of the emotion which surged within him — even his voice was level and quiet like a preacher's voice.

"So," he said, "that's over. Go out. Get out."

Micah did not answer, but bowed and shot the bolt back on the door.

"Peter," Richard Swale said, "send in Captain Haight."

As Captain Haight returned, he heard the old man muttering beneath his breath.

"Haight," said Richard Swale, "have two men seize my grandson and hit him on the head."

"Right!" said Captain Haight, "If them's orders."

"Keep him in the cabin," said Richard Swale, "until you get to sea. And when you join the fleet, give him this." He took his sword down from its peg above the fireplace.

"Ay, ay, sir," said Captain Haight. "And happy days to you, master. And let us have our liquor when we get back home."

"No," said Richard Swale, "you'll not be back. The season is too late. Give my compliments to Sir William Phipps. Say I repeat what I told him in the Council,— that he'll never take Quebec."

It was November when the news came south. Half an hour after the messenger rode in, the church bells began to toll. Men left their work to stand silent in the street or to tell of papish rumors that Indians and priests were gathering on the frontiers.

Richard Swale was standing on the wharf in his black cloak to guard him from the biting wind and the messenger himself rode down to tell him, dismounting and walking toward him and pulling off his hat.

"There's ill news, sir," the man cried out. And, when he told of it afterwards, he said that the old man's face went gray. "The fleet is in; your ship is lost, your Honor."

"Yes," said Richard Swale. "I thought it. The best must always go."

And then Richard Swale stood alone, staring at the river. Though he stood motionless and though his eyes were dry, he must have known that his life was drifting into nothing, like a mass of sticks upon the tide.

"Your Honor," came a voice beside him. "Please, your Honor."

He was not surprised, when he looked up; it was the Scarlet girl beside him, weeping, her hair blowing wild across her face.

"So here you are," he said. "Revile me, if you like it. It is not thy fault, girl."

"No," she said, "I did not come for that, your Honor. I came to be near some one who loved him and I know you loved him, sir."

And, as Richard Swale looked blankly on her, her voice broke in a sob.

"Oh, why did you not tell me before you sent him off? I never would have him marry me."

"How?" said Richard Swale.

For a moment the sight of the weeping girl moved him, when he thought he had lost capacity for all emotion.

"No," she said. "I loved him too much to hurt him."

"It needed only that," said Richard Swale. He did not tell her to go away.

"And yet," he said. "I could have done no different."

And he knew he could not, for at last he knew that he was only vanity. And that he was already gone. He heard the bells from the meetinghouses calling the town to prayer and, all at once, he knew what others were to know at Haven's End,—that his hopes were nothing and that only his town was left.

4

Captain Whetstone

I'd a Bible in my hand, when I sail'd, when I sail'd,
  I'd a Bible in my hand when I sail'd;
I'd a Bible in my hand, by my father's great command,
  But I sunk it in the sand, when I sail'd.

4

Captain Whetstone

FROM THE START OF THE FIRST SETtlement, the Swales and Scarlets have stayed in Haven's End. Their names crop up in every list left in the archives, from landed proprietors and parishioners, from militia muster rolls of all the wars, from shipowners' rosters and prize crews down to the stockholders' list at the gas plant and the cotton mill, and thence to the local telephone directory. "Swale, Dennis, 101-2; Scarlet, John, 17" — you would never guess that piracy once stalked among the Scarlets or the Swales.

When the automobiles go down our main street in the dusk of a summer evening, and when the crowd stands before the Shoe-Shine Parlor listening to the radio, you still can hear them say, "Good evening, Mr. Swale," when a Swale walks by, and still it is only, "Ah there, John," when a Scarlet's on the street. . . .

You have to go back to scraps of recorded fact to get the gist of the whole story, and then piece the facts together with the loose cement of one of those hearsay legends which have not wholly died along the New England coast. But once impaled in type, the early vitality of Haven's End has gone dry as faded flowers, blighted by the plague of meticulous accuracy.

Take the "History of the Swale Family," for example. It is one of those corpulent volumes such as lies on the "S" shelf of any good genealogical library, prepared by Dennis Swale back in 1894. On page 165 the passage stands as a footnote, like an island in a flood of births and deaths:

"It is said," the passage runs, "that the Micah Swale, above-mentioned, whose birth is inscribed in the records of the First Parish Church, as son of Thomas Swale, Esq., and Elizabeth Parlin, from whom the writer is himself descended (see pp. 159-168), engaged himself in a gallant affair, using the term in its broadest sense, with one Submit Scarlet, a town girl beneath his station. It is even alleged that the young man proposed marriage. Upon hearing of this, his grandfather, Col. Swale, the founder of our family (see pp. 49, 50, 67, etc.), forcibly constrained the youth to join the Phipps expedition to Quebec (August, 1690). In the autumn of this same year his ship was reported lost with all hands. Though every investigation confirms this loss, the present writer has come across the rumor that Micah Swale survived, and even visited his birthplace under shadowy circumstances, and there is also talk that a child of his was born. There is no truth in this. In alluding to this matter, the writer hastens to add that he wishes in no way to cast an aspersion on any of the Scarlet descendants, who have always held a most reputable and useful position in our local history. (See odd note on the whipping of Goodman Scarlet, pp. 47, 49.)"

Dennis Swale was not the one to guess how close he was to a tale as grotesque as any you might tell about our town.

You have to go back to 1707, and even then there is the barest rattle of a skeleton within the family closet. You must make a long jump from the "History of the Swale Family" to the last minutes in the life of a Captain Whetstone, as he stood at the foot of a gallows built for his benefit in Boston Harbor, to pay the price of piracy. For some reason, modern histories of Colonial piracy seldom mention this man's name, since the great trial of John Quelch and others of his crew in Boston, which took place three years previous, has eclipsed the feats of Whetstone.

Yet when Whetstone's fourteen-gun sloop was wrecked on Cape Cod near Wellfleet Bar in August, 1707, Whetstone was widely known to crews sailing in the Indies. Though his activities centered chiefly around Spanish and Portuguese shipping, he had captured enough vessels to upset the sugar trade, and at the time he was wrecked there was a price on his head, duly paid by the English Crown. In a southeast gale, according to a survivor's account, "With very Fearsome thunder and lightening Bolts" Whetstone and his crew found themselves among the breakers before they knew they were off the course. Only five survivors, including Captain Whetstone and Nicholas Doane, a forced man from a local fishing boat, reached the beach alive. Doane, who was afterwards cleared by the court, gave information against Whetstone, which caused his arrest near Barnstable, and he was promptly brought to trial.

The details of the proceedings are still extant in a pamphlet, printed at "Boston in New England by B. Green at the Brick Shop near the Old Meeting House 1708." In Haven's End until lately there was a copy of it left. It used to be in the parlor of old Miss Hannah Whistle, between the family Bible and the Book of Common Prayer, and a stranger place for it you could not imagine when the cat was purring on the window ledge and the wet-wash man was whistling at the gate.

"Dear me," Miss Hannah said, "it's one of the family things. Don't ask *me* why it's been kept. Goodness, here's the wet wash coming!"

Even the words of the title were like a muffled bell: "The Arraignment, Trial, Condemnation and Death, being a True Account of the Behavior and last Moments of one Captain Whetstone, who died unrepentant for Sundry Piracies herein set forth."

In the town house of Boston, Captain Whetstone stood, a man with "a long face badly marked by the small Pox and a Blue Scar above his left Eye." The Governor and Lieutenant Governor, who sat on the Court of Admiralty, asked him various questions. Knowing the justice meted to pirates in Massachusetts Bay, he must have known his time was short, for he made no defense and answered tersely. Only a scrap or two of the interrogation is worth recording now.

"Do you then confess?"

"I've been on the account, if that's where you're heading."

"Did you stop the ship of Captain Mellow in the Vineyard Sound?"

"Ay, but she wasn't worth the scuttling."

"The witness hath deposed that before you were wrecked, you entered into a creek or inlet further up the coast, close by the town of Haven's End, and went ashore alone. Is that the truth?"

"It is so."

"Did you go ashore to bury gold?"

"No, I have told you. Mine is off Wellfleet Bar."

"Then why did you land alone?"

"On an affair, your Excellency."

"What affair?"

"An affair that has no bearing in this court."

"Is Whetstone your true and honest name?"

"No."

"Then what is it?"

"Your Excellency, Whetstone will do well enough to hang by."

"The Ministers of the Town," says the pamphlet, "used more than ordinary endeavors to Instruct the Prisoner and bring him to Repentance. There were *sermons* preached in his hearing *Every Day*. And he was Cathecized and he had many occasional Exhortations."

On a Friday of September, 1707, Captain Whetstone, guarded by twenty musketeers, walked to the Long Wharf with constables, the Provost Marshal and other officers, who afterwards spent three pounds in refreshments at the Colony's expense. On either side of the prisoner there walked two ministers, taking the greatest pains to prepare him for the Last Article of his Life. With the Silver Oar, used in those days as a symbol of a mariner's execution, carried in the bow of a longboat, he went by water to the place of execution. On the small island where the gibbet was erected, he walked to the platform and removed his coat. The ministers then stood beside him and spoke as follows:

"We have told you often, yea, we have told you weeping, that you have by sin undone yourself; that you were born a sinner and that you have lived a sinner and that the Sins for which you are to Dy are of no common aggrivation."

"Ay," said Captain Whetstone, "if it eases you, I'll say you've done all that."

"And now," said one of the ministers, speaking as follows, "Ah, unhappy man! soften your heart. As you stand on the Threshold of Eternal Life or Death, put aside your wilfulness. Look on yonder gallows where your body will hang in chains."

"Ay," said Captain Whetstone, "it will hold me."

"Then tell us your true name as you fear the eternal fire."

And then Captain Whetstone spoke as follows:

"A pox on your curiosity. Whetstone, I've been telling you. The tide is flowing in, gentlemen, and only see the crowd in boats. Sure, there'll be all the water I need when I heave up the hook."

After which "he seemed little if at all concerned and said nothing more."

He died without telling his name or of his past. He confessed to landing farther up the coast at Haven's End and, except for that, the record of Captain Whetstone stands blank and white. None the less, his ghost still walks upon our streets as ghosts of greater men are raised by gossip. The story is that a Scarlet could tell his name and a Whistle too, but they kept their lips as tight as his. Yet in a strange perversity the shadow of Captain Whetstone is hovering about the Swale mansion, with the other shadows.

This was the way Hannah Scarlet always told of it, until it became a goodwife's tale. Young Tom Indian, her grandfather's slave, was blowing on his conch horn. Out by the river bank the axes had stopped, where they were laying the keel for a pink. Goodmen and good-wives and indentured men and maids were walking toward the tavern door. The post from Boston was coming in. Old Ezra Finch, who rode the post, was jerking at the straps of his saddlebags, and everywhere there was a smell of drying fish and new pine shavings and molasses.

The shuttle of the great loom where her mother wove moved back and forth, back and forth. Her mother's eyes were on the threads. There was no one like her mother for fine weaving.

"Child," her mother said, "why do you stop the wheel?"

"Please," said Hannah Scarlet, "the post is coming in."

Then she remembered that her mother sighed.

"Go down then," her mother said, "if it's your mind to hear the news."

Downstairs, the great room of the tavern was crowded full. There were laboring men with rolled-up sleeves and leather breeches and Mr. Whistle and Mr. Parlin and the Reverend Mr. White in his black, tight-buttoned coat, gentlemen from higher places.

On the Lord's Day, the Reverend White preached sermons that dealt with the eternal fire,—a pale-faced, ascetic man with gloomy eyes, who seemed to be brooding on new doctrines of sin. Hannah had sat "beneath him", and had watched him turn the hourglass three times upon the pulpit table, while his voice echoed solemnly from the sounding board above him, telling of heresy, of dying witches on the scaffold.

From the Reverend White's sour look she knew Mr. Whistle had been talking. Mr. Whistle was of the established English Church, which stood for all the things old settlers had escaped by a voyage across the sea; and further, Mr. Whistle was a traveled man, who had learned the loose ways of Popish countries. He was a type becoming common in the seaboard towns with the dawn of ready wealth, a man who knew the world and the beguiling ways of evil.

"Marriage?" Mr. Whistle was saying. "There's not the maid yet, parson, who can tie me to a mooring."

"Sir," said the Reverend White, "you're among sober people now. Forget your bawdy ways."

She had never seen Mr. Whistle as fine as he was that afternoon. His coat was new purple broadcloth with silver buttons, and his waistcoat was embroidered with small flowers. When Mr. Whistle saw her, he began to smile, and she remembered he was smelling pleasantly of rum.

"And how," said Mr. Whistle, "goes our wild flower and what's the market for a kiss?"

Hannah laughed because she had to laugh. But when she saw the Reverend White's dark frown, she stopped and grew brick red. Though she was not sixteen, the Reverend White had told her that she had a beauty made for Sin.

"Shame on you, sir!" said the Reverend White.

Mr. Whistle stared at him levelly and took a snuff-box from his pocket.

"Man!" said Mr. Whistle. "Do you see lewdness everywhere?"

She was glad that no one else was noticing. She wished to hide her face.

"Sir," said the Reverend White, "I'll drop my voice for your sake, but I say shame. Will you have her go her mother's way?"

Mr. Whistle took a pinch of ground tobacco from his box and put it to his nose.

"You'd show yourself a kinder man," he said, "if you did not say it to her face."

Goodman Finch had seated himself stiffly at the great table and swallowed at his ale before he spoke, a dour, ill-nourished man. Hannah could see her grandfather, the Goodman Scarlet in his soiled apron, standing at Mr. Finch's elbow.

"Well," said Goodman Scarlet, "can't ye speak out?"

"The track is fearful bad," said Finch.

"Ay," said Goodman Scarlet, "don't we all know that? What of the tawnies?"

"Them?" said Goodman Finch. "They was saying when I left that a family — name of Rucker — was scalped and cruel murdered on the River Kennebec."

There was a pause. The Reverend White was the first to speak, his face alight with glowing rapture.

"What of their tortures?" he inquired; "tell us of their agonies."

Goodman Finch took another pull at his pewter can.

"Scalped," he said, "and Goodman Rucker did have burning splinters in his fingers."

"A lingering death," said the Reverend White.

"Well," said Goodman Scarlet, "they ain't the first ones scalped in the Bay and they won't be the last. On with it, Finch. Sure, you ain't finished yet."

A slanting beam of sunlight came through the western windows, making the room more dingy than it had been, and Hannah Scarlet remembered wishing that she was in the sun.

"Were there no executions, friend?" inquired Reverend White.

"Three men whipped," said Finch, "for bawdy singing on the Lord's night, and Martha Spinnet, that was maidservant, hanged for the strangling of her child born out of wedlock."

The Reverend White drew in his breath and looked at Hannah Scarlet.

"Praised be the Lord!" he said. "And did the poor wretch die in grace?"

"Ay, sir," said Finch. "She died in grace."

"Well," said the Reverend White, "tell us of her agonies. How soon did the woman die?"

Mr. Whistle took another pinch of ground tobacco from his box.

"Scarlet," he said, "fetch the rum. Get on, Finch. Get on to something else."

"Ay, sir," said Finch, "there's more. Word's come from Castle William that Swale's ship, *The Golden Word*, was boarded by a Frenchman."

There was a shuffling of feet. The name of Swale was still a great one in the town. Hannah Scarlet could remember when *The Golden Word* had sailed almost from the foot of their own street, in fine white canvas, with her cargo of dried fish, and at that very moment, through the tavern's open door, she could see the gables of the Swale house. As she looked at her grandfather, she saw that he was smiling and wiping the back of his hand across his lips.

"Ay, them Swales," said Goodman Scarlet. "Them Swales ain't what they used to be."

"Now," Goodman Finch was saying, "don't say I don't bring the news; and that ain't all. There's a pirate off the coast."

It did not seem strange to Hannah Scarlet when she heard, for there had been pirates since the days of Dixey Bull, and fear was everywhere, fear of the present and fear of the hereafter.

"Like as not," said Goodman Scarlet. "Like as not. There's pirates off the coast. But them Swales. . . . I'd like to see his face. Them Swales ain't what they used to be."

Through the other voices and the mutterings in that room, Scarlet's voice seemed to cut like a whetted knife and to carve a groove of silence. She could see the men stare at him, half curious and half disturbed, and then she remembered that something made her turn. Mr. Whistle, partly sitting, partly leaning on the trestle table, was staring at her very hard through narrowed eyes. He was kicking his foot back and forth before him like a pendulum. She remembered how the light struck on the silver buckle of his shoe.

"You've got Swale eyes, my dear," he said softly, so no one else could hear. "You've got their fine straight nose."

She knew enough of tavern ways to know that gentlemen spoke strangely when they took too much. Old Finch was speaking. The stiffness had left his tongue.

"Aye," he said, "right in the Vineyard Sound, and Master Mellow said when he come aboard he acted like a gentleman, for all his ugly face, and like he knew the land. Food was all he wanted. And Mellow knew him — scar on the left temple, puckering the left eye, pock pits on his face. It was Captain Whetstone, as sure as you're alive."

"And I'd admire to know," said Mr. Whistle, "who is Captain Whetstone?"

"Who is Whetstone?" said Mr. Finch. "Don't you read none, sir? There's fine bits of him in the book-shops, which I'll gladly bring you for five shillings come next post, and five hundred pounds on him, dead or alive. It's him who took two Spanish towns as fine as Morgan ever did, and many's seen him at St. Thomas and St. Kitts."

"Rubbish!" said Mr. Whistle. "And don't you frown at me, Parson White. First it's the death of a serving wench and now it's an old wives' tale. Give my compliments to Captain Whetstone and say I'll pull his nose." He turned to Hannah. "Would you care to see me pull his nose, my dear?"

Then she saw her grandfather was still smiling and rubbing at his lips, and she knew he thought as little as Mr. Whistle of pirates on the coast. She knew where his mind was running.

"Them Swales," said Goodman Scarlet. "I wish't I could have seen him when he heard the news. No, them Swales ain't what they used to be."

Then his glance fell on Hannah Scarlet.

"You, Hannah," he said, "polish up the chargers."

The great room of the tavern was still again, growing shadowy and cool as the sun's rays began to slant. Hannah sat by the hearth, rubbing at the pewter with the white wood-ash, and it all seemed like the turning of a page. Goodman Finch was gone to the ferry, and every one had followed to their houses and the farms, except Mr. Whistle, who sat in a corner with a new clay pipe. Yet in the silence of the ordinary room there seemed to be an echo of old voices and catches of old song, for its very silence was a reminder that it was the only place where tongues went loose in Haven's End. A row of pewter drinking cans shone from their pegs, and flitches of bacon and hams swung from the rafters overhead, like figures on a gibbet. Tom Indian came through the doorway, bearing a willow basket filled with sawdust, which he sprinkled on the floor. Once, as he glanced toward her, she could understand the sadness in his eyes. Tom Indian was a slave boy brought up from the Carib sea.

Her grandfather was standing at the open door, staring at the tradesmen's signs above their street, and once again the air was filled with drying fish and new pine shavings and molasses. When Goodman Scarlet had hung a board above his tavern door with a blackamoor's head painted on it, there was more fact than poetic license in his choice. He had dabbled often in the exchange of rum for slaves. The blackamoor's head hung above him, creaking softly as it swung upon its staples. Farther up the street there was a great red glove for Enoch Gates, the tanner, and an anchor for the chandler, a kettle for the tinker, scissors for a tailor, and a pole with a crimson stripe to show where the barber surgeon dwelt. The signs were as crude as the unpainted pine houses. No age had smoothed their newness, but they were beautiful to Goodman Scarlet.

It must have been the silence in the room that made Hannah Scarlet start when she heard her grandfather's soft laugh; and then she saw that a man was passing by the door. She knew the gentleman's gray face and stooping shoulders, and his broadcloth coat, a trifle smooth and shiny at the sleeves. She knew, though he had never looked at her, as long as she could remember, that it was Mr. Thomas Swale who lived in the great Swale house. Mr. Thomas Swale, as he walked by, was staring at the wheel ruts on the street.

"Good evening to you!" called Goodman Scarlet. "Sad news you've had—sad news."

Mr. Whistle, seated in his corner, had laid down his pipe and was listening. Mr. Swale had halted, and Hannah thought the gentleman seemed very tired.

"Scarlet," he said, and his voice was precise, like Mr. Whistle's voice, "you've never wished me well."

"Ay," said Goodman Scarlet. "Ain't I so?"

Mr. Swale did not reply. You might have thought he had not heard, as he turned his back and walked up the street. Something in the way he did it was worse than any answer.

"Now a pox go with you!" said Goodman Scarlet between his teeth. Hannah Scarlet sat motionless, with a great pewter charger across her knees. All at once her hands were cold and her heart was in her throat.

"Steady!" said Mr. Whistle. "Steady! It happened long ago."

It was a time when one believed in spells and in the witches' curse. There was something evil moving in that room when those two were speaking, and she could see its shadow on Goodman Scarlet's face.

"Ah," he said, "and so you know it too."

She did not know what it was that Mr. Whistle knew, but she remembered how those two looked — Mr. Whistle graceful and deliberate, and her grandfather in his soiled apron, as plain as a heap of stone.

"Lord help you, friend," said Mr. Whistle, lifting up his pipe. "It's a small place we live in. Everybody knows, and such things happen. Nature has her way."

Goodman Scarlet spat upon the floor and doubled up his fist.

"Ay," he said. "Yet there she sits in her chamber above this, spinning, weaving, while her life goes by and did you see him turn his back? Did ye see the cursed face to him when he turned away?"

"Steady!" said Mr. Whistle. "Keep down your voice before they hear you in the street. It's their disgrace as well as yours. They sent the lad away."

"Ay," said Goodman Scarlet. His face was deep

crimson and he did not lower his voice, "And gave thanks when he was lost."

"Hush!" said Mr. Whistle. "There's Swale blood in this room."

Then, though she did not look up, she knew their eyes were on her. She had a wish to cry out, but instead she sat very still. The words they had spoken were as meaningless to her then as snatches of voices, and yet her mind was stirring in the silence.

"Now peace." It was Mr. Whistle, speaking coolly, gently. "I know more of the Swales than you. I've played with Swales and sat with 'em. I know what's on your mind, but leave the Swales. The Swales are going down, but you're not the man to push 'em."

"Ah!" cried Goodman Scarlet. "Ain't I so? So help me, there's none in your house shamed to show her face. Give me the whip over 'em, is all I ask, and I'll lay on till their back are welts. Give me one chance to put shame on 'em. That's all I ask—just one."

"Scarlet," said Mr. Whistle, "bring the rum. There's a good man, Scarlet. Now we talk on the broader tenets of philosophy. We talk of a great permanence and balance of the ether, and of eternal ebb and flow."

"Lord, sir," said Goodman Scarlet, "you are took in drink again."

"No," said Mr. Whistle, "no — not that." He leaned his back against the wall and exhaled a cloud of smoke. "I'm speaking of the Scarlets and the Swales, and all the world's made up of them. They live in every town, and there's a promise for you as sweet as any sermon. And what of the Scarlets? That's you, my friend, that's you—heavy on their feet and patient like the cattle. They're the ones who pay the piper for the music. They're the ones who work and build and make two grow where one grew last. They take no risks. They have no ups and downs. They are kind and they are mild and all they want is peace. And what of the Swales? They're the ones who make the music. They take what others may have gathered and toss it over. They lead the Scarlets where no Scarlet dares go first and beat them when they follow. They have no patience and no skill in useful toil and they have no mercy, even for themselves. You cannot bend nor break 'em, or they would have been nothing long ago. Steel for Swale and lead for Scarlet, and steel cuts lead and lead wraps steel. The Swales have no mercy and no fear, but the Scarlets have them both. The Swales go high and fall, but Scarlets die in their beds."

Mr. Whistle paused and smiled.

"And what of the Whistles?" Goodman Scarlet said. Mr. Whistle sighed and took a pinch of snuff.

"The Whistles are not made for a land like this," he said. "We're not lead or steel."

"Ay," said Goodman Scarlet, "talk as you've a mind. You wouldn't be the one to forget. Let me hold the whip. That's all I ask."

Mr. Whistle laughed mockingly and filled his pipe again.

"You haven't got the hardness," Mr. Whistle said. "You'd be too kind to use it, friend."

The room was growing darker, for the sun was going down. From the western windows Hannah could see it sink behind the hills across the river into the loneliness of unknown lands. The tide was at dead

high, so that all the flats of mud and the marshes by
the shore were mirrors of water, reflecting the redness
in the sky; and already the river mist, which always
came at evening, was rising along the shore in curving
ribbons. Hannah walked toward the windows to see it
better. It was blotting out the ugly smallness of the
town and making it unstable and fantastic. There were
small ships at the wharves, being loaded with wood
and fish; and now the mist was rising toward them,
like an army. Ribbons of mist were blowing toward
the ropewalk beyond the tavern windows. Mist was
moving against the sheds where molasses and pelts
were stored.

Shadows were moving from the nothingness where
all things went, Indian men and men in cloaks, witches,
devils, angels, long canoes of birch bark. There was the
train band which had marched to King Philip's War,
and the crews from ships lost at sea, and the souls
of all who had prayed for a peaceful ending. . . .

Then all at once, although her back was turned, she
knew that she and Mr. Whistle were alone. She knew
that Mr. Whistle was looking at her as he would not
have dared to look if they had not been alone.

"Little wild flower," said Mr. Whistle. "Little
wild flower . . ."

As she turned at the sound of his voice, she saw
that his eyes were dark and deep and filled with little
lights.

"Ah," said Mr. Whistle, "don't be afraid."

She did not answer, because she could not find her
voice. Mr. Whistle had not moved. He was sitting in
the corner, leaning against the wall, and yet, for the

first time she had ever known him, Hannah Scarlet was afraid.

"Ah," said Mr. Whistle, "but you're beautiful. Now, thank the Lord for that! Neither you nor I were meant for this."

"You'd best be getting home, sir." Her voice seemed to choke her when she spoke, and all at once in the midst of her fear she felt a sharp resentment. She knew he would not have spoken so to any other maid.

"You should have silks on you," said Mr. Whistle, "and stockings with sweet embroidered flowers. Stand so — just so, that I may see you fair. The Scarlets are lead and the Swales are steel, but the Whistles are like the glass that I have seen in Venice, spun and fine and clear, like the stems of wine goblets. We break, but we're devilish sharp when we're broken. Give me a kiss now."

"It isn't right," she answered. "I thought —" But she did not say what she thought. Mr. Whistle was on his feet, walking toward her, stepping very softly, with his voice as soft as his steps.

"Not right," said Mr. Whistle, "not when you have the beauty? Come and let me show you, and you'll see how I mean."

Then she found that she was crying, choking with harsh sobs.

"I'll call," she said. "I'll call."

"Sweet," said Mr. Whistle, "why call? They'll only know it is the old, hot blood."

And Mr. Whistle had her in his arms and she thought that all the shadows in the room had seized upon her, that she was sinking in deep water, struggling in the dark. Her face was buried in the purple broadcloth of his coat as she tried to wrench away.

"Gad, what a cat!" she heard him say, and he was very strong. He held her so she could not breathe. Then all at once his grasp relaxed.

"The devil!" Mr. Whistle muttered. He must have seen what she could not see. Some one was entering from the street.

Though it was dark, she was certain that she had never seen the man before. Even in the dark she saw his clothes had a strange cut. The man was muffled in a cloak that stretched from his chin well below his knees. A huge felt hat with a loose-hanging brim shaded his eyes and forehead. He spoke at once in a low, metallic voice.

"Is this a tavern," he inquired, "or is it a house of love?"

"It's both," said Mr. Whistle.

The stranger did not raise his voice nor did he move; nor was it possible to see his face.

"Manners!" said the stranger. "Manners!"

The Whistles had always possessed the sort of courage that blunders on until it is too late to stop.

"And who the devil are you?" said Mr. Whistle.

"A soul from purgatory!" the stranger said. "Come back to walk the earth."

"Then you'd better be getting back there," Mr. Whistle answered.

"When I go," the stranger said, "you'll not be the one to send me. Where's the host here?" And he clapped his hands.

Goodman Scarlet came at once, striding rapidly from his private room, with a quill still in his fingers, and Hannah knew that he had been busy casting up accounts.

"Good evening to you, sir!" said Goodman Scarlet, for, like every host, he had an eye for gentlemen and he peered curiously through the dusk. "You, Tom Indian, lead in the gentleman's horse."

"I have no horse," the stranger said.

Her grandfather was astonished then. She heard that rising inflection to his voice, which the Scarlets still own to-day.

"Sure, you did not come afoot, sir? And there's no new vessel come across the bar."

"Does it matter how I came," the stranger asked, "if I bring you trade? It didn't use to matter in these parts, once. Bring me a pot of sack. I wish to rest."

"Right, sir!" said Goodman Scarlet. "Right, your Honor. You come from these parts, then! Will you have some food?"

Those were the days of plenty, such as our town will never see again. "There's oysters from the Little River, sir," said Goodman Scarlet, "that can be roasted before the fire; or a slice of venison that can be grilled. It's fresh in from the woods. There's boiled sturgeon, sir, just out of this here river, and the sturgeon's very fine. There's pigeon if you'd rather, or Indian corn and syrup?"

The stranger listened, standing motionless with his hat brim half across his face. "Bring me the pot of sack," he said. "I'll not eat now."

"Very good, sir!" said Goodman Scarlet. "You, Hannah, bring the candles."

When she lighted the candles on the iron ring above the trestle table, the room became warm and mellow, and it seemed to her that all the light fell upon the stranger and that he was the center of the room, exactly like a figure in a picture.

Mr. Whistle, with his lace and his silver buckles, seemed to fall away before him. Goodman Scarlet was as plain as pine walls when the candles were alight. The stranger's cloak, she saw, was a soft blue with a lining of red velvet. His hat had a clasp on it of red and blue stones. As he seated himself on one of the pine benches, he tossed his cloak from his right shoulder and she saw that he wore a coat of blue brocade that must have been splendid once. She remembered that there was tarnished gold lace on the edges of that coat and that there was a red sash about the stranger's waist which did not belong with the coat at all.

"And what are you staring at?" the stranger asked.

"Your clothes," said Mr. Whistle. "You look like a bird of paradise."

"Give the gentleman what he wishes," the stranger said and tossed a gold piece on the table.

There was no wonder that Mr. Whistle stared. Hannah Scarlet had never seen such a figure in a region where most dress was drab and plain; and it seemed to her that her grandfather had never seen such a man, for his eyes had narrowed and his mouth had fallen open. But, if he wished to ask a question, he thought better of it. The stranger had removed his hat and the light fell on his face, and it was a face to awaken you from dreams. It was neither young nor old, and the marks of weather were on it, making it a reddish brown. The nose was long and straight, the forehead was high and narrow, and about the corners of the lips were little, violent curves, so that you could imagine the whole face changing from placidity to fury. Perhaps the face had been handsome once, but it had been marked by smallpox and a scar above the left eye had half-closed the eye itself into a puckered slit.

"The devil!" said Mr. Whistle very softly. "What a face!"

"There, sir!" said Goodman Scarlet. And Hannah noticed that his face had gone quite white and that he was staring. "You mustn't mind the young gentleman; he's had a drop too much and you know what young men are."

"Yes," said the stranger. But he never took his eyes from Mr. Whistle. "I know what young men are and you'll have your own face marked, sir, before you're through." He raised his cup slowly. "Ah," he said, "the town has changed but the bad liquor hasn't."

"You come from these parts then, sir?" said Goodman Scarlet.

"Damn your curiosity," the stranger said. "Never mind whence I come. And you," he nodded toward Mr. Whistle, "keep your eyes off me or you won't have any eyes to keep. Ay," he raised his cup again, "the town has changed. You've two new wharves and another ropewalk."

"Sure, sir," said Goodman Scarlet, "they've been here the last ten years. The Lord has been good to us.

There's a fine trade with the Indies. I see you follow the sea."

"Friend," said the stranger, "the less you see, the better; and that goes for you, young will-o'-the-wisp," turning to Mr. Whistle. "I know the face of you; you're a Whistle and Whistles are always getting into trouble. Tell me," the eyes in his scarred face were very light in color, as he turned from Mr. Whistle back to Goodman Scarlet, "men come and go; a town like this won't hold 'em. Tell me what of a family here, the Swales?"

"The Swales?" said Goodman Scarlet. "Have you aught against them, sir?"

"Old man," said the stranger, "you must be hard of hearing. Keep your curiosity to yourself. What about the Swales?"

"Ah, sir," said Goodman Scarlet, "the Swales ain't what they used to be. Now you take old Richard Swale, if you should mind him,—him who was with the first plantation. He was a pretty gentleman, if a nasty one and sharp of temper. But now, Mr. Thomas Swale, you might say he has misfortunes. He don't handle men right; he don't hold fast to what he's got, and the old place is divided up amongst other Swales, and what not. The Swales ain't what they used to be."

The stranger set down his pewter can crash upon the table. "Did you hear me, sir?" he said to Mr. Whistle. "Take your eyes from my face."

Mr. Whistle was on his feet. He had reached his hand inside his coat. "Gad," said Mr. Whistle, "I know you now. There's nothing like putting two and two together and you fit it to a T."

The stranger had jumped up and the pine bench crashed behind him.

"Stand easy, sir!" cried Mr. Whistle. "I know you now." And just then Mr. Whistle withdrew his hand from beneath his coat. He was holding a small pistol cocked and ready. "Scarlet," he said, "run for the door and call. We've Captain Whetstone here."

For an instant Goodman Scarlet stood like a pile of stone. "Lord help us, sir," he gasped. "It isn't him, the pirate?"

"Get to the door!" Mr. Whistle was saying. At last his voice was trembling with excitement. "You heard Finch here, not two hours ago, 'pock-marked face and scar by the left eye.' Steady, you; I'm primed and cocked. The Whistles are glass but they're sharp. Get to the door and call for help."

Mr. Whistle was up from the table, his eyes like pin points, his pistol steady in his hand. There was no wonder that Goodman Scarlet still stared fascinated and did not move.

The stranger was also standing; his right hand still grasped his pewter can of sack. There was no doubt, now that Mr. Whistle had spoken. The blue cloak told who he was; all his outlandish, tawdry splendor told it. And even Hannah Scarlet knew there could be no two men with such a face.

The stranger's eyes were on Mr. Whistle's eyes as they stared at each other across the trestle table. The stranger's lips were moving upward.

"Well!" he said. "You're clever. So the hue and cry is got here."

Mr. Whistle laughed lightly. "Clever and sharp,"

he said. "The Whistles are always sharp. Call out the door, Scarlet; he's worth five hundred pounds."

"You're a cool young man," said the stranger. "Yes, I'm Captain Whetstone and I've had pistols at my face before. Do you think in all honesty you can take me, friend?"

"Yes," said Mr. Whistle, "and don't you budge a hair."

"Because you can't," said Captain Whetstone. "There's a trick in every trade."

Hannah Scarlet always said his hand moved so fast you could scarcely see it move. There was a splash and that was all.

"See?" he said. "You should have held up your left hand to keep the priming dry."

He had tossed his can of sack upon the lock of Mr. Whistle's pistol.

"And now," he said, "keep back from that door and you, girl, close it and drop the bar." And he smiled at Mr. Whistle. "Yes," he said, "always let your hand guard the priming when there's liquor on the table."

Hannah Scarlet might have laughed at another time to see Mr. Whistle, but the presence of that man killed humor. He did not move, she always said. He did not even bother to draw a weapon. He had only flicked a cup of wine on Mr. Whistle's pistol, but his immobility held them deathly still. Even Mr. Whistle did not speak.

"Gently," said the stranger, "gently now. Not a scream from you, girl, not a single little shriek. Tiptoe, tiptoe. I'm not made to hang, when I can help it.

And now, old man," he turned to Scarlet, "move beneath the light where I can see you. So; you're not much changed."

Then he moved a step backward very quickly and his head went back.

"So," he said, "we've company. Who's that upon the stair?"

"Please your Honor," Goodman Scarlet's voice was shaking, "it's only — Please your Honor."

"Damn your teeth!" said Captain Whetstone. "Answer me now. Are soldiers out? They hunted Quelch's men like rats, I've heard. No tricks now. Who's that upon the stairs?"

"Please your Honor," stammered Goodman Scarlet, "there's naught I've heard of soldiers. There's no tricks here." And then he stopped.

"It's only my mother, please your Honor," said Hannah Scarlet, and her voice was hardly more than a whisper. "She's the only one above the stairs. They enter from that door."

Just as she spoke, the door to the stairway opened and Captain Whetstone fell back another step. Sure enough, her mother was standing there, staring at Mr. Whistle in a puzzled way, for Mr. Whistle still held his pistol. Then she looked at Goodman Scarlet.

"What is it?" she asked. "I heard the noise."

And then she saw Captain Whetstone, bareheaded in the candlelight, and she knew him. There was no doubt her mother knew him, though her face was still as stone. Hannah heard her mother draw her breath in a quick, sharp gasp.

"Micah!" said her mother. "Micah Swale."

Captain Whetstone's face looked suddenly sunken, all covered by pits and scars.

"Lord," he said. "I never thought you'd know who I was, my dear." And then she would have fallen, if he had not put his arm around her. "Yes," he said, "it's Ulysses come back to Ithaca. I wished to see Penelope before I died."

That was all he said; he never told where he had been.

"There," he said, "are you better now? I am not fit to touch you, but I wanted to see your face."

Goodman Scarlet was the first to speak. "Master Micah!" he was saying.

Then Mr. Whistle also spoke. "Captain, if you'd only said you were a Swale, I'd not have raised my hand."

"Lord," gasped Goodman Scarlet, "strange are Thy ways in the eyes of men. They were glad to think you dead, rather than to wed a girl of mine."

Captain Whetstone looked at him; the color was back in his face. "It was not my fault I left," he said.

"No," said Goodman Scarlet, "not your fault! Curse them Swales!"

The color was back again in Captain Whetstone's face, but he was like a man who had drunk a bitter draught.

"Your pardon," said Captain Whetstone. "I'd have never come here, if I'd thought you'd know."

"Suppose," said Mr. Whistle, and he coughed to clear his throat, "suppose we have a round of rum."

"No," said Captain Whetstone, "I best be going now."

"Going!" Suddenly her mother moved toward him, looking very ill and pale. "Why be you going, Micah, when you've just got home?"

Captain Whetstone opened his lips to speak and closed them once; then he looked sharply, almost pleadingly, from Mr. Whistle back to Goodman Scarlet.

"Business," he said. "Don't ask me what."

"Right," said Mr. Whistle.

But perhaps her mother knew without their telling, for, suddenly, she threw her arms about his neck.

"I wish," said Captain Whetstone, "I wish you had not done that."

"But you'll be back," her mother cried. "Promise, you'll be back."

"My dear," said Captain Whetstone, "I'll do the best I can. The long-boat's by the marsh; I best be going back."

"Lord!" said Goodman Scarlet suddenly. "If them Swales could only hear of it. I'd like to see them Swales."

Captain Whetstone turned slowly toward him. "You hold them in the hollow of your hand," he said. "Tell them. I won't blame you. You can kill the old man if you tell him who I am."

Goodman Scarlet sighed and looked hard at the sawdust floor. "Ay," he said, "them Swales. But rest you easy, Master, I won't tell."

Suddenly Mr. Whistle was laughing beneath his breath. "It's what I said," he murmured. "The Scarlets have the mercy, not the Swales. Are you leaving, sir? I'll walk with you down the track. Keep the brim of your hat well down. You'll want to see the town."

"Ay," said Captain Whetstone, "I'll want to see the town."

Mr. Whistle was moving toward the door, but Captain Whetstone did not follow.

"Wait," he said. "Put up your helm."

Mr. Whistle whirled about, but Captain Whetstone had not moved. He stood with his hands beneath his cloak, looking Mr. Whistle grimly up and down. The scar by his eye made him seem to be winking at some secret jest.

"Here," said Mr. Whistle, "what is blowing now?"

Captain Whetstone moved his left hand from beneath his coat. He was holding a small kid pouch.

"Friend," said Captain Whetstone, "take that and place it in your pocket. You may be alive to open it before I'm through."

Mr. Whistle took the pouch and weighed it in his hand. The color ran out of his cheeks at last, though Captain Whetstone had not moved.

"Now what the devil—" he began. "There's stones inside—"

"Manners," said Captain Whetstone. "Manners." He turned to Goodman Scarlet and for a moment his left eye seemed to be entirely closed. "Go out and fetch a parson." He turned back to Mr. Whistle, "You're going over the side, my friend—one way or the other."

"A parson?" said Goodman Scarlet. "Did you say a parson, sir?"

"Yes," said Captain Whetstone. "Fetch him and his Book."

And then Hannah Scarlet started. Captain Whet-

stone's glance was on her. She could seem to see deep
behind his eyes and behind the pock marks and the scar,
and she knew that he was looking at her kindly, speaking to her kindly, although he did not speak, telling
her not to be afraid.

"You," he said to Mr. Whistle, pointing to a space
on the sawdust floor, "move over there — smart when I
speak, and you, girl, stand beside him. And you, my
dear —"

He turned to Hannah's mother, and his face and
voice were different. "Will you join me behind the
door? It will be the family pew."

"Micah!" asked Hannah's mother. "What do you
mean to do?"

"Hush!" said Captain Whetstone. "It will be as right
as rain. Did you hear me? Fetch the parson, the pale
one I saw when I walked here. And you, my friend,
I'll be just behind the door — stand so until he comes,
and when he comes, ask him to marry you."

"How?" cried Mr. Whistle. "Marry me?"

"Yes," said Captain Whetstone, "right and proper.
You love her. I heard you say it. Stand — I told you
— and when he comes, ask him, and if ye don't — I'll
drop ye like a potted goose." And suddenly he laughed
softly.

"There's been too much here that's been fast and
loose. You'll be an honest man, before I pull my hat
down and we walk out. Mind what I've told you, if you
love the air and sun."

Perhaps Mr. Whistle's blank astonishment, or perhaps his own thoughts made that apparition of a man
break once more into laughter.

"Yes," he said, "the youth of this town is wild, and I'm one who should know it; but I'll save you, friend. I'll save you, though it's too late to save myself. I'm Conscience and I'm Justice, friend, and I'm where they always should be — just behind the door."

5

A Dog, A Woman

A dog, a woman and a hickory tree,
The more you beat 'em the better they be.

5

A Dog, A Woman

THE HUGUENOT LEVESSERS, WHO reached Haven's End from Guernsey in the dawn of the eighteenth century, have vanished like some ugly dream, leaving only a row of tombs in the churchyard by the Common Pasture. You can imagine them breaking upon the House of Swale like a heavy wave and swirling back to sea.

When old "King" Levesser was captain of his own vessel, carrying blacks from the Guinea coast, they say he killed seventeen one night, because their noise disturbed him — an idle tale, but it shows that new, hot blood was entering our town. John Swale was the one who called "King" Levesser a "Foreign Monkey" in a letter still extant. "A Foreign Monkey has come among us," John Swale wrote; "the Lord has turned his back upon His servants for their Sins."

Yet it must have been a good match back in 1738, when Pierre Levesser married Patience Swale, as the Clerk's Book of the First Church shows. The Levessers had grown rich from the African trade, and the Swales were all dirt poor. There is even a story that John Swale was forced to borrow money to keep the family end up at the wedding, but who can tell about it now, when it all has gone to dust and only a sinister echo is left from the wedding bell that pealed?

But, the time does not seem so distant. The bell that tolled for that wedding is still ringing at Haven's End, with a high, thin note, perhaps because the metal is so old. And when you see their portraits, you wonder, you cannot help but wonder. . . . All sorts of curious thoughts come crowding, passages from ancient books, a wharf, the whining of a dog, and water swirling through the pilings, and rain and a southwest gale. . . .

Until very recently the pictures hung in the dark hall in the Swale house, side by side. On the wall above them were relics of the Eastern trade, common in any New England seaport,—a Malay kriss, a panel of carved lacquer. The faces of that pair had sunk back into the canvas behind ridges of cracking paint, which gave them the air of apparitions, impermanent shadows of a day of piety and rum. They were apparitions more than pictures, for there was something in them which was curiously alive. Whoever the journeyman artist may have been, plying his trade at Haven's End, he had caught that fleeting, unnamable expression which gives a face humanity. Pierre Levesser, in a red plush coat, stared from beneath an undulating wig of natural brown hair. It was a wig that would have stirred the ire of any Puritan divine. Its conventionality made the face more startling, for somehow it gave the sense of a man in masquerade, when you clapped eyes upon that picture in the Swales' front hall. Round, unblinking eyes, sharp as a bird's stared oddly into space. The nose was beak-like, typical of the Norman French, and the mouth seemed nothing but a single sweep, done slowly by a very steady hand, with lines about it of a temper more subtle and ingenious than any Saxon brew.

And there beside him, in a frame identical, was Patience Swale, a trifle plain to look at, for the Swales seldom had great beauty. There was no doubt it was a gentlewoman's face, the straight nose of the Swales, level, dispassionate eyes, a proud high neck, and you could almost swear the lips were about to smile and say:

"I am cold, but what if you could make me love? I am cold, but, if I will it, a touch of my hand, a single yielding gesture is enough."

And you could not help but wonder, as you paused and looked, what was it she saw to love, or did love matter when Haven's End was a world sufficient to itself? Did those faintly smiling lips of hers meet his lips gladly? Did her cool eyes soften when she looked upon her husband's face? An answer seemed to come out of the portraits, a hint of clashing wills, gliding side by side and rasping like steel blades, struggling for survival down to the gates of death. . . .

There is no wonder that rumors last in a town like ours, where the past was so vastly greater than the present that everything is a reminder of it, even to the empty river. But Mr. Dennis Swale, who used to show those portraits, had that obtuseness which marked the Swales straight from the First Plantation. He would stand, his hands behind his back, staring down his long nose, which the Swales had never lost.

"Distinguished, don't you think?" was what he said. "Good Huguenot stock, the Levessers, splendid Guernsey family. I wonder why they all died out. Yes, there's a portrait of a gentleman."

That was all he saw, while Pierre Levesser was glaring back beneath that preposterous wig, rakish, venal, evil.

And next a bell was ringing. Its sound was inescapable, sad and out of key.

"Ah," said Dennis Swale, "you hear it? There's the bell from the old First Church — their wedding bell. . . ."

Back in the time of the Levessers and all the rest, there was an assiduous Clerk of Courts, who had a love for sin and scandal. The meticulous details of his records still give that impression, as one turns the pages that he wrote with such an ornate flourish. Ezra Sill, his name was, and he left the beginning, all docketed and filed.

You could have understood his records better if you had read them when they were jammed into the cellar of our public library at home. Steve Higgins, who tended the furnace, would unlock the door, and there you'd be — brick arches above you, a deal table and an electric light. It was a pleasant place to be, cool and quiet of a summer's day; and, curiously enough, the library was originally one of the Levesser dwellings, built in 1780 from privateering profits. Though its paneling and stairs were torn out when it was sold, modern workmen never reached the cellar. You could picture whole hogsheads of rum and casks of Oporto

and Madeira stored there. Though no Levesser had
trod our streets for fifty years, there seemed to be an
inkling of their presence, small-limbed, hook-nosed,
green-eyed, with throaty, foreign speech.

"This day," the record reads, "came Pierre Levassier
and gave payment of 15 shillings the fine imposed by
this Court for his Unmerciful beating of his Dogge
last Sabbath eve in the Publick Square."

It must have been more than an ordinary Sabbath
breaking, for outrage to humanity is specifically
mentioned, as well as outrage to the rules of Puritans.

It seems, in the month of July, 1738, not two
months after the Swale–Levesser marriage was recorded, that Pierre Levesser was crossing the Town
Square on his way from his countinghouse to his dwelling. There is even a picture of our square extant, much
as it must have been in those days, when our town was
young and hard. It is a very rare print now — "A
Panoramic View of the Dwellings, Gaol and Houses of
Worship of the Towne of Haven's End in New England — Cut and sold by John Porter, Printer at his
Shoppe close by Levessers' Wharf, 1762." The bare-
ness of it is what strikes one first. The roofs stood without a single tree above them, and only a few saplings
grew along the streets. Haven's End was like a northern
trading post, and, when one comes to think of it, that
was all it was — when it stood close to the woods,
drawing on a half-known hinterland for lumber and on
a cold sea for fish. In the center of the square, rectangu-
lar and barnlike, stood the First Church, of which only
the bell is left to-day. The gaol, with its stocks and
pillory and whipping post, stood just behind the

church, close to the river and in front of two long wharves.

Against that background Pierre Levesser was odd and out of place. He was customarily accompanied by his spaniel, which was trotting just before him, "A heavy, hairy Beast," the record says, "Employed for the hunting of Marsh Fowl." As Levesser neared the center of the square, two boys drawing water at the pump made a sudden noise that caused the dog to start. The animal, it is alleged, collided with Pierre Levesser, causing him to fall into a puddle near the trough. In so falling, he suffered damage to his clothes, "being of fine imported Cloth and to his Neck and Wrist Bands." Rising from the mire, Mr. Levesser, with a smart swing of his stick, caught the beast a blow upon the head, ripping the hide behind the ear, and causing blood to flow. Whereupon he raised his stick again, raining blows upon the animal, which had set up a horrid yelping, until the noise drew the attention of sundry persons, including the Reverend Nathaniel White, the pastor of that church and an old man then. He hastened to remonstrate, speaking, it is said, as follows:

"Mr. Levesser, I beg you stay your hand. The rod should be used in sorrow, not in anger; and this is Sabbath eve, Mr. Levesser, and this noise is unfitting before God's house."

Pierre Levesser paused for a moment in his beating, and the dog still cowered at his feet.

"God's house or the devil's house," it is alleged Pierre Levesser replied, "I'll teach my dog his manners."

There was once a time when no religious man would

have tolerated such speech, but our town was changing then.

"Friend," said the Reverend White, "it is not the beating to which I raise objection,— but consider the time and place and the language."

Whereupon, it is alleged that Pierre Levesser called the Reverend White "an old black crow", at which the Reverend White hastened off for help. By this time the noise had attracted many persons, but none raised a hand until Matthew Scarlet came forward. He was the Scarlet who owned the ropewalk then, and it was like a Scarlet, since the Scarlets were always kind. Matthew Scarlet remonstrated, speaking as follows:

"Now shame on you, Mr. Levesser. I'll not stand and see a dog beat till he dies. Shame on you, sir, and you not two months married, to make a public spectacle; and many's the time I've seen that same dog guide you on your own pier when you were too far gone to guide yourself. Put up your stick and get home!"

And then one comes to Levesser's reply, and the words are shocking:

"The devil take your impudence!" was what he said. "Damn me, the dog is mine and I'll strike him thus — and thus. And, damn me, my wife is mine. I bought her, which is more than you did, and damn your red face for it; and I'll beat my dog or servant or my wife, and curse you."

There it is in black and white, though the rest is legend now.

Old John Swale looked grave and ill when young Levesser asked for his daughter's hand. It happened at the time when the great Swale house, built by his grandfather, Colonel Richard, the first of all the Swales, had been put upon the market—"To be sold," the notice read in the newsprint, "due to the Misfortunes of a Gentleman." It was like John Swale to phrase the notice thus, for the only consolation left him was that he came of the Swales of Norwich.

When Pierre Levesser called, and entered the paneled room which Richard Swale had built, John Swale did not rise from his chair, and did not bid him sit, because the Levessers were new. He listened, sitting motionless, as young Levesser spoke, watching the color in the young man's olive face. Though John Swale's world was narrow as a plank, he could measure a man by what he knew.

"Sir," said young Levesser, "I'll be round with you as you've been round with me. I want her because she has made me mad. I want her so I do not eat or sleep. She has that way about her that—I cannot help myself—"

"Young man," John Swale answered, "you speak out very strong."

"Sir," young Levesser replied, "I am only flesh and blood. And look you—who else with money would lead her to the church? And she—she loves me too!"

"Young man," John Swale answered, "it's lust!"

"And yet," said young Pierre, "she loves me—and that is that."

"Is it so?" said old John Swale. "D'you think she'll love the likes of you before a year's gone by?"

Pierre Levesser drew out his handkerchief and passed it across his lips.

"I think," he said, "we understand each other—eh?"

John Swale sat looking at him, curious and cold, and he did not move a finger on the arms of his great chair. Who knows? Perhaps Pierre Levesser guessed the hardness that was in the Swales, before he spoke again.

"You do not understand?" he said. "Of course, I will be pleased to pay."

"Wait," said old John Swale. "We'll be more private, if you would close the door."

What they spoke of no one will ever know, but when they finished, the old man saw him out. Patience Swale was waiting in the garden, and she could not keep her eyes off young Pierre, and she touched him before he reached to kiss her hand.

"Lust!" the old man said. "Lust is never love."

"Father," said Patience Swale, "what is it you are saying?"

"Richard shall have a ship," the old man said. "I'm saying that I sold you—and may the Lord have mercy on our souls! And you, young man—I say it in all friendship. You do not know us. Mind you use her well."

There is no doubt that he sold her, though the Swales have forgotten now. He sold her, knowing all the while that Levesser would not forget that money had passed between them.

"Dearest," said Pierre, "is it not a pity? Your father says he will see very little of us after we are wed."

There is no doubt Hugh Penny loved her. Hugh Penny was the bond servant of Pierre Levesser, indentured for ten years, and it was fortunate for Hugh that he knew his place too well to break his silence. He loved her in the shy way of tongue-tied youth, for whom a smile was enough reward, and he may have loved her without knowing that he loved, for no mention of it crossed his lips, when he told of her to his grandchildren and they themselves never thought of it when they told in turn.

It must have been well in the forenoon, for, though it was late September, Hugh Penny remembered the sun was high and warm on his back with the mild heat of autumn. Out on the river the fishing sloops were dancing in the breeze, and the tern were circling, now gray, now white, as the wind took them. Their cries and the smell of drying cod from the frames by the river were mingling with the odor of phlox in the bed where Hugh was working, exactly as life was mixed with sweetness and with death. The Master loved his flowers. Many a time the Master would touch them gently with the tips of his thin fingers, and the Master could not bear to see them die.

When the front door opened, Hugh knew that the Lady was standing there, and the air seemed warmer, once he knew. She would be gazing across the flower beds toward the river. He could fancy her in the carved frame of the front door, with the darkness of the hall behind her. The breeze would be playing at her dress, making her seem light and unsubstantial as a bird above the water; the wind would be pulling at a strand of her hair, perhaps, and her eyes would be steady as a pilot's.

"Joker!" she was calling. "Here Joker, Joker, Joker! Have you seen Joker, Hugh?"

On his knees among the phlox, Hugh looked up and

rubbed his hands upon his leather breeches, and then he wiped his face upon his sleeve.

"Sure, Madam," he said. "Joker do be gone with the Master this hour now to the countinghouse. They're loading the *Michelle* with rum."

"Ah, yes," she said. "He loves his master, doesn't Joker, Hugh?"

"Yes, Madam," Hugh said, "it do be wonderful how Joker loves him. He follows right to his back, come rain or shine or day or night — watching for him when he walks along the planking, in case the Master might fall off. Ay, there's a dog."

Her eyes were on him, pale and gray, and he saw that her face was pale that morning. Her face had often been pale, but it was cool and tranquil, and clear as an angel's face. The Lady had changed since he had known her first, as every one changed when they entered the Master's house.

"Oh, Lady," he wanted to say. "Oh, Lady, don't I know? Oh, Lady, he is sold to Satan and not for the likes of you — an angel lady."

The wind was blowing her hair, and blowing at her gray silk dress, and his voice was lost in his throat and in the crimson of his face. She was smiling at him, and in her eyes there was a light, kind and warm, like a candle in a window.

"Yes," she said. "Yes, Joker loves him."

That was all she said. She was not the one to talk, but somehow it seemed to Hugh that she had told him something.

It did not seem so long ago that he had stood by that very door with the black slave and the three maid-servants and the workmen from the wharf, when Mr. Levesser had brought her home. Her cloak had been about her, a light cloak and a hood. She had smiled as she stepped from the chaise and Mr. Levesser had smiled. He had been very elegant in his blue silk coat and his cane and his peruke.

"The devil!" said Mr. Levesser. "But your hand is cold; you are not afraid?"

"No," she said, "I am not afraid, Pierre."

His eyes were on her, wide and bright and staring.

"So," he said, "you are here at last. Hey? Are you sure you do not fear?"

"No," she said, "I am not afraid, Pierre."

And the Master had laughed in the way he laughed when he was pleased.

"The devil!" he said. "But this is so very fine! You, Penny, it is you I address. Bring me in the eau-de-vie."

"Pierre!" Somehow it seemed that she was suddenly a child frightened of the dark. "Pierre, you are not going to — drink to-night?"

"*Sacré!*" said the Master, and how he laughed and laughed. "Not too much — oh, no!"

Then all at once her voice was different, light and careless.

"As you wish," she said. "But before the servants — I did not know that you were coarse, Pierre."

It was like the Master, Hugh Penny knew, to wish all he owned afraid. That was all, a moment before the doorway, as the new chaise was being led off to the stable; but in that moment Hugh Penny knew that she was a lady, as good as any he had seen at home across the seas.

Now every one knew Master and his ways — our town was too small for secrets then. Every one knew what Pierre Levesser was about down at the Walsings' house, where the captains stayed when they were fresh from sea. When he brought Nellie Walsing home with him to dine, that lady did not blench. Hugh heard him tell of it in the parlor, where the lady sat before her needlework, with all the silks and satins on the chairs, and china on the mantle as delicate as lace.

"You will meet her," said the Master, "as you would meet your sister. Yes? She loves me, do you see?"

The lady laid her sewing down carefully on a little polished table. "Very well," she said, "but there is one thing, Pierre."

"Ah!" said Mr. Levesser. "So you choke upon it, eh? Mind that I bought you. Mind that I paid with money."

A touch of pink was in her cheeks but that was all. There was never a falter in the coolness of her voice.

"Please — not before the servants, Pierre," she said.

"To the devil with the servants!" said Pierre.

"Very well," she said. "I only wish to say I do not care, because — Are you listening? Do you flatter yourself? — I do not love you. That's been over long ago."

Now there was an odd thing, something you could scarce believe. It hurt the Master that she did not love him; he was as perverse and strange as that. The blood ran to his face like a reddish-purple wave. And there she sat, hands folded on her lap, watching him and smiling.

"Oh?" he said. "But you'll love me again, before I'm through. Ah, yes, Madam, on your knees."

And then she laughed, a brittle little laugh like delicate breaking china.

"Dear me," she said, "you must have everything, Pierre. Bring your women to your house. I've made my bed and I must lie in it."

And Mr. Levesser also laughed and bowed. When the Master wished, he had good manners.

Of course Hugh Penny knew. Every one knew that the Swales were poor; every one knew why Patience Swale had become his wife, when commerce was enveloping gentility and birth. He had bought her, the Master had, as surely as he ever bought a cargo of sound wine; and the Master was sharp as a knife at trade and not afraid of risk. The Master had sailed the sea himself; he knew ports and he knew agents and every danger of the sea. He had bought her, but there was something about her as unattainable as the image of an island upon water glassy calm, when the sails hang slack and the yards creak with the ocean roll.

Words . . . Hugh Penny was one who heard them always — words, hot and crackling, like the sparks from a log of pine. Words, but the Master never raised his hand to strike. Often, sitting by the fire, hard-handed, stupid, Hugh Penny wondered what would be left for him to do if the Master raised his hand.

"I tell you." He heard the Master's voice. He was listening and he was not ashamed. Out by the kitchen hearth, Joker, the water dog, had pricked up his ears at the sound of the voice and wagged his bushy tail so that it brushed the ashes on the bricks. "I tell you that I do not wish it."

"Don't you?" he heard the lady say. "But I'll see him just the same, Pierre. Listen, only listen. I'll not tell any tales, Pierre. Have I ever said a harsh word of you beyond this house? I tell you that I'm going. You know that he is ill."

"Not without me," the Master said. "Not to that old man. We go like lovebirds, side by side, or not at all. You understand, Madame?"

"Yes," she said, "but still I'm going."

"I have explained," Master said, "I have affairs to-morrow. The *Michelle* is loading. After that we'll go."

"No," she said, "I'll go before, Pierre."

Then a chair was pushed back sharply. Hugh Penny heard it slide across the floor. Then he heard the Master's voice as he had often heard it, shrill and unbridled as an angry child's.

"Damn your icy face!" the Master shouted. "You'll do what I say. Do you hear me speak?"

There was a pause and then the lady's voice answered. "Put down your cane," she said. "Put it down, Pierre."

There was another pause and Hugh Penny was on his feet, trembling outside the door, and then he heard her voice again.

"I knew you wouldn't dare. No, Pierre, I'll not be beaten."

"My dear," the Master said, "you will be — across the back, just so. Don't start! I simply touch you this time across the back, just so. You will be beaten if you leave this house to see him."

"Nonsense," said the lady; "you wouldn't dare, Pierre."

Then the door opened. Mr. Levesser was in the kitchen, gazing at Hugh Penny.

"Hey," said Mr. Levesser, "what are you making here?"

"Polishing your boots, Master," Penny answered, and a boot was in his hand.

"Did you hear anything?" the Master said.

"No, sir," Penny answered. "The house is that well built. Be you going out, sir?"

"Ay," the Master said, "to the countinghouse."

"Will you want a light, sir?" Penny asked. "It do be powerful dark, sir, down upon the wharf."

"No," said the Master. "Where's Joker? Hey, Joker! He'll be light enough. I'll keep my hand upon his head."

"Will you want me to fetch you, sir?" asked Penny, for he knew the Master's ways. "It's a narrow walk upon the wharf if you take a bit of liquor."

"Get to bed!" the Master said. "Joker will see me home. I keep my hand upon his head, like this. Hey, Joker! Joker knows the way."

The wind was blowing at her dress, making her seem light and airy like a cloud. She was pale but she was a part of the morning, as clear as the morning and the air.

"Yes," she said, "it's wonderful how Joker loves him."

Still on his knees beside the bed of phlox, Hugh
Penny cleared his throat.

"Ay, Ma'm," he said; "there's no accounting for the
ways of dogs or women either."

"Why, Hugh!" She smiled. It was wonderful to see
her smile; it took all the plainness from her face. There
was that about her, Hugh Penny always said, that made
you forget just who she was.

"Your pardon, Ma'm," said Hugh. "I don't know
much of women, please ye. But I know dogs. Yes,
Ma'm. I was the underkeeper of kennels across the
sea in Surrey. Dogs is odd and strange. They stick by
men like women do."

She was listening; it pleased him she was interested.
She had stepped into the garden and was standing
above him, so near that the hem of her dress nearly
touched him.

"Yes, Madam," said Hugh; "take Joker, Ma'm.
Now I've been in this house three years, what with ups
and downs. And now, with all respect, the Master is,
what you might say, solitary. He don't go to the tavern
but to his countinghouse, do you see? And there he sits
by himself, mind, with a bottle, like as not. And there
is Joker every night by the countinghouse door, Ma'm,
just like he was last night, waiting to see the Master
home."

"Truly?" said the lady. "How does he see the
Master home?"

Hugh knew that she was making play of him, but
he did not care. She had picked a bit of phlox and held
it to her face.

"How?" said Hugh. "It's this way, Ma'm. The

countinghouse door opens alongside the wharf, right where the tide is running. There's only a couple of planks between the door and the water. Sure, *you* know Master, Ma'm, when he's had a drop or two. I don't mean offense. He may not be thinking of the water and there's Joker. Joker, he keeps him alongside the warehouse. Joker barks and pushes at him. I've seen it with these eyes."

Then Hugh saw she was not listening; she was looking at him above that spray of phlox.

"Did he beat you this morning, Hugh?" she asked.

"Ay, Ma'm," said Hugh.

"Why?" she asked.

Hugh Penny grinned. "For not taking the dead flowers out of this here bed. You see, Ma'm, he hates to see flowers die."

"Yes," she said, "he loves his flowers. Did he hurt thee, Hugh?"

"No, Ma'm," said Hugh, "not me. We bonded folk, we're used to it. And I'm as tough as a hickory tree by now, Ma'm."

"Hugh," she said, "take this to take the pain away."

He started; she had dropped a piece of gold on the garden path before him.

"Thank you kindly, Ma'm," he said. "I'd take the stick ten times for the like of that."

"And now," she said, "go fetch my cloak. We're walking to my father's house."

Hugh got slowly to his feet and dusted off his leather breeches.

"Ma'm," he said, "it ain't my place to say it, but I wouldn't, were I you."

III

"Why?" she asked, but she knew why. There wasn't much that lady didn't know. Hugh lowered his voice. "Because he'll beat you, Ma'm," he said, "the same as he beat me. I heard him, lady. I heard him last night at candle time."

"Hugh," she said, "were you listening at the door?"

She was smiling at him, standing so near that he caught the smell of lavender and fine perfume from France.

"Sure, lady," he said. "I'll not let him beat you. Mind you that, for you're too fine a lady."

Then he caught his breath, because she had laid her hand on his. It was very light and cool, such a hand as he had never felt.

"There, you're a good boy, Hugh," she said. "Don't worry; he'll not beat me." Her hand had dropped away from his.

"There are some things," she said, "that are not done. Go in and fetch my cloak."

As they walked through the town, Hugh Penny strode three paces behind her, as a servant should, his eyes upon her back. It was good to see her walking; she stepped so light and fast, and folks looked at her when she walked by in a way that made him proud to walk behind her. As they passed the tavern door, which the Scarlets kept, he heard some one speak softly.

"Poor lady," some one said. "Heaven pity her, poor lady."

Enoch Porter, the silversmith, came from his shop and bowed. "Good day to you, Madam Levesser," he said. "Do the tankards suit you still?"

"Yes," she said, "they are noble tankards, sir."

And Israel Lake, the carriage maker, bowed. "Your new chaise will be ready, Madam, before the week is out," he said.

Hugh Penny knew that they would not have spoken so two years before, but now she was wed to a man of wealth, the glitter of which was on her like the sun.

As they left the town and walked along a wooded track, she paused and beckoned him beside her.

"There," she said, "it's better here. I feel sad walking through the town."

"And sure, what would make you sad, Ma'm?" Hugh asked. "There's none there that won't serve you."

"Because I have money," she said, "and that is all. I see the house we used to own."

"What?" said Hugh. "The Swale house, Ma'm?"

"Yes," she said. "The Swales aren't what they used to be."

John Swale, the lady's father, lived a mile from town on a bit of upland near the marshes, which he had lately bought, and Hugh knew whence the money had come to buy it. The house was at the end of the lane. Its southern windows looked across the marshes and the sea.

"Come in, Hugh," she said. "There's no need to wait outside."

Her father was seated alone by the coals of an open fire in an old, high-backed, wicker-seated chair. Hugh could tell he was a gentleman, though his clothes were very plain. On his face was a light and ghostly stamp, such as Hugh Penny had seen on dying men.

"You are better, sir?" she asked, and bent and kissed him on the cheek.

"Yes," her father said, "better in the morning."

Then Hugh saw the old man was looking at her with wide, steady eyes. "Are you happy, dear?" he asked.

"Yes," she said, "very happy, Father."

The old man nodded and stared at the glowing coals. "You shouldn't have wed him," he said.

"I was bound to do it," the lady said. "And I am very happy, Father."

"Yes," the old man said and sighed; "there was no money. When I remember——"

"Hush," she said. "There's no reason to remember."

"Easy come," the old man said, "and easy go. That's been the way."

"I swear," she said, "I'm very happy. Have you heard from Richard?"

"No," the old man said. "He's still at sea. Read me from the Bible, daughter. It was kind of Pierre Levesser to let you come."

"Yes," said the lady, "very kind."

For a long while Hugh Penny sat in a darkened corner, far across the room. Now and then he saw the faces of the old man and the lady and now and then he heard their voices very low. There was something alike in those two faces, Hugh Penny always said: steady, cool and hard.

"Daughter," said the old man, "does he never use thee wrong?"

"No," she said; "set thy mind at peace, sir."

"No," said the old man. "Richard would kill him when he came home."

"Pooh!" she said and laughed. "Richard need never bother." Hugh remembered the sound of that laugh later.

When she called him, the shadows were growing slant, close to the early autumn dusk. The wind was rising, and it was coming on to rain.

"Come, Hugh," she said. "Put on thy hat; it's time we were at home."

It was time and more than time, Hugh Penny knew. "Lord help her now," he muttered. "He'll know she's been away."

The Master knew it, for the Master was on the doorstep when they reached the Master's house. When he chose, he could hide his temper, so that you could hardly know that there was temper there. He was standing on his doorstep, Hugh remembered, looking out toward his wharf. There was a gale in the sky, rising steadily in the whistling of the southwest breeze. The Master was in his wine-colored satin coat, and his face had a dark look to it which Hugh always knew stood as a sign of trouble. The Master's voice was soft and throaty, far too soft, Hugh knew. Joker, the water dog, was at the Master's feet, wagging his tail at the sound of his master's voice.

"Penny," said the Master, "how splendidly you have cleaned the dead flowers out. I do not see a one. And there you are," he said to the lady. "Back from your little stroll, eh? Come, let me help you with your cloak. And you, Penny, get to the kitchen; the evening meal is ready."

Yes, the Master could be pleasant when he chose. Hugh could hear them before the dishes were cleared away and before the door was shut, speaking of this and that. He could hear the lady laugh and he could hear the Master laughing, but Hugh Penny knew the Master and he knew the Master's way of waiting. When the other servants were gone, Hugh still sat in the kitchen, looking toward the door.

The door opened some time later, Hugh did not know exactly when, and there was the Master smiling, with those large eyes of his wide and staring.

"Joker," he said, "here, Joker. Come in here. And you, Penny, get you gone to bed."

"Very good, sir," answered Hugh, and as he turned to go, he looked through the door. There were candles on the table and candles in the silver sconces on the wall. By their light he could see the lady sitting in a carved-back chair, as quiet as a picture.

"Good night to you, Hugh," the lady said.

"And many of them!" said the Master.

As the Master closed the door, there was a sharp, metallic sound which told Hugh that the bolt was drawn. And there Hugh stood in the kitchen, listening at the door, because he could not go away.

"Pierre," he heard the lady say, "what are you going to do?"

"Come, Joker," said the Master. "Where's my stick? Ah, there it is."

"What are you going to do, Pierre?" The lady's voice was louder.

There was a sound and a yelp and a sound and a yelp. Hugh's face was clammy wet.

"Trying the stick on the dog, my dear," the Master said. "It will serve. It's your turn now."

"You don't dare," he heard her voice, a little louder, but still level.

"Don't dare?" the Master said. "Strip off that dress. I'll not have it spoilt."

"Pierre," the mistress said. "I've married you and been a good wife. Take your hand from my shoulder. Don't forget—there're some things I'll not stand."

The Master said something which Hugh Penny could not hear. There was a cry from the lady, a clatter of a chair and the crash of glass.

"Fool!" said the Master. "You're weak as water. Hold still, my lady. Be patient like the dog."

And next minute Hugh Penny heard a sound which he knew well enough. It was the noise of the Master's cane upon the lady's flesh.

To raise one's hand against a master was a heavy crime in those days, but Hugh Penny forgot the danger. An instant later he found himself beating with his fist upon the panels of the door. He was shouting, "Leave that lady be!"

There was no answer. The lady did not cry out, not a single sound. And Hugh could hear the stick falling, falling, falling. A minute later—it could not have been more than a minute, though it seemed much longer—the Master stood before him, with his cane still in his hand.

"Here!" said the Master. "What mean you, beating on the door?"

For once Hugh Penny found his tongue. "You brute!" he shouted. "Ah—you dirty brute!"

Then something, it must have been the Master's

cane, struck him on the head and Hugh Penny was sprawling on the kitchen floor.

"That for you!" the Master said. "Good night, *ma belle*. Sweet dreams! I'll be down at the countinghouse, in case you're feeling lonely."

When the Master opened the kitchen door, a gust of wind came in, which made the candles gutter; the rain was coming with the wind and the night was black at pitch, but the Master did not heed it.

As Hugh Penny struggled to his knees, he saw the Master stride into the black, with a look—Hugh Penny always said—as though he had got the better at last of something. Even Hugh Penny could see that the blows were somehow a victory, the fire from smoldering words and looks, as sure as flame came up from a smoking tinder box.

Hugh Penny could hear him laughing. "That for all the Swales," the Master said, and then the door went slam and the kitchen was very still.

At the same moment with the closing of the door, there was scurrying of feet; Joker ran across the kitchen, whining, for he had seen the Master go.

A Swale had been beaten like a serving wench, one of the Swales who had ordered freedmen whipped when the colony was new. Fifty years ago no man could have dreamed of such an act. Yet a Swale had been beaten by a commoner, while the wind was whistling by the house in the beginning of a southwest gale. It was a time for winds, for all the world was changing.

He got dizzily to his feet, hardly hearing Joker's

whining then, though it always seemed to him afterwards that the whining of that dog and the whistling
of the wind were in back of everything. He walked
softly toward the parlor, where the door was still ajar.

"Madam!" he called. "Madam!" But there was no
answer. He thought that she would cry or sob, as any
woman should, not knowing what the Swales were made
of then.

In the parlor, one of those carved chairs had fallen
over, a wineglass and a crystal decanter had fallen to
the floor, with the wine run from it like blood over the
Turkey rug. The lady's back was to him; she was
seated in another chair, leaning her head upon a table,
pillowed in her arms, her slender fingers tightly
clenched. Her dress was torn, leaving her back half
bare, with red welts upon the soft white skin.

"Madam," said Hugh. "Ah, Lady, God help us
all."

Then she looked up, that thin face as motionless as
stone. Her eyes were wide but there were no tears in
them. Hugh could see the marks where the little
teeth had dug into the lower lip. Forgetting, seemingly,
that her dress was torn, she looked up as though nothing
at all had happened.

"Why, Hugh," she said, and he had never heard her
voice so soft. "There's blood upon thy face, Hugh.
Did he beat thee too?"

"Madam," said Hugh, "it's nothing, Madam. I'm
as tough as a hickory tree, I am. But if he hadn't
knocked me over, I swear I would have killed him for
what he done to you."

"Good boy," said the lady. "Good boy. But we

mustn't mind the Master. The Master's very wild."

Then something was clawing against his leg; it was Joker, wagging his tail and whining. The lady looked at him and sat up straight.

"What does Joker want, Hugh?" the lady said.

As he answered, the wind went whistling through the eaves, and in spite of the closed windows, he could hear the roaring of the sea. "Sure, he wants to go to the countinghouse with the Master, Ma'm. That's where the Master's gone."

"Yes," said the lady, "that's where the Master's gone. Where are Pomp and the maids, Hugh?"

"Sure, Ma'm, they're sleeping in the ell. Rest you easy, Ma'm, they did not hear a sound."

Then Joker was whining again, running here and there.

"Joker," said the lady, "come here, Joker." But Joker did not come; he kept running here and there about the room, sniffing, whining, looking at the lady, looking back at Hugh, raising himself on his hind legs toward the window where the rain was slapping.

"Yes, Ma'm," said Hugh. And he wanted to talk of something else, so that he could forget the lady's back. "Yes, Ma'm, he do be wanting to get to the Master. He knows it's an ill night for the Master to be walking on the wharf. I'll be letting him out, so that he can watch the Master, Ma'm. Then I'll get you a glass of spirits, if you please."

"No," said the lady, "it's too bad a night for Joker, Hugh. Tie him by the fire."

"But, Ma'm —" said Hugh. And then he stopped.

"Tie him by the fire," she said. "And sit up till the

Master comes. And give me a candle, Hugh. I am going to sleep."

"Yes, Ma'm," said Hugh. "I'll tie him up."

The wind was coming to a fearful gale, so that it was like voices outside, all sorts of voices. It made him shiver sometimes, sitting by the kitchen fire, because with all the wind Joker kept on whining. Even when Hugh slapped him, he kept on whining. Sometimes, what with the rain and the wind, he could think he heard the Master's steps coming toward the door, dancing and unsteady, but the Master never came.

It must have been along toward morning, because outside, through the windows, it looked a little gray, when all at once he had a fright.

He had not heard a sound except the wind, when all at once Joker gave a bark and Hugh Penny looked behind him. There was the lady, all in white, and beautiful, oh, beautiful. Her hair was down her back, brown hair which was almost gold.

"Hugh," she said, "bring me a cloak. I'm cold. The wind keeps me awake, Hugh. Has the Master not come yet?"

"No, Ma'm, he ain't come yet."

"I wonder what can be keeping him," the lady said. "Has he ever been so late?"

"No, Ma'm, he ain't," said Hugh.

Then the lady looked toward the gray in the windows and drew a deep breath. Then she looked at Joker and then at Hugh and drew another breath.

"Hugh," she said, "I'll have some spirits now, a very little in a glass. I feel so very cold."

Hugh Penny was the one to open the front door when they brought the Master home. They brought

him on a shutter from the mud flats, where two boys
had found him in the morning, when they went to dig
for shellfish at ebb tide. The Master's clothes were
thick with mud and bits of weed and stone, which made
the Master seem more like a being from the sea than
a man who had walked on land.

The Master's lips were twisted back and his eyes were
open wide and staring up at Hugh, for all that he was
dead.

"Penny," he seemed to say, "did you not let out
the dog?"

They brought him to the great chamber and laid him
on the bed, taking care first to move the coverlet away.
The lady watched them, leaning against the wall with
her arms crossed on her breast.

"Hugh," she said, "go with the men and give them
spirits in the kitchen."

As the bearers of the Master tiptoed down the stairs,
Hugh found himself turning back. The lady was standing by the chamber window, staring out toward the
town, where the houses stood in rows, with the church
spires above them and the weathercocks upon them,
shining golden. What she was staring at, Hugh Penny
could not tell.

"Will that be all, Madam?" he said.

"Yes," she said, "that's all."

"Will you watch with him alone, Ma'm?" Penny
asked.

"Yes," she said, "I'll be with him alone." And then
she paused, looking at the Master. "Wait," she said.

"Yes, Madam?" said Hugh.

"Bring up Joker," said the lady. "Joker always loved
him."

6

Ships Must Sail

"Make yr Cheaf Trade with the Blacks and Little or none with the white people if possible to be avoided. Worter yr Rum as much as possible and sell as much by the short mesur as you can."

— *From Instructions of an early New England Merchant.*

≈ 6 ≈

Ships Must Sail

D ANIEL SWALE HAS LEFT A RECORD
of when ships once crossed our bar at night, in
defiance of the Crown. It was an old man's
recollections — one must remember that.

Yet something of Daniel Swale is still left in the
Swale house. On entering the room where Daniel
Swale drank his wine, after he had left the sea, you
could not help but feel a presence melancholy but
kind. Mr. Dennis Swale, who lived there till very
recently, was the only one who was oblivious. Each
evening after dinner, he would light his cheap cigar and
stare placidly at the picture of Daniel Swale above the
mantelpiece. It was a portrait of a lean man in a sea
cloak, with wide, dark eyes.

"Now there's an old sea dog for you," Dennis Swale
would say, "and, just between you and me, he bought
blacks off the Guinea coast. There's the type to put
fear in a forecastle. Why, when he was a child, he
pulled a lion's tail."

He never saw that Daniel Swale was a man with a vision, who followed visions always. He never thought of Daniel Swale as sitting by his block-front desk in that very room, listening for old sounds that even then were dim.

It was the time of the enforcing of the old "molasses act", just before the Revolutionary War, which Daniel Swale described in his recollections, which used to lie in the block-front desk in the Swale's library.

"The door to Mr. Whistle's private room was open" —the words were written in Daniel Swale's flowing hand—"and I was not a fool, and I heard Mr. Whistle speak as follows, viz:

"'I'll ship in French molasses duty free, as sure as I'll have my rum watered on the Guinea coast, and it's nobody's affair, if you should ask me that. What's trading for? The ships must sail.'

"I asked Mr. Whistle," wrote Daniel Swale, "to ship me as a boy. I came there with John Scarlet. It was before the Lion come to town."

Even as he wrote it, the lion was in his mind, mingling vaguely with the ships, and one can understand it, for the mainsprings had not rusted yet. There are boys in Haven's End right now, who think the same thoughts, and you can hear their voices calling in the streets. Sometimes it almost seems that they are other voices calling through the distance of our town, not the distance of its space but of its time,—calling with an unchanging timbre.

Mr. Whistle's countingroom was empty. Outside, Mr. Whistle's schooner *Sally* was lying by the wharf, high up in the water, for her cargo was all out; and the wind was blowing easterly. There would be rain by night. Hogsheads of molasses covered the wharf, and the air was full of flies. And over everything was a thick, sweet odor, heavy but not unpleasant, of molasses and of rum from the distillery.

They were speaking in the private room, and Daniel knew the voices. One was Mr. Pringle's, the Collector of the Port, and the other was the Reverend Ezra Dole's, who was minister of the old First Church.

"But I tell you," the Collector was saying, "the Commissioner is coming."

"Let him come," said Mr. Whistle. "He hasn't seized a cargo yet."

"But there's danger," said the Reverend Dole. "Thomas Whistle, will you not consider me?"

"You've put your pennies in," said Mr. Whistle, "but you don't steer the ship."

All things seemed possible to Daniel, for he was very young, but even then he wondered what business a minister had on Mr. Whistle's wharf.

"Thomas Whistle——" said the Reverend Mr. Dole.

"My dear sir," said Mr. Whistle, "you should have thought before. Your name is down with mine as owner."

And the door opened, and out came Mr. Dole, with Mr. Pringle close upon his heels. As they passed through the countingroom, immersed in their own thoughts, their faces looked the same, though the Reverend Mr. Dole was large and heavy, all in black, and Mr. Pringle was thin and small, in a blue coat and nankeen breeches. It seemed as though a hand which had held their faces smooth and suave had suddenly loosed its hold. Mr. Dole's heavy cheeks were sagging. The wrinkles about his eyes were deep and loose, and his mouth was hanging relaxed, like a man's mouth in his sleep.

Daniel Swale was the one who knocked at Mr. Whistle's door, because Johnny Scarlet did not dare to knock, but once they were in Mr. Whistle's room, they both stood silent, not knowing where to start. Mr. Whistle was the great man of our town, rich from the Indies and from the African Trade. Mr. Whistle was seated before a table. His coat and wig were off, hanging each upon a peg. His face was very thin, like all the Whistles' faces. His nose was sharp and pointed, and his lips were set in a downward curve.

"Now what brings you in here, boys?" Mr. Whistle said.

Daniel shuffled his feet and twisted his hat between his hands.

"Please, sir," said Daniel, "do you wish to ship two cabin boys?"

"Who are you?" Mr. Whistle asked.

"Yonder," began Daniel, pointing, "is Johnny Scarlet—"

"Yes," said Mr. Whistle, "I know a Scarlet when I see one,—and you're a Swale, I'll wager. Who's your father, boy?"

And Daniel told him that it was Richard Swale, and he remembered that Mr. Whistle pursed his lips.

"Does your father know you're here?" he asked.

"No, sir," answered Daniel.

"Well," said Mr. Whistle, "he wouldn't like it, if he knew. Do you mean to run away?"

"I will, sir, if you'll take me," Daniel answered.

"You, Scarlet, go see Captain Marigold and tell him that I sent you," Mr. Whistle said.

"And me, sir?" asked Daniel Swale.

Before he answered, Mr. Whistle crossed one knee above the other.

"There's kindliness in me," said Mr. Whistle, "Christian kindliness, when I'm ashore. You have not got the strength. We don't ship weak boys on a voyage—"

In his humiliation it seemed to Daniel that his words were lodged fast in his throat.

"Another boy's thought broken, eh?" Mr. Whistle said. "I know. Smash 'em! Smash the lot of 'em as quickly as you can. Listen—there's no justice in this world but strength. Come back when you can pull a rope."

"Will you take me, sir?" asked Daniel Swale. "Will you take me, if I'm strong?"

"Yes," said Mr. Whistle.

He never thought that he was changing the life of Daniel Swale or sending him on a quest among the shadows.

There was a witch in Haven's End then. Her name was Madam Haight, and Daniel knew her. All the children and slaves and bond servants knew Madam Haight. He had seen her often enough walking across the square, an object of derision and superstitious fear. She wore a country woman's bonnet and a billowing gown of rich green satin, patched with red. She had come by ship from Quebec, they said, after the late war, the wife of a British officer who had died on the Plains of Abraham; but others said she was no wife.

It was raining, Daniel remembered, when he reached Madam Haight's house. It stood on the edge of the cedar swamp, where deer still wintered, a dwelling of a single room.

"Come in, Dan Swale," she said.

He stood close to the threshold, shivering from the rain and wondering how she knew his name. Her hair was jet-black, streaked with gray, and her face was rough with whiskers like a man's. The wind was blowing through cracks where the clapboarding had fallen. A row of dresses hung on pegs along the wall, all silk, but torn and soiled.

"Come in," she said.

Now that he was on the threshold, Daniel remembered that he was half ashamed.

"Thank you, Madam," he began.

But he could not finish. He could see the rafters heavy with bunches of dried twigs, and with roots like old hands, and in the darkness he saw a kettle upon the embers of the hearth.

"Herbs," she said, "herbs and roots, those be. The selectmen cannot move me on, while the roots are growing. Yonder's bay leaves and sweet fern, and the daisy root for deafness. The gentlemen and ladies come here and the doctors too. Sure, I know gentlemen and ladies, and I know the stars—"

"Madam," said Daniel Swale, "may I ask a question, if you please?"

"Sure," she said. "I know questions and the answers to the Alpha and Omega."

Daniel cleared his throat, but he could not ask the question which he wished.

"Madam," said Daniel Swale, "is it true you know the dark spirits of the air?"

He saw her smile, and her eyes were like dark water.

"There are light ones and dark ones. I've seen 'em both," she said, "since I was pretty."

The rain was louder on the roof when she had finished speaking. Pomp, the black slave at home, had his spirits too. Daniel had heard him calling on them by rattling bones at night. The Reverend Mr. Dole himself confessed to spirits. Daniel had heard him when the church was still.

"Oh, Lord," Mr. Dole would pray, "save us from the tyrannies of unjust laws and save us from the Dark Spirits of the air."

"Sure," the witch was saying, "you'll not hear the spirits till you get old. What do you want, Dan Swale?"

"Madam," said Daniel Swale.

But he could not say it, for she was only like a poor old woman.

"Speak out," she said — "speak out. Every one is wanting something who comes here — love or health, and you're too young for love."

"If you please, Madam," he said, "I want strength, if you please, to go to sea."

And then she began to laugh.

"Sure," she said, "you won't need no strength. — The rain is over. Get on home."

He never told where he had been. He would not

have dared to tell, when his last hope was gone that night.

"Wait," the witch called to him, just as he turned to go, and he could see her in the shadows, laughing.

"Wait," she said, "I'll tell ye. When next you see a lion, pluck two living hairs out of his tail, and those will make ye strong."

"But, Madam," Daniel answered, for he could still be literal, "there are no lions here."

"No," she said, "there are no lions—and no charity either, hereabouts."

Only the next morning, when he was standing in the square with Johnny Scarlet, he knew she was a real witch. There was no reason that they should have been there, unless it was pure destiny. It was high noon, and warm for early summer, and the river was flat calm, so that all the wharves and ships were double. Two ships were in from the Indies, with specie in their cabins, and you could hear the sailors singing, as they warped them up to Scarlet's wharf.

"Chi'lly," you could hear their voices shouting, "Chi'lly . . . Chi'lly!"

Then a hand bell was ringing, jingle, jingle. It was the town crier, coming down the street past the shops with their swinging signs, and as he walked, he tolled his bell and shouted in a sing-song voice.

"Hear ye! Hear ye!" he was shouting. "For those who be curious at the wonders of the world—there be a lion at the New George Inn, a lion new come from Barbary. A lion brought in from Africa. His cage is on a wain drawn by two yoke of oxen—a monstrous lion—"

Daniel Swale never forgot the crier's voice, echoing in the still, warm air.

"A lion. A wondrous beast, the size of a calf and twenty times the weight. There be hair on his withers, and a shaggy mane, and the eyes and nose of a cat. He is worth the examination of all the curious—for a shilling a head. A lion at the George Inn yard—a shilling for a sight you may never see again!"

It seemed to Daniel Swale that the square was suddenly silent and that he was standing all alone. Then the buildings and the square seemed very close, and the ships' masts in the river were like towers.

"John Scarlet," he said, "have you a shilling?"

"Yes," said Johnny Scarlet, "and that's more than you."

"John Scarlet," said Daniel Swale, "will you play me at chuck farthing? I want to make a shilling."

"Why do you need a shilling?" Johnny Scarlet asked.

"To see the lion," Daniel answered. "I need to see that lion."

There had been a trained pig before and two trained dogs, and once a dancing bear, but there had never been a lion.

John Scarlet made a hole with his heel and marked a line four paces off.

"Chuck," he said. "What are you shivering at?"

"I'm not shivering," said Daniel Swale. He forgot that he was playing chuck farthing in the public square, and all he saw was the brown ground and broad copper pieces in the dust, until a hand seized his collar and jerked him backward off his feet. And then he turned to see the Reverend Mr. Dole.

There was no gentleness with children then, and Mr. Dole was earnest in his duty.

"So the children are at it too?" he said. "Pick up that filthy money."

As Daniel stooped to pick it up, Mr. Dole dropped his collar and seized him by the ear.

"Eightpence, eightpence," Mr. Dole was saying. "You'll thank me when you're older. The money must go to the poor, Daniel. It is not fit to keep."

Mr. Dole's fingers were very strong. He had twisted the ears of other boys. The pain made Daniel wish to cry aloud. The tears were starting from his eyes, but even in his pain he thought of Mr. Whistle's counting-house.

"Wait," he said, "I wished to see the lion."

"Daniel," said Mr. Dole. "Take that!"

Daniel took it, for there was nothing else to do.

It was a blow and nothing more, and it was a time when blows were freely given, but that blow was different, though Daniel could not tell why. It gave him a sense of indignity and of grave humiliation, because Daniel knew that Mr. Dole would not have struck if he had been a strong boy. The air seemed filled with flashing lights. There was a taste of brimstone in his mouth, and all respect and decency were lost to him in a wave of hate. His foot lashed out before he thought, and he had committed sin.

"You imp!" shouted Mr. Dole.

"Then give me back my eightpence!" Daniel shouted back. There seemed to be a swarm of bees buzzing in his head, but he heard another voice.

"Leave him," some one was saying. "Leave him for the moment, Mr. Dole."

As Daniel looked up, he saw that two gentlemen were standing very near him. One was Mr. Whistle, very thin and tall, and beside him was a heavy, red-faced gentleman, whom Daniel had never seen, dressed in a riding cloak and boots.

"Yes," he said, "leave down the brat. I've come to speak on business."

"This is Mr. Dickey," Mr. Whistle said, "who has come to see how our collector runs the port."

Mr. Dole's face twitched and Daniel saw him dig his fingers against his palms. Mr. Dole did not answer, and Mr. Whistle cast a quick, hard glance at Mr. Dole.

"Well," said Mr. Dickey, "every one's gone mad in this cursed country. It's not so odd to find a minister breaking law."

"Sir," said Mr. Dole,—and Daniel saw that his face was long and white. "Fifty years ago, you'd be in the pillory for half that speech."

Mr. Whistle waved his hand, still looking hard at Mr. Dole.

"Hush, Ezra," he said. "Mr. Dickey, in this wild place where all of us have our wrongs, we have to live. I trust you'll report them, Mr. Dickey, when you sail for home."

"Sir," said Mr. Dickey, "I wish to heaven you were with me there and I'd have you safe in Newgate."

Mr. Whistle raised his eyebrows.

"Sir," he said, "you use harsh words. You say we have made a false declaration, but your collector, who carries His Majesty's commission, has passed our cargo."

"And I tell you," Mr. Dickey raised his voice, "the collector is a piece of all the rest of you. I tell you — don't stop me while I speak — your schooner came in deep-laden from the Indies. You made declaration on five hogsheads of molasses. Do you take me for a fool? There were twenty hogsheads in that hold, if there was one. Now where's the rest?"

"Can you find it?" Mr. Whistle asked.

Mr. Dickey drew in his breath and turned to Mr. Dole.

"Sir," he said in a different tone, "this is no dealing for a minister. If you make a full confession, I'll leave you out."

"Mr. Dole gave me a small sum for a venture. I told you he knows nothing about molasses," said Mr. Whistle very quickly.

"Thomas," Mr. Dole said, "Thomas —"

"Ezra, leave this to me," said Mr. Whistle. "Mr. Dickey, your government does wrong to interfere with trade. We've made this land, and there'll be bloody revolution."

Mr. Dickey smiled and blinked.

"D'you think I'm to be threatened by a lot of smugglers?" he said.

Mr. Whistle smiled also.

"Whistle," Mr. Dickey said at length, "will you

open your warehouse doors, or will you have me smash them down?"

Mr. Whistle took another pinch of snuff.

"May I ask," he inquired, "just how you're going to smash them?"

"Did you ever hear of a writ?" asked Mr. Dickey. "I've got one in my pocket with rights to break and force."

Mr. Whistle rubbed his chin, and he and Mr. Dickey stared at each other for another moment.

"Thomas," said Mr. Dole, "Thomas—"

"Ah," said Mr. Whistle, "one of those writs of assistance? Who'll help you, Mr. Dickey? I can only think of one man with the courage in this whole town."

"So you'll resist the law, will you?" Mr. Dickey raised his voice again, until it rang across the square. "I've a dozen troopers following. They'll be here in town by night."

"My dear sir," said Mr. Whistle, "there's no use being round. I've told you there were only five hogsheads in the hold. The rest were water casks for ballast. Isn't that enough?"

"And I say," Mr. Dickey answered, "we'll look at those water casks to-night, as soon as my men ride in."

There was always talk in those days of the "sugar and molasses act", and every boy there knew that rum and sugar and molasses made Haven's End. The lines on Mr. Dole's face were deeper, and he seemed almost ill, and then Daniel saw that Mr. Dole was looking at him strangely.

"Get you home, boy," said Mr. Dole. "I'll report it to your father before the evening meal."

Then the bell of the town crier was ringing, and Daniel heard his voice above the other noise.

"Hear ye! Hear ye! A Lion in the George Inn yard . . ."

Mr. Whistle sighed, looking about the square. From a distance men were staring at them, standing in small groups and whispering. Daniel Swale thought nothing of it then. He only knew much later that he had witnessed an event of a turbulent time, that was destined to lead to the war of the Revolution. He was thinking of the lion, and he wanted to be strong.

It was Pomp who told him when he got home. Pomp was the Swales' black slave, and the story was that he had been a king, but Pomp was carrying a load of wood, like any other man, toward the kitchen door.

"Master Dan," he said, "the prayer man — he been here."

"Did he see my father?" Daniel asked, "Is my father angry?"

Pomp showed his white teeth. They had been filed to points before he left the Guinea Coast, and there was a great hole in his flat nose from which had hung a ring.

"Pomp," said Daniel, "there's a lion at the Inn. Tell me, Pomp, is it true that hairs from a lion's tail will make you strong?"

Pomp showed his teeth again and scratched the matted hair upon his head.

"Mebbe so," he said, "black man no can tell. When

I was boy like you — me, I had the lion claw from witch fella. Me — he made me strong."

When Daniel reached the dark front entry, he heard his father calling him from the parlor. It was a small room, which was simple and unpainted. The furniture was mostly oak, such as richer families had discarded for mahogany. Upon the wall by the chimney hung a steel cap and breastpiece, which his great-great-grand-father had worn when he led a regiment in King Philip's War. His father was standing by the window, in threadbare, snuff-colored clothes, and his Aunt Levesser was there also, sitting in an old oak arm-chair. She had come to live with them after Daniel's mother died.

"Daniel," said his father, "is it true you kicked our minister?"

Before he answered, he saw his aunt was looking at him with a half-smile on her lips, which seemed to tell one everything, yet nothing.

"If you please, sir," said Daniel, "he took my eight-pence and wrung me by the ear."

"Take off your coat," his father said, "and fetch the birch from behind the door."

It was like his father, that even, melancholy justice, which stood above adversity and joy. Daniel always remembered him as he rose and took the rod, testing it in his heavy hands, without a change of feature.

"Daniel," he said, "Mr. Dole is an honest man. Come here and take your stripes."

Richard Swale laid the birch smartly a dozen times across Daniel's shoulders, while Daniel held his breath. Though he felt the gross injustice, he could feel no resentment against his father for it, but instead a growing anger against the Reverend Mr. Dole.

"Richard," his aunt said, "you always strike too hard."

"There," said his father. "Daniel, why were you so late in coming home?"

"If you please, sir," said Daniel, "there's a lion at the Inn. Please, sir, may I have a shilling to see the lion?"

His father walked to the window and stood looking out, his hands clasped behind his back. Richard Swale always pondered over small things as though they were important.

"And why do you wish to see a lion?"

"Fiddlesticks!" said his aunt, "I'll give the boy a shilling."

Richard Swale turned from the window and walked across the room and back.

"Dan," he said, "you'll have no shilling, and you, Madam, you shall give none to him. You shall go to the minister instead, Daniel, and make him your apology. That will cost you nothing, and he shall be your lion."

Only long afterwards Daniel knew there was a similarity between his father and himself, the same harsh humor, the same unbending will. And that was when their wills clashed for the first time and the last. Daniel heard his own voice, thin and high, and it did not sound like his own.

"I'll not go, sir," he said. "You can beat me, but he wronged me as much as I did him."

There was a long, dull silence. He could clearly

hear the thudding of the wood, which Pomp was piling by the kitchen door. The look on his father's face was very strange, and his aunt was first to speak.

"Why," she said, "there's still life in the Swales."

His father had laid his hand on a chair back.

"Madam," he said, "do you taunt me, because I obey the law?"

Madam Levesser had risen. There was something in that room which Daniel could not see, but he could feel it in the silence.

"Richard," she said, "even the boy sees clearer. Will you send him to make apologies to an — informer, Richard Swale?"

"Daniel," said his father, "leave the room."

And Daniel left, and he was glad to go, but even in the passage he heard his father speaking.

"Madam," he was saying, "I am an honest man. If any one is an informer, it is I. Mr. Dole came here to ask me my advice. What was there for an honest man to give? I told him to lodge information with authority. I told him to tell what he knows and be free of it — that the molasses will be moved to Mr. Whistle's barn to-night."

That was how Daniel knew, and he knew that his father was an honest man. All at once he could see it very clearly. He could see why Mr. Whistle had taken his snuff and had smiled in the square that noon. There would be no molasses when they smashed his warehouse door, because he would move it after dark. He knew that Mr. Dole would tell, and that telling would be right, and yet his heart was beating faster.

Then he was standing in the dooryard, and the wind was blowing toward the trees, softly as it sometimes did toward evening, and, from where he stood, he could see the river and the wharves and the masts of all the ships, like a strange, small forest along the river bank. The new clock in the First Church was striking out the hour of seven when he turned and saw his father standing near him.

"Daniel," said his father, "Daniel—" Then he stopped as though he could not go on, and Daniel remembered how tall his father seemed and how the wind blew at his wig.

"Daniel," said his father, "will you go to Mr. Dole?"

"No, sir," he said, "I will not."

His father stood looking toward the river, not a muscle moving on his face.

"Daniel," he said, "if you do not go, you will not be welcome in my house."

And Daniel knew his father spoke the truth, as surely as he knew that he could not go. The wind was blowing from the sea, as salt and bitter as the tears that filled his eyes.

"Father," he said, "Father—" He knew his father loved him in a way, and his father laid a hand gently on his shoulder.

"There," he said, "that is better."

He did not know why Daniel wept. He did not know, because the Swales were endowed with a peculiar stubborn blindness.

"That is better, Daniel," said Richard Swale. "Let me know when you come back."

As he turned and walked away, Daniel watched his father's shadow on the grass. It was dark and very long and ugly. He was turning from the dooryard, when a thing happened which he was never to forget.

"Daniel," he heard some one calling, "stop a moment, Daniel."

It was his aunt who was calling. She was coming down the path, past a cluster of sumac bushes.

"Daniel," she whispered, and pressed something in his hand, "here's thy shilling, Daniel."

Then suddenly her voice broke, and he remembered that her voice was sweet like running water, and that her arms were about him, and that she pressed him to her close; and then he found himself sobbing, his head buried in her gray silk dress.

"Poor Daniel," she was saying. "We love bright things."

The George Inn stood on the main street, then some distance away from the shipping. It had the same simplicity of line as the older tavern by the water, but it was larger, with fine, panelled chambers and a high, carved doorway. Instead of one great room with a sanded floor, there was a ballroom where a fiddler sometimes played, and a parlor and a taproom which opened to the yard, where the Boston stage changed horses. On the street outside Daniel was surprised to see so many people, most of them mechanics and sailors.

"Curse the Customs," he heard some one saying.

"Ay," said a voice that Daniel knew. "Speak up

and stand for your rights. Now there's the bully boys!"

It was Captain Marigold who was speaking. Captain Marigold was one of Mr. Whistle's masters, a small, broad man in canvas breeches. His hair, already white, was done up in a clubbed eelskin, and the whiteness of his hair seemed to bring out all the sly wrinkles that surrounded the Captain's eyes and mouth.

"Sure," said Captain Marigold. "Now there's the bully boys. There'll be rum enough when you finish up tonight."

Their voices were low; they kept staring at the inn door as they spoke, but farther on at the Anchor Tavern, Daniel could hear other voices that were louder.

Some one was shouting down the street: "Free trade and rum!"

Captain Marigold cocked his head to one side, and the wrinkles deepened about the corners of his mouth.

"Look lively, boys," he called. "Here comes Mr. Whistle! Give him a helping hand."

Sure enough, Mr. Whistle was walking down the street, bland and smiling, with a gold-headed walking stick tucked under his right arm.

"Marigold," he said, "does everything go well?"

"Sure sir," said Captain Marigold, "fine as silk. The boys are ready."

"Right," said Mr. Whistle. "Then get moving."

And Daniel knew as sure as he was standing by the inn that they would move Mr. Whistle's molasses from the warehouse as soon as it was dark, over to his barn. He was sure with some intuition of his own that Mr. Whistle did not know that Mr. Dole had told. His heart was beating wildly as he walked through the tavern door and turned into the taproom. It seemed to Daniel that he had never been so small and weak. Should he tell Mr. Whistle when his father had not told?

The taproom was already lighted by candles on every table. Two boys in white aprons were carrying bowls and pewter cups to all the gentlemen. William Scarlet, the owner of the inn, was in his apron, standing by a trestle table, where a dozen men were seated, smoking long clay pipes, talking in low voices and staring across the room. Mr. Parlin was there and one of the Levessers, and Mr. Busk.

"Look," said Mr. Parlin. "Here comes one of Swale's brats now."

"Ah!" said Mr. Levesser. "Here's a toast for him. Telltales — Tar 'em and roll 'em in a feather bed!"

Goodman Scarlet glanced across the room.

"I beg you be more easy," he said. "There's trouble here enough."

Daniel followed his glance and saw that he was looking at a gentleman seated all alone, who was drinking placidly at a glass of flip. It was Mr. Dickey, whom Daniel had seen in the square. Mr. Dickey was still in his riding cloak and boots, and his look made Daniel sure that Mr. Dickey had been told. Mr. Dickey was only waiting until his troopers came.

"Now," said Goodman Scarlet, "what do *you* want, Dan Swale?"

"If you please," said Daniel, "I've come to see the lion."

Goodman Scarlet took his shilling.

"Then get out and see him," he said.

Outside in the inn yard it was growing dusk, but four pine knots were lighted, so that any one could see. Some men stood about a great cage upon a heavy wain. The wheels of the wain were painted red and yellow. There was a cage upon the wain, like the Sabbath-breaker's cage upon the square, and in the cage Daniel saw the lion.

Now that he saw, he felt a disappointment, which was often to come upon him, when he saw the other wonders of the earth. The beast was nearer the size of a dog than a calf, and his coat was mangy. He was pacing back and forth inside his cage and staring out with sleepy eyes.

"I warn you," his owner was saying, a mangy-looking man like the lion; "I warn you not to come too near the cage."

Then some one began to laugh, but Daniel hardly heard, as he edged nearer. He knew that all his life was in the balance.

For a moment he hesitated, close to the cage, where there was a sharp, unpleasant odor, like the smell of a thousand cats, and then he seemed to be as cold as ice. His eyes were on the beast's tail that was moving softly, like a great rope cable frayed upon the end. He was as cold as death, but it seemed to him that something inside him made him move without his own volition, and he could never tell exactly what occurred.

He heard the keeper shout, and then he heard a snarl that was like a clap of thunder. He had snatched for the lion's tail between the bars, and next he was staggering backward. Some one had pulled him back.

There was a gash upon his arm. All at once his sleeve was red and moist, but he could see, even though his sight was dizzy, that he held a tuft of hair.

The next he knew he was in the taproom, where they must have carried him, seated on a bench, leaning against the wall. It was as if a curtain were drawn from before his eyes. A roar of voices was about him, first blurred, then clearer, and Mr. Whistle's face, and Goodman Scarlet's and Mr. Levesser's and Mr. Dickey's were all staring at him. Some one was binding a cloth around his arm, and the lion's owner was speaking.

"I tell you," he was saying, "he stepped straight up and tweaked his tail."

"Now!" said Goodman Scarlet. "It's what I tell you, gentlemen; there's a devil in them Swales."

"Give him a dram!" said Mr. Dickey. "Why would he want to be pulling at a lion?"

"Ah, Mr. Dickey," Mr. Whistle said, in that pleasant voice of his, "we may twist a greater lion's tail, before we're through with this."

"It's what I tell you, gentlemen," Scarlet repeated. "There's a devil in them Swales."

"Here," said Mr. Dickey. "What's the noise out yonder? Do I hear a wagon rolling in the street?"

"Mr. Dickey," said Mr. Whistle, "I'd advise you not to look for any wagon. It's a hard walk to the door."

"Very well," said Mr. Dickey; "but may I add my troopers will be coming?"

But Daniel Swale hardly listened. He was looking at his hand. It was still tight clenched, for all the blood upon it, and the lion's hairs were in it, dripping with the blood.

"Daniel," said Scarlet, for he was a kindly man, "are you feeling better now?"

"Yes, thank you." Daniel got to his feet. The floor seemed to move beneath him, but he kept his balance, and he seemed very light, as though a burden had been lifted from him. He knew that the witch was right. The lion had made him strong.

He remembered, not so long before, that he had sailed a small boat to the river mouth. He remembered how still she had been, dull and loggish, tied against the wharf, but she had been like a living thing, once he had pushed her free; and now he had the same freedom. The lion had made him strong. His arms were the same; his cheeks were thin, but he had dared to pull a lion's tail.

"Mr. Whistle," he said, "may I see you in the private room?"

Then they were alone in a small white room. There was a table in the center, Daniel remembered, covered with cards. Though cards were forbidden by the law, every one knew that gentlemen played them every night.

"Well," said Mr. Whistle, "what is it, boy?"

Daniel drew a hard, deep breath. His head was light, but his thoughts were very clear.

"Mr. Dole has told, sir," Daniel said. "They know you are moving the molasses to your barn. They'll seize it there to-night."

Mr. Whistle was looking at him, and as he looked, he reached to the table, took up a card and tore it sharp in two. Daniel Swale looked back at Mr. Whistle. He knew what he had done. He could never return to his father's house.

"Thanks," said Mr. Whistle. He did not seem surprised. "I'll move the molasses on."

"Please, sir," said Daniel, "I've been thinking you might do this: You can take the lion's wain. It is in the yard here. It's painted red and yellow. Draw out the wain, sir, and the lion's cage. Leave the lion in your barn, and put the hogsheads on. They'll think it is the lion, moving out of town."

"May I ask," said Mr. Whistle, "how you thought of that?"

"Please, sir," said Daniel, "it came to me — when I pulled the lion's tail."

7

Jack's the Lad

For Jack's the lad when maids are sad
To kiss their tears away.

1

Jack's the Lad

HAVEN'S END WAS LIKE A PIRATE'S rendezvous in 1778. The list of its privateers, though incomplete, covers a dozen pages in the county records of the Revolutionary War. You can find the *Charming Nancy* with the rest. She was known chiefly because her crew, when prisoners, rose up and seized the *Enterprise,* of British privateering registry. She was named, one supposes, for some girl in Haven's End, and was built in one of the river yards. A sloop, she was called, though the term is vague in that day of pinks and snows and other archaic rigs, and the classification of the merchant shipping is nearly impossible to follow; but she was called a sloop, burden: eighty tons; master: Daniel Swale; owner: Messrs. Whistle, Scarlet and others.

That was when the Swales grew rich, when the *Charming Nancy* sailed. The *Charming Nancy* brought in the first money to Daniel Swale for the building of the brick Swale house on the ridge, and the Swales are guarding what is left of that fortune still. That was when cannon lay before the warehouses, when every wharf had its prize ships, and when goods were up at auction almost daily. Any morning you could have heard the fife and drum calling for new crews. Whistle and Company made a million, before they took their losses; and the Scarlets cleared four hundred thousand, before patriotism ceased to pay hard cash.

And even now, little waves are lapping against the piling of the wharves, small, sparkling waves when the sun is bright and when the sky is blue above the marshes and the sand dunes. "Money," they are saying, "money, money, money"; but there's no money in blue water now.

And Haven's End is cool and empty now, chill in an autumn of threadbare meagerness. A poverty has reached the elm-lined street above the river, where the old square houses stand. It is a poverty so like the austerity of the first plantation that it is difficult sometimes to believe that our town once was rich enough to produce a culture of its own, drawn by itself from the sea. Only the houses are left to tell of that moment of its greatness, and now and then a bit of silver or a Chippendale chair.

In the president's office of the Ten Cents Savings Bank, Dennis Swale used to keep a heavy, dog-eared ledger that was the *Charming Nancy's* log. Upon the battered calf cover was a round mark where Captain Daniel Swale had once set down his grog, and there were also little parallel cuts of a sharp knife blade, where Seth Scarlet had shaved off a twist of tobacco for his pipe, when those two shared the *Charming Nancy's* cabin.

There was no romantic reading in the pages. Daniel Swale, at the time he had reached his late twenties, was under no illusions.

But indefinably, above the harshness of that age, hovered the presence of a lonely man, self-reliant and aloof; and over all that record of loss and gain and bloodshed was a simplicity close to greatness. There was an innocence between those lines that was almost gentle, and the vague imprint of a belief, close to the realm of mystical, — the tranquil, unstained credulity of the man who dreams.

On a stray leaf between the pages were the crew's names, signed to the articles — the patient, trembling signatures of hard-handed illiterates; blots and scratches, crosses. The Christian names were like a genealogy from the Old Testament. It was that strange piety of violence and godliness which no one but a Yankee could ever understand.

"The crew," wrote Daniel Swale, "is indifferent bad."

But there was another passage in that log.

"We brought aboard the chest of specie. It will run to twenty thousand pounds. Also one sack of silver service, very good. Also brought aboard the Honorable Amaryllis Denby, passenger for Halifax — deeming she would be safer on our vessel than aboard a prize."

And then there was another passage, still more amazing for a privateering log. It was written off one of those small West India islands which New Englanders in those days knew so well. "After dark," it read, "put off in the longboat and back two hours later, married. Grog rationed to the crew."

And there was all that was left that was tangible of the love of Daniel Swale, which one may believe or not. But the pride of our town was in it and that unbridged gap between the Scarlets and the Swales. A broken heart was in it, and money that came easily and went fast. And a secret was in it, half spoken now and half forgotten, and a man's honor and a family's honor. They all lay in the pages of the *Charming Nancy's* log.

It happened this way, Job Willing said, when he was an old man and his speech was free. And Job Willing must have known, for he was cabin boy in those days.

They had changed the name of the George Tavern to the Liberty, but the gentlemen were the same hard-drinking, genial gentlemen, ready to buy up a boy's prize share, in whole or part, before he went aboard, at a price depending on the master and on the tonnage of the vessel.

Down by the river they were working by lantern light, loading the *Charming Nancy* by Mr. Whistle's wharf with her last supplies, and groups of men were standing listening in the dark, for the *Charming Nancy* was a fast sloop and Daniel was a lucky master. A misting rain was beginning to fall and the night was very dark.

"Boy," said Captain Swale, "where are you, boy? Go down to the cabin and fetch my cloak that's lying on the chest."

The cabin was in disorder, because nothing was put to rights as yet; the captain's pistols and cutlass were on the table above the captain's books and papers. There were four great folios of charts with inky covers, North and South America, Africa, the British Isles and France, and then the captain's note and navigation books, and a heavy Bible and a volume of Milton's poems. Opened, where he must have been reading, was the seaman's "Vade Mecum", London, 1744, "Shewing how to prepare a Merchant Ship for a close fight by disposing of their Bulk-heads, Leaves, Coamings, Look-holes, etc." At the foot of the companion ladder was a chest which must have just been left aboard by the new first officer, who would share the cabin. "Scarlet", Job Willing could read in new red paint, upon the broad pine cover. The lockers were covered with the captain's clothes and sea boots, but Job Willing found the cloak.

"Will you have it on, sir?" Job Willing asked.

"No," said the captain. "Follow me to the tavern, boy. It's the last you'll see of land."

He walked up the street quickly, with his hat drawn over his eyes. He was a slender, nervous man, who appeared to pay no attention to the sounds and sights.

"Good evening, sir," said some one on the street. "Good luck go with you, sir." The captain did not answer; he did not turn his head. He was as proud and as close-mouthed as all the other Swales.

He walked quickly toward the tavern, his hat pulled over his eyes, unconscious of the gentle rain. In the taproom it was very bright with candles; a fire of birch logs had been newly lit and the air was full of the scent of birch smoke, sweet and oily. The taproom was filled with gentlemen, all talking; owners and merchants, not masters, and the social difference was strong in those days between the master and the owner of a ship. In that company Job Willing felt out of place.

The captain was standing very straight, looking here and there.

"You wished to see me, did you, Mr. Whistle?" he asked.

Then every one was turning, looking. The captain was not a handsome man; he had the long Swale nose and their thin, hard mouth. His clothes were plain and drab; with none of the embellishments of embroidery and lace that all the gentlemen wore who were seated at the tables.

Mr. Whistle looked up and laid down his long clay pipe. He was an old man in those days, whose face was wan and wrinkled below his powdered wig. There were two strange gentlemen beside him, urbane and beautiful, whom Job Willing had learned that afternoon were merchants from Boston and part owners in the *Charming Nancy's* venture.

"Ah," said Mr. Whistle, "here he is, gentlemen."

One of the strangers stood up, young and well-proportioned, in a white satin waistcoat which was edged with bright gold braid.

"So that's the little fighting-cock?" he said.

The captain looked at him but he did not smile.

"Gentlemen," said Mr. Whistle, "he's as good a man as you could find. He's been sailing for me ten years, mostly on the Guinea coast, and you know what that is, gentlemen. He's the one to fight a ship. Manly and O'Brien are no better."

"And Swale his name is, is it?" said the tall man. "Here's at you, Captain. Come here. Sit down."

"Thanks," said the captain, "I have not the time."

"Sit down, I tell you," said the tall gentleman. And he reached forward, seizing the captain by the collar of his coat.

"Take your hand off my coat," said Captain Swale. "I tell you, take it off."

Mr. Whistle rose hastily, dusting the tobacco ash from his vest.

"Mr. Jenks," he said, "Captain Swale comes from an old family. We all have our ups and downs."

The other gentleman spoke. He was older, with a mellow, booming voice. "The captain is a patriot," he said. "To the devil with distinctions, when you meet a hero — yes, a hero. If I were young enough to strike a blow, I'd be with you, Captain, working at the guns."

The captain shrugged his shoulders.

"We're not patriots," he answered; "we're all in this for money."

"What?" said the other gentleman. "What do you mean by that?"

And for the first time the captain smiled.

"It's money," he said. "That's what ships the crews, because men want money."

"Daniel," said Mr. Whistle, "don't you want it too?"

"That's why I'm going," said Daniel Swale. "Because I want my own house up on the high street. I'll have it and a coach, before I'm through."

"Gad!" said Mr. Jenks. "I hope so."

The captain looked down upon the floor and clasped his hands behind his back. "There's no glory in it," he answered. "That's what I mean to say. We take the weak vessels and run from the strong. That's the owner's order."

"And now," said Mr. Whistle, "is the crew aboard?"

"Yes," said the captain, "a mangy crew. All the good ones are aboard the prison ships."

"Well," said Mr. Whistle, "you've sailed out with worse. And now about the mate, Daniel. We have a mate signed on for you."

"Who is he?" asked the captain.

Mr. Whistle coughed again. "It's Seth Scarlet," he said.

The captain bit his lip.

"Him?" he asked. "You mean the landlord's son?"

"Now, Daniel," said Mr. Whistle; "steady, Daniel. Mates are hard to find."

"He drinks too much," said Daniel Swale, "and talks too much."

"Now, Daniel," said Mr. Whistle, "Mr. Scarlet wishes him to go and Mr. Scarlet is part owner."

"Very good," said the captain. "Will he mind my orders?"

"Yes," said Mr. Whistle. "You'll find he is a good one. Knows the sea. And besides, it's better he was gone because —" Mr. Whistle whispered something in the captain's ear.

"So he's wenching again?" said the captain.

Mr. Whistle looked at Daniel Swale beneath his heavy brows.

"Seth knows women," said Mr. Whistle. "Seth

knows when to run, and that's the thing, believe me, —to know when to run away."

The captain did not answer. It was clear he had no desire for the refreshment on the table.

"Well," he said, "where is he? We're leaving on this tide."

"He's waiting here," said Mr. Whistle.

"Well," said the captain, "bring him in." And then Job Willing saw the new mate walk across the room, a red-faced, heavy-handed man, like all the Scarlets. He was grinning and bowing like some one anxious to please.

"So I'm sailing with Danny, am I?" he said. "Now there's a rare one, gentlemen. I used to whip him when we were at school."

"Hold your tongue!" the captain said.

"Listen to him," said Seth Scarlet. "We've never pulled on the same rope yet, Danny Swale or me."

"Now come," said Mr. Whistle. "You're shipmates now. Fill the glasses up and here's one to the cruise."

They stood about the table with glasses of Madeira in their hands, and just as they were about to drink, some one must have jostled Seth Scarlet on the elbow, for an instant later every one was looking at a stain upon the table where half the wine had spilled from Seth Scarlet's glass. For a moment every one looked at each other, because times were uncertain and they were superstitious men; and the captain spoke.

"There's the sign," he said, "for an unlucky voyage."

They went to fight the British aboard a vessel of eighty tons, with sixty men as crew and an improvised battery of twelve six-pounders, which were lashed beneath tarpaulins, behind ports cut in the bulwarks. They went to sea in a vessel scarcely more than a fishing smack, and even that crew of gawky country boys, unversed in the subtleties of life, knew that the *Charming Nancy* was not large enough to hold a Scarlet and a Swale.

Long before there was danger, there was trouble; for the sea, in spite of all its space, was about them like bare, narrow walls, against which wills and wishes beat and gave back hopeless echoes. All those nameless attributes that make a personality were bound to strain and creak in tune with the complaining of the *Charming Nancy's* timbers.

They were cooped up in the cabin aft, eating together off a swinging table, sleeping each upon a mattress thrown upon a locker. There they were in a dismal, dripping place, with stands of cutlasses and small arms along unpainted bulkheads, in a space not more than eight by twelve feet, with a deck so low that Seth Scarlet struck his head if he stood upright. It was no place for a Scarlet and a Swale. Even the crew could tell that they were different breeds; the captain cold, aloof, and Mr. Scarlet boisterous and friendly, like an ordinary man.

If even the crew could guess it, Job Willing was the one who knew, because Job was the boy who brought the meals aft and who set the place to rights; and a boy with sharp ears heard things which no one was meant to hear. Yet what he remembered afterwards was the silence of Daniel Swale, long, implacable silences while Seth Scarlet talked until all conversation died, and the captain was left sitting staring at the wall; or standing at the rail alone, looking at the sails. Even when he gave his orders, he was lonely, a thousand miles away.

"Evening to you, Danny," Mr. Scarlet said, when they sat down to table early on that cruise.

"Seth," the captain said, "it's no matter here, but I'll have you to call me 'Sir' when we're on deck."

"There you go," said Mr. Scarlet; "putting on airs, ain't you?"

The captain made no answer.

"You're here to fight this ship, ain't you?" Mr. Scarlet said. "Not to bully me."

The captain stared over Mr. Scarlet's head at the small-arms racks and drank his drink in silence.

"D'you hear me?" Mr. Scarlet said. "My father's part owner, so don't you put on airs with me. What have you been, lad, but a skipper on a stinking nigger ship? — you remember that."

The captain did not answer.

"Damnation!" Mr. Scarlet said. "Aren't you going to speak?" And then he laughed, for he was not a man to stay angry long. "You've got the manners, Dan. I haven't. But the Scarlets have the money."

"Yes," the captain said. And he stared beyond Seth Scarlet at the wall.

"Lord," said Mr. Scarlet, "I'd give a piece of it right now to know what's on your mind. Are you always this way, never speaking, always thinking, Danny Swale?"

"Seth," the captain said, "I'll tell you this. The Swales will have money before I'm through."

"And here's to it," said Mr. Swale. "Tip the glasses up. Here's to money and the girls."

"Drink for all you're worth," the captain said; "you won't find any here."

Captain Swale would sit beneath the swinging lamp, writing in his log.

"Clear weather," he wrote, "fair, northwest breezes. Cleared ship for action twice. Crew indifferent poor."

"Boy!" he shouted. "Boy — fetch out my blankets. What are you crying for, boy?"

"Nothing, if you please, sir," Job Willing said.

"No?" said Captain Swale. "Don't lie. You're crying to be back to Haven's End. Do you mind the way the church bells ring?"

And all at once his voice was kind, and all at once the light was brighter, which had always played behind his face.

"And you heard the fife and drum?" he said. "Don't be afraid of me. I was young when I first left. Tell me where you live, boy. I know Haven's End."

"Sail sighted S.E.," was all that Daniel wrote, as though it were an everyday affair. "Proved to be British brig *Eclipse*. Kingston to Halifax. Struck when we boarded after engagement of one glass. Lost fore topmast. Five killed — ten wounded."

That was all he wrote, but by the time they boarded, every one knew why seamen's shares sold at a premium when Daniel Swale was captain. Daniel was the one who led them, with Seth Scarlet just behind him, but the fight was nearly over when the grappling hooks were thrown. The late afternoon sun beat on a deck covered with blood and splinters, and a knot of men stood at the mainmast, but the rest had gone below. Daniel Swale was in his shirt sleeves, with a cutlass in his hand, but even then he seemed apart from all the rest, unshaken by the excitement of it, methodical, precise.

"Daniel," said Seth Scarlet, "it's true what they say. You're a great captain, Danny."

"Seth," said Daniel, "you'll please to call me 'Sir' on deck. Where's the ship's master? Go down with him and see what's in the cabin."

"Very good, sir," said Seth Scarlet. "Well, it don't make any difference. You know how to fight."

It was like a hundred affairs, up to then. Swale had been in enough before to know the whole routine. As Seth Scarlet and the master of the brig, a middle-aged man, who might have been a shopkeeper, moved away, Daniel Swale looked forward. The crew of the *Charming Nancy* were by the forecastle, where the prisoners were emerging one by one.

"Stop there!" shouted Daniel Swale. "Don't take their money from their pockets."

"Huzzah for the captain!" some one shouted.

"Be silent forward," roared out Captain Swale. And they obeyed him because they were afraid of him, and because the prize shares would be handsome, if the *Eclipse* should gain a port.

Already the *Charming Nancy* was cast off. Already men were busy with repairs, when Seth Scarlet, came back on deck.

"Captain," called Seth Scarlet, "will you please to step up here?" He lowered his voice and his broad red face was puzzled. "There's a woman in the cabin.

Ho, did you mind what you were saying,—there'd be no women here?"

To every man who lives there comes a moment sometimes of strange illumination, when all the world becomes a wish turned true, regardless of the truth. Seth Scarlet could not understand it, for he knew the type she was, that parody of stateliness, that unreserved complaisance which was old as time, when Babylon was young. It flashed between those two in a look of recognition. He knew what she was. She knew he knew. It was not for him to see the sublimity in Daniel Swale's unworldliness.

All he remembered was Daniel Swale in a dripping shirt, no longer white, with a smudge of powder on his cheek bones, staring at that lady from the sea.

"By thunder!" the captain of the *Eclipse* was saying. "Don't take on so, Ma'am. They'll use you right." And then he lowered his voice. "Blimme!" he murmured. "If you wouldn't think she'd never seen a man."

The ship was rolling on a gentle sea and the dying sun was reflected from the water through the cabin windows in a fitful way, like the light of a faintly burning fire. That was how Daniel saw her first in that flickering, uncertain light, as stately as a vision, without the hollows in her cheeks, without the patient weariness in her eyes. The light played like a halo on that lady's yellow hair, giving her a beauty like a white light against the hardness of a thousand meager days.

And there he stood staring at her, and no one guessed that he was staring at a wish of his own, conjured up from silent watches. He stared at her like a country boy, for her dress was all blue satin, embroidered with little flowers in vines and sprays. And where could one find a standard for a lady such as she, when there was not her like in all of Haven's End? But the courtesy of Daniel Swale overcame the rudeness of staring. The silence was over in a moment. He took his eyes from her face and looked down at her hands, slender and white, with half a dozen rings.

"Madam," he said, "do not be afraid."

"No," said Seth Scarlet, "you wait and see if we ain't the bully boys."

"No," said the master of *Eclipse*. "There, there, Ma'am. I told you when you shipped, times was uncertain-like. Why, look at this gentleman — if he is a Yankee, damn him, he won't let the crew lay a finger on you. There, there, Ma'am."

"Lud," said the lady. Her voice was as soft as though she sang a song, and she looked at Daniel Swale as though she could not understand him, and perhaps she never did. "Excuse me, sir; I didn't mean to take on so. Are you a Yankee, sir?"

"Yes, Madam," said Daniel Swale. And he bowed with a touch of color in his face. "And you, Master, will you give me your name and the papers?"

"Jenkins," said the master, "Herbert Jenkins. And it wasn't my fault the men wouldn't stand to it, once you come aboard. I done my best for the owners. The lady's a passenger." He looked at them and nodded. "None of my affair, except a passenger, passage paid for. Name, Denby — Honorable Amaryllis Denby, so she says. From the Jamaica station, bound to meet Sir Rodney Burke at Halifax."

Then Seth Scarlet began to grin at the light of his own knowledge.

"Honorable?" he said. "*Honorable*, did you say?"

The lady looked at him with level eyes and turned her head.

"Yes," she answered, "Honorable. And Sir Rodney Burke's my — uncle, if you have to know."

And then Seth Scarlet started. He was staring at Daniel Swale and there was no wonder that he could not understand. Daniel Swale was bowing again.

"Madam," he said. "I am very sorry."

"Thank you, sir," she said, but she was looking at Seth Scarlet. "Will you have some refreshment while your man is pulling things about?"

"Thank you, Madam," Daniel bowed again, "but we are pressed for time. Madam, we have no way to entertain a lady, but you will be safer with us than on a half-manned prize. If you will pack a box, it will be carried aboard. I — " he paused and shook his head, "I have my owner to think of, like any other captain."

She looked at him and nodded very graciously. It all was like some fantastic play, when she nodded to Daniel Swale.

"Well," she said, "beggars can't be choosers, sir."

In the meanwhile Seth Scarlet stared, and moved about the cabin, looking here and there, but suddenly he paused and bent above a chest.

"Here!" he said. "There's no manifest for this. What's in it? Where's the key?"

Captain Jenkins frowned and cleared his throat.

"Only personal gear," he said. "That's all."

"Is it so?" said Seth Scarlet. "Now, don't you trick

us. Don't we know you were in a convoy before the blow? Open it up or we'll smash it in. It's what Goldilocks here said — beggars can't be choosers."

The captain drew a bag from his pocket, and then the cabin echoed with Seth Scarlet's shout.

"Danny!" he said. "Blast us, but we're rich men, Danny!"

There was no wonder that Daniel Swale's eyes narrowed as he looked. The box was full of gold — more than he had ever seen or hoped to see. The light from the gold seemed to shine upon his face, and for a moment his lips trembled.

"It's specie," said the master heavily. "I told them fools it wasn't safe. Twenty thousand pounds of specie — and they wouldn't hold the deck."

And then, suddenly, his face sagged and his body sagged, and he bent his head above the table and began to weep. Daniel Swale drew in a breath that was almost like a sigh, and he, too, seemed shaken by some emotion.

"Lock up that box," he said. "Send four men down to get it."

Daniel Swale, himself, was smiling, once he came on deck, but his eyes moved here and there. He had a way of seeing everything at once, and already his mind was moving forward. Yet somehow, any one could tell that he had changed, because that cloak of loneliness had left him before some unknown spell.

"Ah!" said Seth. "But you're a cool one, sir, and it's manners all the time. It was all I could do not to bust out laughing, you bowing and scraping as though she was a lady."

"What!" the captain said, "what do you mean by that?"

"No," said Seth Scarlet. "What's she doing on a trading brig, traveling all alone? You've been born long enough to know just what I mean."

Daniel Swale stared at him for a moment, and once he opened his lips, only to close them before he finally spoke.

"I don't," he said, "and perhaps it's just as well, but you mark this. You mind your manners when she comes aboard, if you can't tell good blood when you see it."

Then Seth Scarlet must have known, because his broad, heavy mouth fell open, and his eyes grew wide.

"Danny," he said, "have you lost your wits?"

And then he stopped, because the look of Daniel Swale made him stony silent, and he stood as though he saw an amazing sight that lay beyond his furthest thoughts. He was staring at what stood behind the hardness and the silence. It was there where any one might see — the ignorance and the gentleness of Daniel Swale.

She must have marveled too. He was beyond the realm of her sophistication and of the brilliance that shone from her, when she talked of this and that in London; and she had seen it all. And she was beautiful, even to one who did not long for land, that lady from the sea. As she sat in the *Charming Nancy's* cabin, it seemed like a fantastic place, which even swayed Seth Scarlet's judgment. There was no hope for Daniel Swale, and the end was very clear.

They put her in the cabin, all alone, and the officers slept forward with the crew. But they ate with her in the cabin of the same boiled, salt meat the crew ate, ending with pasty raisin pudding, washed down by rum and water.

It was a marvelous picture, that cabin with the smoky, fish-oil lantern swaying overhead, the small arms rattling in their racks and Amaryllis Denby with rings upon her fingers seated before a wooden trencher, while Seth Scarlet chewed his victuals savagely and Daniel Swale drank his rum and water.

The captain never asked her how she came upon a trading brig, traveling alone in time of war, because he accepted her like the sunrise after a stormy night. It was marvelous to see the captain rise and bow.

"Madam," he said, "we will leave you now. No one will disturb you unless we sight a sail."

"No," she said, "I'm lonely. Captain, stay and smoke your pipe."

"Ay," said Seth Scarlet, "to be sure he'll stay." Even when he believed the innocence, he could not believe the chivalry of Daniel Swale.

But Daniel Swale did not touch her; he would as soon have touched an image of the Virgin.

"Captain," she said, "tell me who you are."

For a moment he looked at her diffidently.

"I am a Yankee trader, Madam," he said. "Mostly toward the Guinea coast until the war began. But I'll be a ship's owner some day, unless I die."

She sat with her chin in the palm of her hand and for some reason he was not ill at ease when she gazed at him thoughtfully, with a wrinkle between her brows.

"But you're a gentleman, if you are a Yankee," she said. "Not like that officer of yours!" She shrugged her shoulders and made a face, but he did not see because he did not dare to look at her for long. He could not forget that they were in the cabin all alone.

"Madam," he said, "I've always bought and sold. I know the value of this and that, but the Swales are gentle people. We are the Swales from Norwich."

"Oh," she said, "the Norwich Swales? When I stayed at Dean Manor once, there was a Swale."

"Was there?" said Daniel. "Was there now?"

And then he told her of the Swales at Haven's End, of Colonel Richard Swale, who had led his regiment in King Philip's War; he told her of the great house that Colonel Swale had built, and of the Colonel's steel cap and breastplate that hung above the chimney at home. If she was amused, she did not show it, because she had skill enough for that, but there must have been a transparency in him which amazed her from the very first, as he talked of the grandeur of the Swales. "We're poor now," he said. "It's a trading town."

All the while that lady seemed lost in some thought that puzzled her. She kept looking at him curiously from beneath half-lowered eyelids, as though she waited for something that did not happen, and finally she pointed at the chest upon the cabin floor.

"And how much of that will you have?" she asked.

"Madam," he answered, "I should have two thousand pounds when I get home."

And then he told her of Haven's End, because her glance was kind. He told her of the marshes where the wild fowl came in and of the sturgeon in the river. He told her of the sleigh rides on winter nights and of the dancing in the tavern. He told her of the great houses that were being built and of the prizes that were coming to the wharves and, as he spoke, he seemed to see the streets in a new glory which had never yet descended upon Haven's End, and all the while she listened, half perplexed, because she did not understand.

"And are there any red Indians?" she asked. "I thought the Americas were forests, always filled with Indians. Is it true that all the men sing psalms?"

"Madam," said Daniel Swale, "the Indians come in, with deer and beaver pelts, but only a very few. Listen —you can hear the watch singing now, the Hundred and Third Psalm from the old music book."

And then they were silent, for he could think of nothing more to say, and all about them was the creaking of wood and all the noises of a ship at sea. And he felt that her eyes were on him, though he could not look. He could not look because of her nearness and her helplessness and because the softness of her voice was temptation, though she was so fine a lady.

"You'll be a great man in your town," she said. "I know it, Captain Swale."

"Madam," he said, "you have seen so many greater men."

"I am not so sure," she said. "Good night to you, Captain Swale."

She held out her hand, covered with its rings of red stones and of green, and they flashed like fire before his eyes. At the touch of her hand, as he bent over it, his blood was like fire. She seemed to be drawing him beyond himself, into a place of laughter and shining floors, where candles shone on diamonds and where there was an odor of lavender and roses.

"Good night to you, Madam," he said.

"Captain Swale," she answered, "you are a very gentle man."

When he was on deck, he stood for a long while looking at the sea, where the bows cut the black water into a feather of light.

"Ah, Captain," said Seth Scarlet, "will you be in the cabin to-night?"

"You fool!" said Daniel Swale. "Can't you tell a lady when you see one?"

"Maybe not," Seth Scarlet said, "but I'll tell you one thing straight, and it's bad, black luck for you. You love her, Danny Swale, and you're the fool, not me."

Seth Scarlet was the one who needed more than a lady's hand to kiss and Daniel Swale was the one who heard her scream. It was past midnight and black, rainy weather, when Seth Scarlet had the watch on deck. Daniel Swale was in the cabin in a moment, and there was the Lady Amaryllis Denby, white-faced, wide-eyed, struggling in Seth Scarlet's arms.

"You!" said Daniel Swale. "Go up on deck."

Even in his anger, his voice was level, but Seth Scarlet must have known that anything might happen. Nevertheless, he tried to laugh in the absurdity of that moment.

"Danny," he said, "easy, Danny. Don't you see she likes it?"

"Go up on deck," said Daniel Swale. But even then, Seth Scarlet tried, purely out of kindness, to tell him. There was no use, but still Seth Scarlet tried.

"By thunder," he cried, "don't you see what she's after? She started screaming just to get you here."

Daniel Swale reached toward the arms rack.

"Seth," he said, and still his voice was level, "I don't want trouble over this. I'm being patient, Seth."

"Very good," Seth Scarlet's voice was thick. "Very good, sir, but don't say I didn't put in my word — and you'll be sorry until the day you die."

Daniel must have been the only one who did not know what was to follow, because, by then, it was as inevitable as time. Yet to the very end, he stumbled in his diffidence.

"Madam," he said, "I've been afraid of this. You must not blame him too much. Men are like that. It's — the loneliness —"

"Yes," she answered. Her hands were trembling, as she twisted up her hair. "Yes, I know."

Daniel Swale cleared his throat.

"Our course is close to the islands," he said. "I can put you ashore, perhaps. I think you would be safer there, unless —"

"Unless?" she took up his word haltingly, and Daniel bowed his head.

"I suppose you'll laugh," he answered, "because I'm very plain. Will you forgive me? I was about to say — unless we married."

There was not a sound but the groaning of the *Charming Nancy*'s timbers in that eternal complaint of ships, a moaning, dirgelike sound, but the sweetness of her voice was what he heard.

"I'll make you a good wife, sir. I swear I will," she said.

And next, before the thing seemed possible, her head was on his shoulder and her soft gold hair was on his coat.

Although he was a trader, who knew short weights, he never asked her who she was. One can imagine what Seth Scarlet must have thought. He did not see the beauty of it or the sadness of it. When the longboat came from shore that night, Seth Scarlet watched it, grinning, and he bowed before her in a parody of pleasure.

"My congratulations, Madam!" he said. "You have found a good man."

And he turned to shake the captain by the hand. In the happiness that was upon him, how should Daniel have noticed that his lady's face had blushed scarlet? Her hand had closed tight on his, with a new ring on it of plain gold.

Then Daniel Swale was laughing; all his loneliness and all his repression were gone for a little time, lost in that dream of his that was as wild and poignant as any lover's thought. It was not for Daniel Swale to guess what she was, and he would have died sooner than believe it. And when he believed, he wished that he was dead, but it was too late to die.

When His Majesty's privateer *Enterprise* came up

with the *Charming Nancy* after a six hours' chase, Daniel Swale would have fought her, if his crew had stood up to fight, but they were only country boys, who were making their first cruise. They ran below at the first broadside, forcing Daniel Swale to strike, and the boats of the *Enterprise* brought them off, a frightened lot of boys, with Mills Prison staring them in the face.

Daniel Swale, his lady, Seth Scarlet, the box of specie and the *Charming Nancy*'s log crossed in the last boat and Captain Bligh of the *Enterprise* received them on his deck. Captain Bligh, in his middle thirties, with puffy eyes and small, plump hands, was in dress uniform when they arrived, smiling at them when they climbed on deck.

"Gad!" said Captain Bligh. "So you didn't choose to fight your ship? I'd have fought, if I were you. Oh, gad, what have we here?" He had seen Daniel Swale's lady, but he did not remove his hat. "Gad!" said Captain Bligh, "Now here's a pleasant meeting. Damme, if it isn't Lady Amaryllis—and in a Yankee boat. Oh, Amaryllis, tell me, aren't you true to your first loves?"

Disgrace had made Daniel Swale silent until then, but anger gave him back his tongue.

"Have you no courtesy, sir?" he said. "The lady is my wife." And then his face went white, for Captain Bligh was seized with a sudden fit of laughter.

"Capital," said Captain Bligh, "that's capital. But it does not go with me."

"Sir," said Daniel Swale, "what do you mean by that?"

"Don't be a fool," said Captain Bligh. "She's everybody's wife. Damme, I know Lady Amaryllis, don't I? There's no ensign in Portsmouth who doesn't know her."

"Sir," said Daniel Swale, "I tell you she's my wife."

Captain Bligh's mouth fell open. "Oh, good God, you didn't marry her now, not Amaryllis? Amaryllis is an officer's lady. Speak up and tell him, dear."

Daniel Swale took one look at her, and one look was enough, even for Daniel Swale. It seemed as though the words had dragged her in the dirt. She was not weeping; instead her face was drawn into lines ugly and horrible, and her voice was a shrieking discord.

"You beast!" she cried. "You filthy beast, Bob Bligh."

Then Seth Scarlet began to laugh, although he should have known it was not a laughing matter.

"Ho!" he cried. "There's one for you, Dan Swale."

Daniel Swale stood for a moment staring, while Seth Scarlet laughed and Captain Bligh began to laugh again, and then he must have forgotten where he was, for he jumped at the captain's throat. It was so quick and unexpected that they fell to the deck together, but in an instant it was over. The second officer of the *Enterprise* ran up, fetching Daniel Swale a blow on the temple with a pistol butt, and Daniel Swale lay deathly white, face upward on the deck.

"You beast!" screamed Lady Amaryllis. "Oh, you beast!"

Captain Bligh was getting to his feet, dusting at his coat. "Put both these men in irons," he said. "Iron them in the hold with their crew. Lady Amaryllis, shall you and I be sensible? I would, if I were you."

When Daniel Swale opened his eyes, he was in the hold with the crew of the *Charming Nancy* and the hold was very dark. Seth Scarlet was leaning over him.

"You're alive, are you?" Seth Scarlet said.

"Yes," said Daniel Swale, "yes, I'm alive."

Then Seth Scarlet began to laugh, not because he was merry, but because his nerves were shaken. "The joke's on you," he said. "I wish you could have seen your face. The joke's on you, Dan Swale."

Daniel sat up and his voice was very faint. "Laugh again and I'll kill you," he said. His head sank back against the planking. "I — " his voice was hardly more than a whisper, "I'm going to take this ship."

Like all the other Scarlets from Haven's End, Seth was plain and plodding. He could not know the torment in the mind of Daniel Swale.

"Dan," he said, "you've not got your senses back. You're lying here with your head broken, aren't you? Haven't you been gulled by a little painted hussy that any man could see was no better than she should be? Wait till they hear about it back at Haven's End. Remember you're in irons, Danny Swale."

Daniel Swale sat up again, weak in body and weak in voice, but it startled Seth Scarlet to hear him, because he could not understand the driving force of will, or the sublimation of stubbornness that was speaking in the dark.

"These irons," said Daniel Swale, "these irons," and he shook them on his wrist. "We have better irons in the Guinea trade and I've seen the black boys pick the locks. I've seen them. I know how."

"Are you crazy?" said Seth Scarlet. "Are you crazy, Danny Swale?"

"There's a nail in my pocket," Daniel Swale answered. "When my head is better, I can pick the locks."

Seth Scarlet stared at him in silence through the dark, and all the crew were listening, swayed by the contagion of that feeble voice.

"If I get you free," said Daniel Swale, "where do you want to go, men — to the prison or back to Haven's End?"

Then, if they had never known it before, they felt his spirit, rising from the embers into flame.

"Scarlet," he asked, "did you see? Where did she go?" He was thinking of her still.

"Lord, sir!" said Seth Scarlet. He was swayed at last by the unreality of it. "She's up there in the cabin. Now don't take on. Just sit quiet, Captain."

"Is she?" said the captain. "Is she so? Now listen. Do what I tell you and I'll have you out of this. D'you hear me? I tell you I'll get you out of this . . ."

Long afterward, when Daniel Swale told of it, the thing did not seem strange, only a combination of audacity and luck, distilled from his imagination. He and his carpenter ripped off the hinges from the bulkhead door one night, which led to the cabin aft. They worked it back a foot, and Daniel Swale got through and pulled the bolts, and went for Captain Bligh. Captain Bligh went down without a moan, and, with the small arms in the cabin, all the rest was easy.

Even when it ended, he did not seem to realize

what they had done. He stood on the deck in the lantern light, staring at the dark.

"Damn you for thieves!" he shouted. "Don't take their money from their pockets. Boy, serve out a round of grog. Mr. Scarlet! Scarlet—are you there?"

"Aye, sir," said Mr. Scarlet. "Give him a cheer now. Have you lost your tongues?"

"Stop your bellowing!" That was the only answer the captain made. "Mr. Scarlet, set a watch and come with me to the cabin. I haven't finished yet."

There was no wonder that Seth Scarlet could not understand; it was the way always with the Scarlets and the Swales.

Captain Bligh still was dazed by the time Daniel Swale reached his cabin. One of his officers was tied there with him and two lay dead on deck.

"Take out the other gentleman," he said. "Where is the lady gone?"

"She's here, confound her!" groaned Captain Bligh. "She held a pistol on me. And so help me, I wish she'd pulled the trigger, if you want to know."

Then Daniel Swale saw her, standing there, with all her airs gone, wide-eyed. He looked at her and back at Captain Bligh.

"Untie him, Mr. Scarlet, if you please," he said and rested his hand upon the cabin table. "It's all right, my dear. It's quite all right."

Though Daniel was never a handsome man, every one stared at him. The wound on his head was unwashed and black.

"Captain Bligh," he said.

"Yes," said Captain Bligh. "What do you want now?"

"When I saw you last," said Daniel Swale, "you made some remarks on this lady, my wife."

"By gad, sir!" said Captain Bligh. Seth Scarlet had untied him and he was on his feet. "I did not know she was your wife."

"But you know it now," said Daniel Swale. "And we held different opinions, unless you've changed your mind. I hold she is a lady of unblemished reputation."

"A what?" said Captain Bligh.

"A lady of unblemished reputation," repeated Daniel Swale. "Do you agree with me?"

"I'm damned if I agree!" shouted Captain Bligh. "What the devil are you doing now? Do you mean to kill me, sir?"

Daniel Swale had primed two pistols and had placed them on the cabin table.

"Captain Bligh," he said, "take your place at the end of the table, please. Mr. Scarlet has not a handkerchief; will you kindly lend him yours?"

"Yes," said Captain Bligh. "What do you mean to do?"

"Sir," said Daniel Swale, "we are sailing for Haven's End. My wife shall be what I say she is when I reach there. When Mr. Scarlet here says three, we will reach across the table, take a weapon, cock and fire."

"Sir, it's murder," said Captain Bligh.

And then the lady spoke. "Daniel," she began.

"My dear," said Daniel Swale, "will you please be still. Mr. Scarlet, will you please count three and drop the handkerchief?"

Seth Scarlet's hand was trembling and his voice was as unsteady as his hand.

"Daniel," he said, "there's no need for this. The gentleman will give his word."

"I'll be damned if I will!" shouted Captain Bligh. "She's a common light of love. Count out and I'll stick to it."

At the last number they both reached forward and straightened back, but as they did so the vessel gave a lurch. The lantern, swinging from overhead, wavered; both men lost their balance, but Captain Bligh regained his first and fired. The cabin was a roar of noise and smoke and they both were standing by the cabin table, and Scarlet asked:

"Are you all right, Daniel Swale?"

"Load the pistols, Mr. Scarlet, if you please," Daniel said. He was leaning forward against the table, gripping it hard with both his hands. Captain Bligh had taken a step backward and his eyes were round.

"Man!" he said hoarsely. "Haven't you had enough?"

"No," said Daniel Swale. "Load the pistols, Mr. Scarlet, if you please."

Captain Bligh stared through the smoke as though he saw a ghost.

"Have I hit you, sir?" he asked.

Daniel Swale gazed back. And they all must have had a glimpse of what went on behind his eyes.

"I'm able to stand," he answered, "and will go on with it. I'll have my wife a lady if I'm to take her home."

Then they must have understood, for his wish no

longer seemed absurd. Though they might not have known it then, he was a sublimation of the Swales, with all their stupidity and with their stubbornness. All at once nothing seemed impossible, as Daniel Swale stood clutching at the table's edge with his thin white hands.

"My dear sir," said Captain Bligh, and his manner changed without his own volition, "I was mistaken. I never knew your wife. She, as far as I'm concerned, she's as pure as the driven snow."

"Thank you, sir," said Daniel Swale. "I see you understand."

"Certainly," said Captain Bligh. "There will be no word spoken of it, not a word. If you'd put it to me plain, there'd have been no need to fight about it."

"Thank you," said Daniel Swale. "And now, no doubt, you'll beg the lady's pardon."

"How?" said Captain Bligh. "Must I do that?"

"If you please!" said Daniel Swale.

Then all three were looking at her, where she stood with the color back in her cheeks again. The words of Daniel Swale had made a change in her; she was taller, more aloof, like a fine lady on a Gainsborough canvas.

"Madam," said Captain Bligh, "I mistook you for some one else, an unpardonable mistake, of course, but I ask your pardon."

"Thank you, sir," she answered, as if the words had been written for her to read. "The captain is very kind."

"And you, Seth Scarlet," Daniel Swale turned slowly to his mate, "there'll be no error back at home,

you understand? Madame Swale comes of an old
county family."

Seth Scarlet must have understood. He must have
understood and, like the other Scarlets, he was a
kindly man.

"Heaven help me!" said Seth Scarlet. "She'll be
a princess, if you say so, back at Haven's End."

"Thank you," said Daniel Swale. "Take Captain
Bligh on deck."

Daniel Swale sank down upon a locker. Blood was
dripping from his left sleeve, but he did not seem to
notice; he was staring at the cabin wall, watching some
vision which his own thoughts made.

Down on her knees beside him that lady was reaching for his hand.

"Daniel," she said. "Daniel."

"Yes, my dear," he answered, and he touched her
bright head softly.

"Daniel," she said, "it's true. You know it's true."

His answer was like the Swales. "It was," he said,
"but it's not true now."

"Daniel," she asked, "are you going to cast me
off?"

"No," he answered. "Why do you ask me that?"

"It was the money," her voice broke. "That—box
of money. And you were such a gull, Dan Swale, so
easy and so good. I'm not even as pretty as I was once.
Couldn't you have seen?"

Daniel Swale did not answer, but sat looking at
the wall.

"My dear," he said, "it's fair trading. I've been
sharp in trade, so that I can't complain when one is

sharp with me. And besides," his eyes grew bright, and he began to smile in a mild, contented way, "one can be anything, if one dares enough. I'll have a fine house for you on the high street before we're through, and your own coach, if I live. You are a lady when we get to Haven's End."

8

Slave Catcher

8

Slave Catcher

IT SEEMS ONLY A YEAR OR TWO AGO that Washington Cuffy would be standing beside his hack to meet the evening train at Haven's End. His hair was gray and kinky; his old silk hat had faded to a rusty color, not unlike his face, and he was the end of one of those strange tales which are half alive in our town still.

The fifties and the abolitionist era hovered uncertainly about him, and the Missouri Compromise and all the glowing periods of Webster and of Hayne. And there was something else, older by far than that.

When the train came in, all the wrinkles in Washington Cuffy's cheeks and eyes would curl upward, each one in a smile, and up would go his hand to the brim of that preposterous hat in a gesture of the old régime.

"Evenin', Master Dennis," he would say, and his voice would be clear and deep like a bar of music.

And there would be Dennis Swale, his evening

paper rolled like a diploma in his hand, stout and middle-aged. His face was growing identically like the face of Matthew Swale when he was old. The resemblance was surprising, if you recalled the portrait in the dining room of the Swale house. The turned-up collar of Dennis' overcoat was like the great white collar of Matthew Swale. The nose of Dennis Swale was the same long nose, sharp and slightly sinister. The mouth was the same, small and close; the eyes the same, deep-set and keen.

"Good evening, Washington," Dennis Swale would say, and sometimes he would add, "so there you are."

And there they were upon the station platform beneath the smoky lamps, the son of Malachi Cuffy and the son of Matthew Swale. They must have recalled the story, sometimes that white man and that black man, for the memory of it was the sort that could not blur.

You could find the letter which Matthew Swale once wrote in the files of the old *Gazette*, December, 1852. The Swale money, like other New England fortunes had turned from the sea to the cotton industry. It was natural that Matthew Swale should take a conservative stand, when the Fugitive Slave Act was passed a decade before the Rebellion. Whenever there was a conservative side in our town, one could always find a Swale.

Sir:

I am criticized for holding views contrary to the theories promulgated by certain abolitionists. Do those gentlemen —

I use the term with hesitation — forget that the production of cotton is founded upon the institution of slavery? If that institution is the error of our forefathers, it is a necessary evil now.

I paraphrase the words of a clergyman when I say that I should feel it my duty to *turn from my door* a fugitive slave, *unfed, unaided in any way*, rather than set at naught the law of the land.

"Yes," Dennis Swale would sometimes say, "father was a hard old man."

It never occurred to Dennis that he might be hard himself.

"Yes," Dennis Swale would say, and he would tell the story as accurately as an antiquarian, "I was too young to understand it, of course, but my brother Richard gave me the facts. It seems that a man named Scarlet headed the mob. They came up from those cabins by the railroad tracks, called Little Guinea."

And there was a strange name for you. All the pieces came together once you heard that name — Malachi, and the letter, and the face of Matthew Swale. Beside the railroad tracks, hidden from the older streets, you could see the unpainted houses of Little Guinea. They named it Little Guinea when there was a Guinea coast — but those were matters which one seldom speaks of and only the name is left to hint of a forgotten business.

"Yes," said Dennis Swale, "they came up from Little Guinea. . . . Now I wonder why they called it that."

The Swale house must have been a fine place for a boy. It was becoming an old house, when Dennis' brother Richard was young, and Richard Swale was old enough to die at Fredericksburg.

When Richard told Dennis about it, Dennis was of an age when sights and sounds stay clear. Dennis could remember his brother's uniform, with the state shield on its buttons, and the slope of Richard's cap, and the hopeless look in Richard's eyes. Richard must have known he would not see the house again.

"You mustn't mind the old man," Richard said. "Why, damn it, you'll miss his hiding you some day. This is a fine place for a boy."

The shadows of the Swale house and the peace of the gardens were like sounds to Richard Swale, and he was a part of it when he was a boy, as much as the elm trees on the lawn and the eagle on the cupola. The Swale house was like a country then, and that country was his own. All the narrow passageways were his, and the attic filled with discarded Chippendale and cowhide trunks, where the dust would dance in the sunbeams, never wholly still.

"Forever poking in the attic, forever nosing in the passages," Richard said to Dennis. "Brother, you ought to know. Don't the hinges always squeak? Don't the halls grow very large at dusk? And in the morning — there's the time, the very early morning. . . . Lord, the old man was angry . . . and he was heartier then."

It was very early in the morning, Richard said, when he woke with a sense that time was moving fast; and there he was in his trundle bed in his little room that looked from under the cornice toward the river. It was April, and down below — it seemed a long way down — the lawn was sodden and weary from the winter — and the air was damp with mist beneath the early sun.

Dressing was no long matter in those days when he was fourteen. In not much more than three minutes he was in his boots and breeches, and he was thinking — it seemed natural enough:

"You're going to the attic," he was thinking. "You've time to see the attic before the breakfast bell."

There was still a grayness in the hall, as though the night had not escaped as yet, and by the landing he could look over the balustrade down the three flights of flying staircase. He could hear his father's voice and then the voices of the children from the nursery, but the attic was asleep, always, day and night, asleep.

That morning was when Richard found those iron things in the faint, fresh light. He could remember the heavy coldness of them and the clinking of the chains, musical and soft, and all the morning went about them like a frame. They were in a pine chest, he remembered, the lid of which was branded, "D. Swale, 1769", and there was a smell of camphor and old leather and unpainted wood.

It was the sea chest of Captain Daniel Swale. Richard had never ventured to open it before. First there were some volumes of charts, such as were in the library downstairs — giving directions for the African coast. The compass bearings on the maps were like the lines of a spider's web, and profiles of the land were like a child's book of pictures, showing "The Ivory Coast, New Callabar and the Islands of Fernando Poo"—in the silence of the morning those names might have been of lands as distant as the moon.

"When you see the highest of the cliffs," Richard read, "with a crooked Tree appearing like an Umbrella NE. by N. and NNE. from you, then you are not far from the shore in 17 and 15 Fathom of good sandy Ground. You'll see also a great Forest beset round with Palm-Trees. From thence The *Blacks* will bring fresh water in pots. They come a great Way aboard with little Boats."

In the silence of the attic he had the strangest feeling. The words were like a voice—exactly like a voice.

His hand, as he groped in the box, encountered something hard that rattled. He pulled and pulled again. As he did so, that smell of pine and camphor and decaying leather was all about him and in his hands were two chains. They were crossed like an X, fastened at the intersection, and at each extremity was an iron ring that locked. They clanked and rattled as he dragged them on the floor.

A shaft of sunlight was coming through the window and the dust was swirling in the light in nervous little eddies.

There was no sound, but all at once his heart had started to his throat, because he could have sworn there was something in the attic besides himself. His heart was in his throat and then the breakfast bell was ringing.

His father was in the dining room, seated before the silver coffee urn, reading from a heap of letters. His high, flaring collar held his head up very straight; his watch and fob were on the table, and he held his cup of coffee halfway to his lips.

"You're late," said Matthew Swale. "Can't you hear? Do they have to ring the bell fit to wake the dead to bring you down?"

"Father—" began Richard.

"Sit down," said Matthew Swale. "Breakfast's getting cold."

"Father," said Richard, "what are these things?"

"What things?" said Matthew Swale. And then he saw them. Richard was holding them up so that they were dangling against the background of the sideboard and the silver. There was a minute before his father spoke, or the time seemed as long as that.

His father wiped his fingers with his napkin very carefully.

"Where," he said and stopped to clear his throat, "where did you come on that?"

"Up in the attic, sir," said Richard. "I found them in a box."

His father wiped his lips with his napkin very carefully.

"In a box?" said Matthew Swale. "What box?" Then his voice had dropped almost to a whisper. "Get up. Put 'em back where you found 'em, boy, before the servants see 'em. No, wait. Here comes your mother. Give those things to me."

He snatched them out of Richard's hand and tossed them clanking beneath the table.

"Don't mind what they were; they were your great-grandfather's," he said. "Did I tell you or did I not, not to meddle in the attic?"

"Yes," said Richard. "Yes, you told me, sir."

His mother moved to the table in a rustling sound of silk. Her black, plaited hair made her look very pale, and you could imagine that she was floating on that rustling sound. She was poorly that morning. Richard could tell from the way she smiled, and he had heard them say that very soon she would not come downstairs at all.

"I'm sorry, dear," she said, "that I'm too late to pour your coffee."

Matthew Swale looked at her without speaking, but she must have read his look.

"Don't worry," she said. "I'm feeling better. And you can't help it, if I'm not."

"Can't I?" said Matthew Swale. "Can't I? Richard, pull back your mother's chair."

She was laughing, and she seemed to draw away on the sound of her laughter until she was wiser than them all.

"I wish to God," said Matthew Swale, "you wouldn't laugh about it."

Her lips were still half parted in a smile, and, in that instant, she seemed very young.

"Matthew," she said, "I wish to God that other people knew that you were kind."

Matthew Swale's lips relaxed. She had a way with him, because she had never been afraid.

"It doesn't matter," he said slowly, "what other people think."

"I suppose," she said, "that you know what they're saying."

Before he answered, his father walked to the fire-place and back, with his quick, nervous stride.

"It makes no difference what any one says," he answered. "The only thing to do in these days is to stand by one's conviction, and I'll stand."

What he would stand for, Richard could not guess, but his mother must have known.

"It makes no difference where one stands," she said. "It's all the same, as long as one is kind."

His father did not answer, but all at once he did a startling thing. He lied. It was the first and only time that Richard heard him lie. He picked up the chains from beneath the table and wrapped them in his napkin, and Richard noticed that his face flushed into a wintry pink.

"The chain's snapped on the hitching post," he said. "I'll have to get another. That's the trouble with this house. It's getting much too old. Everything keeps breaking."

"Matthew," said Richard's mother, "Matthew."

"Yes," his father answered quickly. "Yes, what is it?"

"Pomp is ill," she said, "down in Little Guinea."

"He's getting old," said Matthew Swale. "Everything's too old. Richard, come with me."

His mother turned; her head was raised in a question before she spoke, and all sorts of words were in her eyes. The beauty that was leaving her and the strength that was leaving her were in her eyes.

"What do you want with Richard?" his mother asked.

"I want to speak to him. That's all," his father said.

"What," she asked, and her shoulders shook with one of her noiseless fits of coughing. "What has he done wrong?"

"Nothing," he said. "The boy's all right."

"I'm glad," she said. "You must be gentle, Matthew, when I'm not here to make you."

His father drew a deep breath as though he were about to speak, but the pantry door had opened before he could begin. Bridget, one of the Irish maids, was standing in the dining room, twisting at her apron.

"If you please, sorr—if you please, there's after being a big black man, a negur like, in the kitchen wants to see you."

"Well, what does he want?" said Matthew Swale.

"About caring for the horses, sorr," said Bridget. "Pomp being took sick, sent him down."

"Send him to the library," said Matthew Swale. "Richard, come with me."

He closed the door of the library softly. The chains were still in his hand, bundled in his napkin. Before he spoke, he strode over to his block-front secretary, tossed the bundle into the lower drawer, locked it and placed the key in his waistcoat pocket.

"Richard," he said. "Richard."

"Yes, sir," Richard answered.

"You'll not tell your mother what you found."

"No," said Richard. "No, I'll not tell her, sir."

The colored man of whom Bridget had spoken came

into the library and closed the door behind him, brushing at his frayed, patched coat.

The man was tall; his skin was the same color as the black mahogany of the block-front desk, and it glistened in the light. His face was broad, the mouth like a scar, the nose flat, the eyes wide and melancholy. Negroes were not a strange sight and yet Richard always remembered that the man seemed strange. As he stood there, the whole room seemed unfamiliar, and something went stirring in Richard's mind, and then he recollected what it was.

"They come a great way aboard with little boats."

Matthew Swale stood beside the desk, looking the black man up and down.

"Well," said Matthew Swale, loudly as one speaks to a foreigner, "what do you want?"

The Negro shuffled his feet and moved his head and sighed. The door was just behind him, and on either side were cases filled with books, and then there was the portrait of Daniel Swale in his sea cloak, and pictures of two ships done in oil. The black man sighed again.

"Pomp sent me, sah," he said. "He say fo' me to 'tend the hosses." His voice was low and even when he finished speaking, it left an echo in the room.

"Well, what's your name?" said Matthew Swale.

"Malachi, sah," the black man said. "Malachi Cuffy, if yo' please."

"Where do you come from?" said Matthew Swale. "You don't belong in town."

"From Virginia, sah," said Malachi. "I done come from Virginia way."

"Well," said Matthew Swale. "What are you doing here?"

"Searchin' fo' work, sah," said Malachi. He smiled, so that his face all turned to wrinkles. "I knows horses, I do. I've driven for the quality."

"What quality?" said Matthew Swale.

"I'se 'ud rather not say, if yo' please, sah," Malachi Cuffy said.

"Why?" said Matthew Swale.

"Sah?" said Malachi.

"You heard me," said Matthew Swale. "Do you think I'll hire a servant who won't say where he's worked?"

"Sah," said Malachi, "I'm powerful good with horses. I be so."

"Yes," said Matthew Swale, "and you're a powerful good black liar. You tell Pomp from me not to send any more black tramps here."

"Yes, sah," said Malachi. "Pomp, he done send me. Pomp, he says yo' might help me, if yo' please, sah. I come from very far."

"And they're looking for you," said Matthew Swale; "I'll wager that."

The black man did not move at first, but his expression changed and Richard remembered how it was. His eyes became sharp with a sudden glint of fear. His hand made a quick, spasmodic gesture and he shrank backward until his shoulders touched the door.

"Please, sah," he said. His voice was low and soft.

"Be off with you," said Matthew Swale.

"Please, sah!" the black man said, and Richard was

frightened then. Malachi's eyes were glowing. They were suddenly hard, intent.

"Be off with you," said Matthew Swale.

Then he was gone. A moment before, he had been standing in front of the gray panels of the library door and next, though the door was closed, Richard could almost believe he saw him still, tall and black, with that strange light in his eyes.

"Father," said Richard, "what made him look like that?"

His father must have had the memory too, for he also stood looking at the door.

"The man's a runaway," his father said. "And confounded ugly too. Go out. Your mother's calling."

His mother was in the dining room, seated just as they had left her. When he came in, she gave her head a little shake and brushed quickly at her shawl.

"Richard," she said, "there's a basket in the kitchen. Will you take it down to Pomp?"

"Yes," said Richard. "Now?"

"It's Saturday," his mother said; "you have no school. Yes, you know the house in Little Guinea."

Richard knew the house. As long as he could remember anything, Pomp had been working at the harness and brushing down the horses as he sang beneath his breath.

"Yes, I'll go," said Richard, but, as he turned, his mother called him back.

"Richard," his mother said, "did your father see that poor black man?"

Richard nodded.

"He's gone," he said.

"Gone?" said his mother. "I saw him in the hall. I wonder where he's gone." But how should Richard Swale have known?

"He was like a lost soul," she said, "a poor lost soul, and he was frightened. I can tell, because I'm frightened too. There's something — something terrible going to happen. Richard, I'm afraid."

The Unseen Things were moving. Not the wind, but unseen things were hurrying through the streets, and Richard felt that sense of hurry. The sun was out in a soft blue sky. A northwest breeze, still bearing on it the sharpness of the winter, was making the river dark and rough, and making the puddles on the lawns and streets like little rippling seas. A row of muddy buggies was tied before the West India Store; smoke curled from the chimney of the old distillery on the river street, and smoke was coming from the engine house of the new granite cotton mills. There was a humming from the mills, a new and restive sound.

Old Mr. Nevins, who was preacher at the old First Church, was walking toward the main street. His long white hair made him very venerable; his thoughts were so far away that he walked through the puddles, splashing as though he did not see them.

"Where have you been, Richard Swale?" Mr. Nevins asked.

When Richard told him that he had been to Little Guinea, Mr. Nevins laid a hand upon his shoulder.

"Be merciful," he said. "Mercy is the best of all."

The frost was oozing from the main street, leaving it all mud and ruts; steam from wet shingles was curling from the old First Church. A carriage had drawn up before the tavern; a single man, a stranger, was standing on the porch, and a group of men were gathered on the sidewalk ten yards or so away. The strange thing was that Richard could hear their voices a long way off.

"There's trouble," said Mr. Nevins. "I do believe there's trouble."

The men on the sidewalk were staring at the tavern and their voices rose and fell with a curious intensity. A man in a tall beaver hat was speaking to them and Richard knew him well enough. It was Mr. William Scarlet, who owned the rigging lofts farther down the street — a heavy man, like all the Scarlet family, wearing a greatcoat buttoned to his throat. As Mr. Scarlet spoke, he would wipe his face with a red handkerchief and then thrust it in his pocket and pull it out again.

"William," said Mr. Nevins, "what's the matter?"

They all turned when they saw Mr. Nevins, as if they were glad to see him.

"There's matter enough," Mr. Scarlet said. "A slave catcher's come to town."

"Yes," said one of the shipyard men, "and he'd be a damned sight wiser if he was to get out again."

"Quiet," said Mr. Nevins. "Speak more gently, friend."

He turned to Mr. Scarlet and a look passed between them. When that look passed between them, both their faces changed.

"William," said Mr. Nevins, "is there —" and his sentence ended with another glance.

"Yes," said Mr. Scarlet. "Yes, a new colored man's in town. You know where. And look on the porch; there's the one who's after him, him in the black slouch hat, and the marshal and two deputies are up the street."

As Mr. Nevins glanced toward the porch, you might have thought that the excitement pleased the stranger. His face beneath his whiskers and his drooping brown moustache was thin and yellowish. His eyes were yellow and unblinking and his voice was very smooth. He took a long cheroot from his mouth and spat at a knothole.

"Wherefor's all the noise?" he asked. "It's what I tell you. I'm here to get a nigger, a low, no-account nigger. Holler, if you like. I'll get him."

"Nigger catcher!" some one shouted.

"White trash," said the stranger, "shut yore face!"

Mr. Nevins drew a key from the pocket of his coat. It was the key to the old First Church.

"It's time," said Mr. Nevins. "Open up the door and toll the bell."

Then Mr. Scarlet made a sudden gesture and looked narrowly up the street.

"Here comes Swale."

"He'll do no harm," said Nevins. "I'll speak to Matthew Swale."

Then Richard saw his father walking toward the tavern; his head was stiff and unbending, supported by his great white collar. His gray beaver hat was freshly brushed and smooth; the pin in his cravat, his watchchain and the top of his walking stick all glittered in the sun. The mechanics touched their hats and Mr.

Scarlet looked ill at ease and mopped his forehead with his handkerchief.

"Good morning, Matthew," said Mr. Nevins.

Matthew Swale bowed, but before he answered, the bell began to ring.

"What's wrong?" he said. "Has some one died?"

"No," said Mr. Nevins. "Since you ask, it's a call. The time has come."

Mr. Nevins' voice rose higher. The sound of the bell went pulsing through the blue like heartbeats, stirring all the sleep and all the peace of Haven's End.

"You're a just man, Matthew," Mr. Nevins said. "I've known you and I've known your father for fifty years. You won't see injustice done. There are officers here, looking for a poor black slave, and the bell is ringing for a signal."

"A signal?" Matthew Swale said. "Do you mean to start a riot?"

A crowd was gathering in the street. A minute before the place had been empty, and now, before one noticed, it was filled until it seemed that all the town was there, shouting questions and elbowing toward the tavern steps.

"Parson," said Matthew Swale, "do you know what you're doing?"

"Yes," said Mr. Nevins, "and you'll be with us, Matthew."

"No, I won't," said Matthew Swale. "There's one honest man in town. Who's that on the porch?" He was pointing to the stranger in the black felt hat.

Mr. Scarlet stepped up and mopped at his forehead. "Now, Mr. Swale," said Mr. Scarlet, "you leave him to us. Hey," Mr. Scarlet's voice rose to a shout, "do you see him, boys? There's a slave catcher in town!"

"Git him!" some one shouted. "Ride him on a rail."

Then Matthew Swale's voice also rose, harsh and clear above the ringing of the bell.

"Stop that howling," he shouted. "Don't you know the law?"

Next there was a silence, and every one was staring.

"Look!" Richard heard some one mutter. "Yonder's Matthew Swale."

"Don't he lay it on, though?" some one was muttering. "You might think he owned the town."

The noise of the bell was filling the air with a throb of excitement, until the air seemed full of angry waves. Matthew Swale walked up the steps, and every one was watching.

"Good morning, sir," he said. "My name is Swale, and I'm at your service." He glanced down at the sidewalk. "Don't mind them," he said. "Something like this was bound to happen, and cheap sentiment won't help it."

The man in the black felt hat stretched out a lanky hand. "Proud to make your acquaintance, sir," he said, in that soft, smooth voice. "I'm Joe Lacey, sir, from Calvert's plantation, Mr. Calvert's agent with full attorney powers. I've come to fetch a nigger back."

Mr. Swale did not appear to notice Mr. Lacey's hand suspended indecisively between them.

"Very good," he said. "I'll do what's right, you understand. How do you know your man is here?"

Mr. Lacey spat over the porch rail. "Mister," he said, "we traced him on from Boston. Niggers are powerful stupid; I reckon I know, and he's a downright ordinary chattel."

"What's he like?" said Matthew Swale.

Mr. Lacey chewed on the end of his cheroot.

"A big buck, powerful and prime," he said. "Field hand purchased by Mr. Calvert in Mobile. Goes by the name of Malachi Cuffy, if he ain't changed it."

Matthew Swale's cane dropped from beneath his arm and clattered on the veranda boards.

"Have you chanced to have seen him, sir?" said Mr. Lacey.

Richard's father cleared his throat and then his words came harshly, loud enough for every one to hear.

"He was at my house this morning," Matthew answered. "He should be in Little Guinea now."

"Don't you fret, sir," said Mr. Lacey. "We know that. The marshal's gone to fetch him. Heigh, now look yonder! Here he comes."

There was a murmur in the street that was growing louder. Every one was turning, pushing, staring, and the sight was strange enough, for Haven's End. Half a dozen men were walking down the street, led by a heavy-bearded man who wore a badge upon his coat. A black man was in the center of that group and the eye clung to him, Richard always said, as though he stood alone. His shirt was in tatters; the whites of his eyes were gleaming. The blood was running from a cut upon his temple and his hands were tied with rope.

"It's him," shouted Mr. Lacey.

"And now," shouted Mr. Swale, "there's going to be trouble. Marshal, bring that man up here."

The sound in the street had risen until there was a roar. How it happened you could never tell; first there was the knot of men walking down the street, and then the crowd was all about them in a rush of tossing hats and sticks.

"Run!" some one was shouting. "Run!" It was old Mr. Nevins' voice. His hat was off and his white hair was flying.

"By God!" shouted Mr. Lacey. "He's got away. Look there, he's running yonder."

Sure enough, the black man was running up the street and Matthew Swale was watching.

"Yes," said Matthew Swale, "he's got a pair of legs."

"Git the slave catcher," the crowd was shouting. "Ride him on a rail."

"Don't worry," said Matthew Swale. "He'll not run far; they'll take him up again. He's tired; he's very tired."

"Fetch the slave catcher!" they were shouting. "Ride him on a rail."

"I think," said Matthew Swale, "you had better come to my house. You'll be safer there."

He pushed his hat more firmly on his head and walked down the steps of the tavern porch. "Get back," he said. "Get back."

They did not touch him, though Richard could not tell why.

"Shame!" some one was shouting. "Shame on you, Mr. Swale."

At the head of the street, Matthew Swale stopped

to look behind him. Mr. Lacey's breath was coming fast; Mr. Lacey's hands were trembling like his voice.

"Damn 'em!" he said. "Did you hear 'em? They want to ride me on a rail."

But Matthew Swale still did not appear to hear. He was gazing at the crowd which was growing larger by the old First Church; the mechanics were coming from the rigging lofts and the shops, and mill hands and shipwrights were walking from the river.

"He'll not run far," said Matthew Swale. "The man was very tired and weak."

He sighed and looked at Mr. Lacey.

"You can only do what you think is right in these days," said Matthew Swale. "We all must stand by that."

"You're a gentleman, sir," said Mr. Lacey.

"Richard," said his father, "take Mr. Lacey to the guest room and bring him whisky. I'm going back to town. We'll have to find that man."

"Shame!" some one had shouted. "Shame on you, Mr. Swale!"

But there was no shame upon him, even Richard could see that.

It must have been after four when Matthew Swale got back home. Richard could remember, because the shadows were growing long, and the sunlight in the front hall was growing soft, as always in the afternoon, before the sun went down.

As his father stood beside the table in the hall, taking off his coat, he seemed very tired.

"Ah," said Matthew Swale, "what are you doing here?"

"I was waiting, sir," said Richard.

His father laid his cane beside his hat and looked sharply up and down the hall.

"What the devil were you waiting for?" he asked.

"I don't know," said Richard, and it was true, he did not know. "Have they caught him, sir?"

"No," his father said. "They saw him down at the Scarlet's wharf and he broke clean away. Where's that overseer? Did you bring him back?"

"He's in the guest room," said Richard. "He's got the whisky there."

"I'll be bound he has," said Matthew Swale. "Does your mother know he's here?"

"No," said Richard. "Mother's in her room."

"Good," his father said. "Has any one been asking for him?"

"No," said Richard. "Nobody's been here." As he answered, he could imagine that his father was listening to some noise out in the street.

"Well, they will be," said Matthew Swale. "They're coming. Come into the library. Don't stand mooning there. Come into the library. I want to think." His father was very much disturbed; and his face was all sharp lines. Richard went back to a chair by the window and glanced out at the sodden lawn. His father was pacing quickly about the room but finally he sat before his desk and leaned his head upon his hands.

"Father," said Richard.

"Be quiet, boy," said Matthew Swale. "Be quiet, I want to think."

It was getting on toward dusk and there was not a sound except now and then a creaking noise in the front hall and the rustling of the wind in the trees outside.

There was the portrait of old Daniel Swale upon the wall; his face seemed to sink back into the canvas but his eyes seemed brighter in the dusk. There seemed to be all sorts of people who moved about that room. You could almost imagine that all the other Swales were back in the Swale house, when the dusk was coming on, whispering of all sorts of things which every one had forgotten, and voices were saying, "Don't be afraid. We're here."

The blacks would come out in canoes to meet the ship. Richard could see them coming over violet water, through the dusk, against a coast line of dark, misty trees. He could almost hear their shouts as they came alongside the ships from Haven's End. It did not seem strange when he looked up to see a black man there, because he seemed a part of all the shadows, an unseen thing grown real.

He stood in the center of the library, as noiseless as a shadow, but he was alive; Richard could see the gleam of his eyes and the rise and fall of his black skin beneath his torn, checked shirt. He was in a shirt and breeches, barefoot, with a blood clot on his cheek.

Richard Swale remembered clutching at the arms of his chair and shutting his eyes, but when he looked again, the black man was still there, breathing noise-lessly through his open lips.

"Father," said Richard, "father."

And then his father saw him. Richard saw his father turn very slowly and saw his eyes grow wide and his face turn white as paper. Somehow some spell had broken, when his father turned, and all the shadows vanished.

Malachi Cuffy, the runaway slave, was standing in the library.

As Matthew Swale moved, Malachi Cuffy moved also, and as he did so, Richard saw that he had a billet of wood in his hand.

"White man," he said softly, "white man."

Matthew Swale got up, holding the back of his chair, but he did not speak; his face was still as white as paper, just as though he had seen a ghost.

"White man," said Malachi Cuffy, "don't yo' move. Yo' done tole on me, did yo', white man?"

Then Matthew Swale found his voice, and it did not surprise Richard that he was not afraid.

"I told," he said, "but they'd gone to get you before I told. How did you come here?"

As Malachi Cuffy answered, Richard could remember his white teeth shining through the dusk.

"I come through the back window," Malachi Cuffy said. "They'll know that no one will help a poor nigger here. And white man, yo' done told."

Richard always remembered how his father stood with his hands resting on the back of his chair and though his face was white, his voice was steady.

"You've been running a long way," he said.

"Yes, white man," said Malachi, "I been running; I been running."

"Put down that stick," said Matthew Swale.

"White man," said Malachi, "don't yo' move. I'll kill yo' if yo' move."

Matthew Swale was very quick. He must have known

all the while what he would do, and the chair he held was light enough to handle. He swung it upward, and its upward arc landed clean on Malachi Cuffy's jaw. There was a thud and a rattle of the chair, as the two men rolled together on the floor. Then Matthew Swale had his hands on Malachi's throat and his knee on Malachi Cuffy's chest.

"Richard," he was saying, "take this key and get the irons from the desk, and close the door. Don't hurry; there's no need to hurry. The poor man's weak as water. You could have knocked him down."

There was one thing besides, which his father said. Richard could remember it, though he was taken with a fit of trembling.

"They work," said Matthew Swale. "Now who would have thought they'd work?"

Malachi Cuffy was sitting on the floor, with manacles on his wrists and ankles, and Matthew Swale was on his feet, and looking still as though he saw a ghost; and the picture of Daniel Swale was staring at them and all the room seemed filled with people, although they were all alone.

"This house is old," his father said. "Lord, but it is old. Richard, fetch the brandy and wet that poor man's lips. Take the brandy, black man; don't you be afraid."

Matthew Swale, himself, must have known the room was filled with other people, for he looked around him exactly as though he saw.

Then Richard heard some one running down the stairs.

"Mr. Swale," some one was calling. "Mr. Swale."

"Here," called Matthew Swale, "don't shout like that. You'll wake the dead."

Richard was the one who opened the library door, and there was Mr. Lacey, smelling strong of whisky. His hair was matted; he was twisting his long hands together, and he did not appear to notice that anything was strange, because it was very clear that Mr. Lacey was afraid.

"I seen 'em from the window," Mr. Lacey said. "There's hundreds coming up the street! You won't let 'em take me, will you, Mr. Swale?"

"No," said Matthew Swale. "Stay here and watch this man."

As though it was an everyday occurrence he walked into the hall and picked up his hat and cane. Even then, that experience must have been fresher in his mind than the news of the crowd upon the street, for he turned toward the library again and spoke out a thought, though there was no need to speak.

"He wanted to kill me," he said. "I'd have done the same."

Then his voice was drowned out by the thundering of the eagle knocker on the front door.

Matthew Swale opened it and walked out upon the granite steps. The first thing one felt, Richard said, was the imminence of danger that made the skin creep, and then one saw the crowd.

They were filing through the gate of the high fence by the street, an orderly lot of men who made but little noise. You could easily see their faces through the dusk. There must have been a hundred, enough at any rate to be beyond the grasp of ordinary thought.

They were talking in low voices, but they stopped when they saw Matthew Swale. Two men who must have knocked upon the door were standing on the gravel walk, Mr. Scarlet, mopping at his face, and Jonathan Hume, a foreman from the shipyard.

Matthew Swale looked at the crowd and then at Mr. Scarlet and then at Jonathan Hume, seemingly getting it all in his mind as one might memorize a row of figures.

"Well?" he said. "Well?"

Mr. Scarlet mopped his face again, and Jonathan Hume thrust his hands in his jacket pockets.

"Don't you want to know what we're here for?" he inquired.

"No," said Matthew Swale, "but I'll tell you this. I'll give you two minutes to get off of my front lawn."

Mr. Hume spat on the gravel path. "It don't do any good to talk like that," he said. "Scarlet and me here, we're heading the Vigilance Committee."

"Now, Mr. Swale," said Mr. Scarlet, "we don't want to make any trouble for you."

"You won't," said Matthew Swale, and smiled. "When a pair like you heads anything."

Mr. Scarlet's voice was thick. "I guess we're just as good as you."

"Ah," said Matthew, "did you come here to tell me that?"

"We came here to get that damn slave catcher. That's why we've come. Will you give him up or must we bust in to get him?"

It was clear that Matthew was growing angry, though he did not raise his voice. "So, it's a mob, is it?" he said.

"A tar-and-feather mob. Get off with it, Mr. Hume. And mind you don't come here again until you're asked."

"Don't you put on any airs now," Mr. Scarlet said. "We're just as good as you — you nigger catcher."

"Nigger catcher," shouted some one. "That's what Swale is, boys!"

Richard never dreamed what would happen next; even when it had happened, the action seemed incredible. Matthew Swale had raised his cane and had struck Mr. Scarlet diagonally across the face. Mr. Scarlet staggered a step backwards; involuntarily his hands went up.

"There," said Matthew Swale, "that'll do for you." Suddenly his voice rose to a shout. "Listen, you," he shouted. "Hold your tongues and listen. The man in my house is acting according to the law. Do you understand what that means? He's in my house and he'll stay in my house as long as I'm in it. Now move off of my front lawn."

Then some one threw a club. It went crashing through a window and then the air was filled with stones and the noise was suddenly terrible, indistinguishable, derisive, jeering. Every one upon the lawn was sneering at Matthew Swale.

"Come on," Mr. Hume was shouting. "Come and git him, boys."

And they were coming, swarming up the thirty yards of lawn. Richard could see them, black faces and white faces, crouching bodies, and awkward, shambling feet.

"Richard," Matthew Swale was saying, "go inside and lock the door."

The time was too short for accurate impression, but it could not have been more than a few seconds after his father raised his cane when Richard was aware that his mother was on the doorstep. She had come there as illogically as a figure in a vision, but the sight of her was very clear, her white hooped skirt with little flowers printed on it, her shawl with the cameo pin.

"Matthew," she was saying, "what is it, Matthew?"

He remembered her voice, clear and very sweet, and next instant she lay on the doorstep in a rumple of white muslin, broken and without a word. And next, his father was kneeling over her, holding up her head.

Somehow everything had stopped and there was only his father's voice, breaking with a sob. "You cowards!" he shouted.

He was lifting her in his arms; his back was to the lawn as he carried her through the doorway. Richard followed him, but when he turned and looked, just before he closed the door, there was no one on the lawn. Every one had gone; they must have started leaving when they saw her fall.

Richard remembered when she opened her eyes, though he could not tell how much time had elapsed. She was lying on her four-posted bed, covered with a Paisley shawl. There was a decanter of brandy upon the candle stand, and old Nora, the children's nurse, was laying a hot towel on her head.

"Matthew," she said, "whatever is the matter? I should drink that brandy, if I were you."

Richard had never seen his father so. He was nearly ashamed or afraid to look long at his father's face; he could not tell which. Matthew Swale had been kneeling by the bed, but when she spoke, he got up slowly and drank the glass of brandy very quickly and then he wiped his eyes.

"When I find the man who did this—" he began, but he stopped when she smiled at him, softly, mockingly, for she was never afraid of Matthew Swale.

"It's just as well I was there," she said. "You couldn't have stopped them. Could you, Matthew?"

Matthew did not reply. The old lines were returning to his mouth and eyes, but he must have known that never in the world could he have stopped them.

"It's what I said," she was still speaking. "None of them know that you are kind."

When his father answered, Richard understood him, because he himself had the same feelings; yet perhaps his father never knew exactly what he said.

"You can't help what's inside you," said Matthew Swale. "I have to do what I think is right. Don't you understand? I have to do what I think is right."

She sighed and turned her head. "I know," she said. "Please don't lecture, Matthew. The Swales always do what they think is right. It makes no difference, if one is kind."

"You'd best be leaving now, sir," Nora said. "You and the young master. The lady's very tired."

Matthew Swale walked down the stairs very slowly. You could not tell what he was thinking, because the lines were back upon his face. The lamp in the hall was lighted and its yellow light went up and up into the blackness of the landings, making his shadow grotesquely long against the wall.

"There's too much rubbish in this house," said Matthew Swale, and he opened the library door.

There they were, just as he had left them. The black man was crouching on the floor, with his face buried in his hands, as Mr. Lacey sat watching him, smoking one of his cheroots. The air was very thick with the cigar smoke, thick enough to make you cough.

"The marshal's coming in a carriage," said Matthew Swale, "to take you out of town."

"Well and good, sir," said Mr. Lacey. "It can't be too quick for me, and once I get this black boy back—" And Mr. Lacey began to swear.

Matthew Swale crossed the room toward Malachi and slapped him on the back.

"Stand up," he said. "I want to have a look at you."

"Yes, sah," said Malachi. "Yes, sah."

"And how do you feel about it?" said Matthew Swale. "Are you ready to go back?"

Malachi looked at Mr. Lacey and looked away. "Yes, sah," he said.

"Ah," said Mr. Lacey. "He'd kill me if he could, the black—" And Mr. Lacey began to swear again.

Matthew Swale placed his hands behind him and looked at Malachi and cleared his throat.

"I stand for law and order, do you understand?" he said.

"I reckon," said Mr. Lacey, "when I get back, I'll tell 'em there are gentlemen in the North."

"Lacey," said Matthew Swale, "I stand for doing what's right, but I've never seen a black man chased before."

"You ain't a planter, sir," said Mr. Lacey, and he laughed. "But you know niggers, that's what I've been saying: 'These are gentle people, and they know niggers, and they've got the fixings in the house.'"

"Yes," said Matthew Swale, "we know them, and this one looks like a good strong hand."

"Ah," said Mr. Lacey, "he'll be prime when he gets the cussedness beat out of him. Yes, sir."

"Do you want to sell him?" said Matthew Swale.

Mr. Lacey started and took his cheroot from his mouth. "No," said Mr. Lacey, "I ain't his owner, sir."

"No," said Matthew Swale. "But you have attorney powers. You have them in your pocket and fifteen hundred dollars is the top price of field hands now."

"Well," said Mr. Lacey, "I don't aim to sell. I didn't come on to sell no niggers."

"Very good," said Matthew Swale. "You, Malachi, hold out your hands. Mr. Lacey, you don't own these chains. My grandfather owned these."

"Here, now," cried Mr. Lacey. "What do you aim to do?"

Matthew Swale began to smile.

"I said," he repeated, "that you don't own the chains. He's yours. Take him, if you want him. Richard, let us step outside."

"Here, now," cried Mr. Lacey. "That ain't right."

Matthew Swale stepped toward him. "Don't tell me what's right or wrong. There he is; now take him."

"Here, now," cried Mr. Lacey, "don't go out. Don't leave me with that nigger here."

"Perhaps," said Matthew Swale, "you'd rather sell?"

"Yes," said Mr. Lacey. "Yes, I'll sell."

"That's better," said Matthew Swale. "Richard, light the candle on my desk while I draw my check. Malachi, come over here. You're my nigger now."

9

Obligations

≈ 9 ≈

Obligations

NEARLY EVERY ONE IN HAVEN'S END
could tell you how Dennis Swale grew poor,
but Dennis Swale himself would be the one
to tell it best, you'd think, until you tried to ask him.
Dennis had that tight mouth of all the portraits in the
old Swale house. Nothing could shake a word from
Dennis Swale on such an affair as that, because the
Swales were proud.

Yet he must have known that everybody knew, because the story was too good to be forgotten. It had
the harshness and the narrowness of a port which had
lost its shipping. Though Haven's End was growing
very small and bare by then, the old currents still were
running.

The landmarks still exist, though it happened nearly
forty years ago. The Swale mills were in it, and the
granite buildings of the mills are by the river. The
engines in the power house were made in '72, when
old Matthew Swale knew that shipping was finished;

and not a spindle has turned for fifteen years, but they were moving, back in '93. And the Deene place was in it, rising paintless and gaping now from its overgrown shrubbery, farther up the river, devoid of a graceful line, for there was no beauty in Haven's End back in '93. And the Penny Savings Bank was in it, a brownstone façade among the old brick buildings on the street.

You may have seen Dennis Swale, a pompous, dull, stout gentleman, walking in the evening past the stores down by the river, a long-nosed little man with a tight-shut mouth. The crowd in front of the Shoe-Shine Parlor would stop its talk. Their voices would drop to a murmur involuntary and low, but if Dennis noticed, he never gave a sign.

"Good evening, Mr. Swale," some one would say, and Dennis would give a gracious nod, while every one stared after him, as he walked quickly by. Then there would be a silence, half constrained, as though every one had met with something odd and out of place.

"Say," some one would say, "he's getting older. . . . Yes, that's Swale — getting older. Don't he look old-fashioned, though? Say, do you remember —"

Something preposterous in his manner, which took for granted an unmerited superiority, gave him that archaic air.

When Dennis ran for mayor against John Scarlet in the fall of '92, you have the beginning of it, as much as anything in our town can begin, where the Colonial era kept rising from its grave. You can imagine Dennis Swale speaking in his thin, harsh voice to a sea of strangers who had never known a Swale. You can imagine the brass bands and the torches weaving down the street and what the mill hands said. Dennis had no sympathy for mill hands and they had none for him.

You can imagine what John Scarlet said, waving his arms, shouting through the autumn night. Dennis Swale could never gain that common touch, which the Scarlets could not lose. John Scarlet ran a shoe shop after he sold the tavern and he could handle men. You could imagine him mopping his red, perspiring face and shaking his heavy fist, lost upon the sea of his own eloquence. His speech is still in the files of the old *Gazette*, ringing with a bitterness rising from the solid type.

"Friends,—I call you friends, because you know me and I know you. I know what you think and I know what you want. Does Mr. Swale know that? No, friends, he don't know anything and what's more, he don't care.

"'But he's Mr. Swale,' you say. 'Of course, Mr. Swale would never think of us.' Now, who are the Swales? Don't be frightened; I can tell you. There's been a Scarlet in this town as long as there's been a Swale. Who are they and what? I can't think what— they've lived so long on dead men's money. They've lived here on other people's work, and the work of folks like you and me. And what have they given back? Nothing, no friends, nothing. Is Mr. Swale here now? I'm not afraid to say it to his face. He's nothing but a name."

Dennis was in the directors' room in the Penny Bank

when the last returns came. The gaslights flickered against the black-walnut woodwork and in the street outside a band was playing very badly. Mr. Deene was there, of course, being president of the bank in those days. He kept looking out the window at the torch-lights; he kept tapping on the sill and whistling through his teeth.

"Dennis," said Mr. Deene, "you can't compete with Scarlet. You can't swim against the tide."

Dennis sat in his chair, motionless and stony-faced.

"It's Scarlet's fault," he said, "that blackleg's made them vote me down." Then he rose with sharp, deep lines about his mouth. "Do you hear them yell?" he said. "That's Scarlet. I'm not finished with Scarlet yet."

Mr. Deene turned from the window with that same bland look; the story goes that Alfred Deene was a handsome man, heavy and broad-shouldered, with dark, deep eyes and a high white forehead. Alfred Deene had the golden touch and he knew life as well as he knew money.

Outside in the street there was a burst of cheering; the noise made Dennis start.

"There," said some one, "there goes Scarlet now."

The gaslight flickered against the dark woodwork and flickered against the face of Alfred Deene, and one can imagine how he spoke when Dennis Swale was gone — with half-concealed amusement and half-concealed contempt.

"Can you believe it?" said Alfred Deene. "He thinks he's living in the eighteenth century. He thinks he can hurt Scarlet. Can you imagine that?"

Then Adam Munn spoke up. He always said he

never liked the smartness of Alfred Deene. He seemed
to be speaking for a lost cause, for politeness, or for
something that was leaving Haven's End.

"I don't know," he said. "No, I don't know. There's
something in them Swales."

Though Alfred Deene did not answer, one could
imagine what he was thinking behind his deep, still
eyes. Alfred Deene could juggle figures and he could
juggle facts; he must have been thinking, even then,
how he could juggle Dennis Swale.

"Yes," he said, "Scarlet's made him mad and
when a man's mad he's a fool. I don't get mad ever."

There is silence now in the Penny Bank, except for
the money talking; the sound of the money rings behind the counters, hollow and secure, above the pains
of life and death. The adding machines click with a
sharp, staccato note, like machine guns in a front-line
trench, followed by the rustling of treasury paper and
the rippling of the silver, but all the rest was silence.
Nevertheless, until a little while ago, Adam Munn
used to sit behind the counter, working at the ledgers,
and Mr. Munn could tell about it because he had
been there for a long time. He had grown thin and
light and noiseless, like a genius of the place, and his
voice would echo from the black-walnut carvings of the
directors' room, so that it sounded like the rustling of
a sheaf of bonds. Mr. Munn would twist his eye-shade
back and straighten his alpaca coat and stare at the
photographs of the presidents on the wall, all hard-
faced, whiskered men of an older generation, but all
with a common stamp, like the members of a family.
Adam Munn could pick their voices from his memory

as one picked music on a banjo's strings. He could imitate their footsteps and their gestures with a mimicry more like an actor's than a clerk's, if the directors' room was silent and the bank's front door was closed.

"Yes," he would say, "in the big gold frame — there's Denny Swale. It don't seem so long that he was younger. Matters don't move much hereabouts. The slower the place, the quicker the time, is how it seems to me."

And he was right. Haven's End was very slow.

"Yes," Adam Munn would say, "you can tell him from his nose. The Swales have always had long noses, as I've heard tell — comical, like this — but he wasn't president then, only a director, serving without pay. Alfred Deene was president back in '93. No, his picture isn't on the wall. The slower the place, the quicker the time. It don't seem so long ago that Mr. Deene left town —"

And Adam Munn's voice would go quavering and keen, turning the old secrets up which were a part of other secrets which one could feel but never know.

"He walked right in here," Adam Munn would say. "He wasn't fat the way he is now, Mr. Dennis wasn't, and you couldn't tell what he was thinking, no more than you can now. He walked in — like this — slowly, like he owned the place — you know how the Swales do — and he sat down — like this — right where you're sitting now, with his hat still on his head. And then he looked around the room, squinting up his eyes."

It was curious — when Adam Munn went on, he could make the whole scene real, because he had the actor's gift. A sudden grimace, a quick turn of his wrist, and Adam Munn was Dennis Swale, and the directors' room was filled with a new, tense stillness.

"'Give me a sheet of paper and a pen,' was what he said, 'and now go fetch the gluepot, and paste that on the door.'"

And that was all that Dennis said. He was like all the Swales, without a sense of drama but with a code of manners, or an instinct, if you care to call it that.

Adam Munn could remember the morning when Alfred Deene called on Dennis Swale, but only later could he piece it all together, even to imagining what both those men were thinking, so that all their words seemed finally like draughts on a checker-board, moving with a purpose, but meaningless, like most words, until hidden thought was clear. It was the year of the panic in 1893, when the nation was tossing in its economic throes and when banks were falling down like ninepins. The noise of it reached even to Haven's End in those days, carrying an uncertainty upon the air, which was very close to dread.

It was a stormy morning, Adam Munn remembered, and the east wind was blowing hard, driving a cold gray rain, hissing upon the windowpanes of the office in the Swale mill. The hissing of the rain and the moaning of that wind were mingled with the humming of the cotton spindles, which made a sound so constant that it was like a background to all living. The private office was vibrant with that sound, even on that windy morning.

Through the grimy windows facing north, one could see the river, slate-gray and wintry, because the spring was coming late. Beside the river, like wreckage almost, was the lost endeavor of Haven's End. The last of the wharves, right below the window, had degenerated to a coal pocket, and the rain could never wholly wash the soot from the sagging buildings around it. The roof and chimney of the old rum distillery, which had been closed ten years before, thrust themselves out of that blackness in sullen disrepair, and the gray piling and the rusting machinery of the disused shipyard were like a patch of forest blackened by some fire. The granite foundations of the Swale mills seemed to be standing on that wreckage, like a last endeavor of the town to cope with change, and even the Swale mills were growing old and dark.

Adam was making entries in the private account books, standing in his shirt sleeves in front of the tall clerk's desk, when Mr. Dennis called him. Adam could write with a beautiful hand in those days, when penmanship was nearing its zenith of perfection. His figures and his letters had fishtails and shadings like a copperplate engraving; but his pen shook when Mr. Dennis called.

"Did you hear me, Munn?" said Dennis Swale.

"Just a minute, sir," said Adam. "I made a blot upon the page."

Mr. Swale looked up quickly from his roll-top desk and straightened the purple folds of his cravat.

"That's the second time this week you've blotted those accounts," Mr. Dennis said.

"I'm sorry, sir," said Adam.

"It does no good to be sorry," said Dennis Swale. "You're lucky to be earning ten dollars a week. Come here and write down this notice. I want it pasted on the doors."

Adam Munn was angry. There was something steely and meager in Dennis Swale which was enough to stir one's anger.

"Ten dollars isn't much," said Adam Munn.

"It's enough for these times," Mr. Dennis said. "I can get a dozen men like you."

"No wonder every one leaves town," said Adam Munn. "You're the sort who makes 'em."

For a moment he could almost think that Dennis Swale was surprised at that. He looked at Adam Munn and then out of the window toward the river, which was flat and empty beneath the rain.

"This place is good enough," said Dennis Swale. "Leave it if you want to go away."

Mr. Dennis was looking at him and he was not angry. "But you won't," he said. "I want you to bring the books to the house to-night at half-past seven o'clock. Now write down this notice. Are you ready?" Dennis Swale cleared his throat; he seemed to be listening to the humming of the mill. "Owing to uncertain business conditions," he said, "this mill will be closed, beginning to-morrow, March 10th, until further notice. Signed, Dennis Swale. Make a dozen copies and tack them on the doors."

He turned away as though he had dictated an ordinary letter, but Adam Munn was startled.

"Are things as bad as that?" he asked.

"Yes," said Mr. Swale. "Copy out these notices. The wind's freshening; we're going to have more rain."

It must have been almost at that minute that Mr. Deene came in, and it was good to see him. Mr. Deene was always rich and easy; he came in smoking a long cigar and smiling at Mr. Swale, but even when he smiled, his glance was steady and his face was a poker face. In spite of his frankness, you had a baffled feeling always; you could not tell what was going on behind his eyes. He slapped his hat on the table by the letter press, sat down and twisted his heavy watch chain around his fingers.

"Have you seen the wires from New York?" he said.

Mr. Dennis leaned back in his swivel chair, looking thoughtfully at Alfred Deene. "Yes," he said, "I'm glad I'm not playing the market. Deene, are you all right?"

"Yes," said Mr. Deene, "yes, I'm all right. Look at me. Do I look worried?"

"No," said Dennis Swale, "nothing ever worries you. I wonder how you do it, Deene. Nothing ever worries you. What do you want? I'm busy."

Alfred Deene began to laugh and flipped the ash from his cigar.

"How do you know I want anything?"

Then Adam Munn remembered a look that passed between them, a wordless, watchful look, as though they both were thinking of something which they did not say.

"Because you're always wanting something," Mr. Dennis said. "You're the kind who never goes anywhere unless there's something he wants."

Mr. Deene laughed again, but his eyes were very

blank and there was something happening which Adam did not know about. All at once Adam felt a twinge of dread and a suspicion of Mr. Deene; he was watching every move which Mr. Dennis made, as he sat there smoking his cigar. All at once, Adam Munn could tell that Mr. Deene was sharp, with a sharpness that Mr. Dennis would never match.

"Dennis," he said, "you're sharp, I always said you were sharp. So you're going to close your mill?"

"Who told you that?"

There was a pause for a moment; there was not a sound except the hissing of the rain upon the window.

"Scarlet," said Alfred Deene. "Scarlet told me that."

There was a sharp creak from Mr. Dennis' chair. "He did, did he?" Mr. Dennis said. Mr. Deene was watching all the while, behind his blank, clear eyes.

"Yes," he said; "and Scarlet said, 'It isn't right. You ought to think about your help,' he said."

Mr. Dennis cleared his throat. "Why should I think of them?" he asked. "They've never thought of me."

"Swale," said Mr. Deene very softly, "are you still angry, Swale?"

"Yes," said Mr. Dennis. "He's the one who made them hate me. Yes, I won't forget."

"No," said Mr. Deene, "I thought you wouldn't." He smiled and leaned forward, so that his voice was very low. "I've got two notes on Scarlet's shoe shop. They're falling due to-morrow and I'll sell 'em to you cheap. I won't take 'em up again. There isn't a bank in the State that will take 'em up to-morrow."

Mr. Dennis' voice was steady but he was leaning forward too.

"Due to-morrow, eh?" said Mr. Dennis.

"Yes," he said, "and I won't take them up. Did you see the bank this morning? There's a run. They're drawing out deposits. There's a line of women on the sidewalk, waiting in the rain. I won't renew." Mr. Deene leaned farther forward. "He can't meet them, Swale."

Dennis Swale was not pleasant to look at, though his expression had not changed. Suddenly all the narrow harshness of our town was written on his face, a fanatical, unreasoning harshness. Adam Munn stood staring over his account book; he did not dare to move, because he knew that he was watching something that he was not meant to see.

"What do you want beside the cash?" said Dennis Swale. "Put your cards on the table. Don't keep them up your sleeve. You want something, Deene."

Mr. Deene sat motionless, watching Dennis Swale. "Listen," he said. "The bank's all right, as right as rain." And as he spoke, the rain went swish against the window. "I don't like Scarlet any more than you. He isn't our kind, Swale, and you're a director in the Penny Bank."

"Yes," said Mr. Dennis, "a Swale's been a director since 1849."

Then, suddenly, they both looked up, startled, though Adam Munn could have sworn he had not made a sound. Suddenly their eyes were on Adam, Mr. Dennis' startled, Mr. Deene's bland and opaque.

"Munn," said Mr. Dennis, "go out and wait in the other room."

Then Adam Munn was standing in the outer office

by the door, and all at once he noticed that his forehead was very moist. Though the door was a blank
pine panel, he still could see Dennis Swale and the
face of Mr. Deene, and he still could see Mr. Deene's
forefinger twisting at his watch chain. There he was
in the private office, twisting Dennis Swale around his
finger. And Mr. Dennis never knew.

"Munn." It was Mr. Dennis calling. "Munn, come
back in here."

There they were by Mr. Dennis' desk, seated side
by side. Mr. Dennis was looking at a paper lined with
figures; he folded it, as Adam Munn came in, and
passed it back to Mr. Deene.

"Munn," he said, "take this down. Are you ready?
— As a director of the Penny Bank, I have examined
the figures, and to the best of my belief, the bank is
sound. — All right, bring it here. I'll sign it."

Mr. Deene rose slowly from his chair and took his
hat. "Thanks," he said. "I won't forget this, Swale."
And probably he never did.

Adam Munn could always remember him standing
in his newly pressed clothes, tall and handsome, looking down at Dennis Swale, smiling. Though one could
not read his thought, Alfred Deene must have been
laughing inside himself, laughing at his own despair,
in his knowledge that he was fighting grimly beneath
his smile, like a drowning man struggling for one more
day of grace.

"Good-by, Dennis," said Alfred Deene. "They may
not like you, but they know you tell the truth."

Dennis Swale looked up at Adam Munn, but he
could not meet his eyes; it was conscience, Adam knew.

"Keep this to yourself," said Dennis Swale.

"Yes," said Adam Munn, "I'm not a talker."

"No," said Mr. Dennis, "you're not a talker. What the devil are you waiting for?"

"Mr. Swale, sir," Adam cleared his throat, surprised at his own voice. "You hadn't ought to have signed that, Mr. Swale."

"Signed what?" said Mr. Dennis. "What the devil do you mean?"

"Mr. Swale," said Adam Munn, and he forgot to be afraid of Dennis Swale, "don't you see he was fooling you? You shouldn't have signed that about the bank. He's a slick one, Mr. Deene is. Twice as slick as you. He—he's fooled you somehow, Mr. Swale."

"Stop your talk!" said Mr. Dennis. "Get back there to your books." And Mr. Dennis turned, looking through the window across the street, and Adam Munn knew what he was watching; he was looking at Scarlet's shoe shop, dripping in the rain.

Tom Low had come in from the outer office; he was shifting nervously from one foot to the other, because, in spite of all his talk, he was afraid of Dennis Swale.

"Well, what is it?" Mr. Dennis said.

"Mr. Scarlet's out here, sir." Tom swallowed in his nervousness, as Mr. Dennis stared at him. "Mr. John Scarlet from the shoe shop. He wants to see you right away."

"Scarlet," said Mr. Dennis, "Scarlet? The town is full of Scarlets. Why don't you show him in?"

John Scarlet was like all of them, a solid, red-faced man with bushy hair, and he looked embarrassed, like the clerk almost, when he stood in the center of the office.

"Hullo, Scarlet," said Mr. Dennis, "what's the matter now?"

"Mr. Swale," said Mr. Scarlet, "I sort of thought I'd come in here, Mr. Swale, because there has always been Swales and Scarlets in this town, and we've got to do what's fair."

"Yes," said Mr. Dennis, "yes, of course."

Now Adam did not know what to think when he saw them standing there. There was a significance about it, without relation to the time and place, as John Scarlet must have known, when he said that there had always been a Scarlet and a Swale. You had a feeling, Adam said, that they could not help what they said next. They were like the figures in his ledger in black ink and in red, each in an opposite column separated by a rule of ink, always truthful, yet in a contradiction which never struck a balance. Somehow, as Adam saw them, his mind went back to endless pages of red and black and black and red, mingling with all the days and nights which had passed over Haven's End.

"Now it's this way," Mr. Scarlet said. Mr. Scarlet was a good man and not afraid to speak his mind. "I see you're going to close the mill. Couldn't you carry it for a week or so? I'm keeping the shoe shop going, running at a loss."

Mr. Dennis seemed surprised; he looked at John Scarlet with an added interest.

"And why, are you doing that?" he asked.

"Look here." Mr. Scarlet also seemed surprised. "Aren't you worried about your help?"

"My help?" said Mr. Dennis. "What about the help?"

"What are they going to do? That's what I mean."

"They won't do anything." Mr. Dennis was always dull. "I've made plans, in case there's trouble."

Mr. Scarlet drew out his handkerchief and wiped his forehead, and for a moment he seemed at a loss for anything to answer.

"Say," said Mr. Scarlet, "listen. You don't grasp what I'm trying to say. You've got to think about these people, haven't you? They're human, like you and me. You're responsible for these — these fellers, Mr. Swale. It ain't right, now is it, to throw 'em out without a bit of notice?"

A flash of light came over Mr. Dennis; Adam could see it come.

"Look here." Suddenly Mr. Dennis' face was a cold, light pink. "Are you coming here, telling me what to do? Are you telling me what's right or wrong? Is that it? This is my mill, Scarlet, and I'm running it. I'll mind my business, and you attend to yours."

"Now here, now," said Mr. Scarlet, in a louder tone. "That ain't no way to talk, Swale. You get off your high horse, Swale. I've come here the way any decent party would, to talk things over. It ain't right — that's all."

Mr. Dennis rose from his swivel chair, and Adam hurried from behind his desk, because Mr. Dennis had an ugly look.

"Confound your impertinence," Mr. Dennis said. "Do you think I care a continental what people like you think?"

"No," said Mr. Scarlet. "That's right, you don't;

but I guess I'm just as good as you. You don't care if men are dying starving, so long as you're all right; and every one knows that. You're a hard man, like your father. The whole tribe of you is hard, but you keep this mill going, or you'll be a dirty skunk. You're a skinflint, for all your airs, and I'll say it to your face."

There was a silence broken by the humming of the mill and by the splashing of the rain. Mr. Dennis drew a deep, sharp breath and touched his purple cravat softly with his finger tips, and Adam knew if Mr. Scarlet tried a hundred years, he could not look like Dennis Swale. He was beyond the anger of Mr. Scarlet's voice, in some land of his own. A thousand men with sweating brows, a century of shadows had built that land.

"Scarlet," said Mr. Swale, "listen to me, Scarlet."

Adam Munn set down his pen because his hand was shaking.

Mr. Dennis' fingers were moving over his purple cravat and he had begun to smile. It was almost like a play, the end of which Adam knew already.

"You've made me into — what did you say? — a skunk. You've interpreted me to every one, you've lashed me with your tongue. Yes, you've got a nasty tongue, and I've sat here and taken your lashing. Did you think I was always going to take it? Were you such a fool as that? You've been meddling with my affairs. I'll meddle with yours now. I bought your notes from Mr. Deene this morning. They're due to-morrow noon."

Mr. Scarlet passed his hand across his forehead. "He sold me, did he? Deene did that?"

"Yes," said Mr. Swale, "Deene did that. Can you

raise ten thousand dollars by to-morrow morning, Scarlet? Think! Think hard! Will you keep your shop going and owe me ten thousand dollars? Think hard, Scarlet."

"Ah," said Mr. Scarlet, "you're laughing at me, are you?"

"Yes," said Mr. Swale, "I'm laughing at you and everybody like you. You've laughed at me long enough. But why discuss it, Scarlet? You wouldn't understand."

"Don't I?" said Mr. Scarlet. "I understand, all right. I understand the way you got them notes, because you wrote a piece saying the bank was sound. Deceiving people when a bank is going busted! All for personal spite! Oh, you're a fine one, you are, and I thank the Lord that made me that I'm not like you. If I've said anything about you, I've said it right, and I'll say it again about a man who knows a bank is going busted."

"Just a minute," said Dennis Swale. "What bank?"

"The Penny Savings Bank!" roared Mr. Scarlet, "And everybody knows it, the same as you!"

Dennis Swale sat down again and shrugged his shoulders.

"Scarlet," he said, and his voice was almost pleasant, "I suppose it takes all sorts to make a world. You and I are different sorts. I regret that there are more of you than me. I don't like you, nor you me, and there's no reason that you should. I've never liked you, nor what you stand for. I don't like demagogues. Did you ever hear the word? That's what you are. You're the loud-mouthed Cleon, who splashes mud upon the marble wall, and you belong in mud — but I never knew until now you were a liar. Don't double up your fist, Scarlet. There's been scene enough. Munn, show Mr. Scarlet out. He'll be leaving now."

For a moment, Mr. Scarlet stared at him open-mouthed, without an answer. He seemed bewildered, bereft of anything to answer.

"Here now!" cried Mr. Scarlet. "Don't tell me you don't know!"

"Munn," said Mr. Swale, "show Mr. Scarlet out."

Nevertheless, Mr. Dennis was upset when Adam Munn came back. He was standing, staring at the worn pine floor, his lips as tight as though they had been sewed together, breathing through his long, thin nose. He could not keep his hands still; his fingers were clenching and unclenching, long, graceful fingers like the hands of all the Swales.

"Damn his insolence!" said Mr. Dennis. "I should have horsewhipped that man. Post those notices on the door and bring the books at half-past seven to-night. Munn, I am going home."

Then Adam Munn was running after him. "Mr. Swale," he was calling, "you've forgotten your coat and hat. It's raining, Mr. Swale."

There was no doubt that it was raining; the wind had shifted to the northeast and the streets were running water, but Dennis Swale did not answer; he was walking through the mill yards, past the picket gates, with a quick, nervous stride, bare-headed in the rain.

It was strange how small Haven's End seemed, once the wind shifted to the northeast and the rain was coming down; even now, on a stormy, blowy day, one still has that sensation — that our town stands aloof and small, beyond the aid of all the land behind it.

Haven's End was small and drab and weary when the rain was coming down; the mist of the rains cut off the hills behind the river and the marshes and the mud flats, leaving only the streets and the houses entirely alone. There was a railroad in those days and a telegraph and even several telephones, but none of these made a difference in the northeast wind; the houses were small and sodden in their dampness, and the streets seemed narrower, and a futility was over everything as the rain came down in sheets.

Adam Munn could feel the sadness because the town was going down; all about the mills the streets were lined with slack, small houses, crowding against larger dwellings, which were falling to decay. The streets were filled with strange voices, speaking in foreign tongues. The tide of emigration had left swarthy faces, rising like the river tide, soiled and dark like the river. Adam Munn hated the sight of them, regarding them with sharp distrust, as every one did who was sprung from native stock.

"Look at 'em," said Adam Munn. "They're reading the signs on the door."

The mill yard was filled with men and women, standing in the rain; they were talking in a babel of voices, wholly meaningless, raised in volatile excitement.

"Look at 'em jabbering like a lot of monkeys," muttered Adam Munn.

There was a shuffling and stamping in the outer office and a pounding on the door. When Adam Munn opened it, Michael Towhig, the foreman of the lower spinning room, was standing on the threshold, and behind him were half a dozen men in overalls and ragged shirts, whitened by the cotton dust. They stared at the office, inarticulate and bereft of speech, all except Michael Towhig, who cleared his throat and wiped his hands on the side of his breeches.

"Where's the boss?" Michael Towhig asked.

"Who?" asked Adam. "Mr. Swale?"

"Sure," said Michael Towhig, "sure, I'm after meaning Swale. Is he gone? Ain't he the dirty sneak? What we want to know is, is it true the mill is closing?"

"That's no way to talk," said Adam. "It's Mr. Swale's mill; he can do what he wants with it. You saw the signs — of course the mill is closing."

"Ah," said Michael Towhig, "and so he run away, did he, without looking us in the face? How do we eat without work? Suppose you tell me that."

"Boys," said Adam Munn, "I can't tell you that, and don't you yell at me, Mike. I'm not Mr. Swale. I don't own the mill."

"Ah," said Michael Towhig, "ain't he the dirty sneak? Isn't he up the street, living in the fine house of his, with his pair of horses and his nigger to drive him, living on dead men's money, so he is? He didn't build this mill, did he?"

"Oh, shut up!" said Adam Munn. "What's the use in yelling? Times are bad, and I guess they're bad for rich men too. Work somewhere else, if you want to. The mill is closing up."

"Sure," said Michael Towhig. "He'll laugh to see us starving, setting there behind his two horses. All right, if he ain't here, we'll go to his house to-night to see him, and I guess he'll see us there."

When they were gone, Adam Munn could hear their footsteps still and the voices in the yard were louder. Yet in spite of the voices, there was a silence. The engines of the mill had stopped, the spindles had stopped turning, and the mill was closing down. It was as though some hand, immense and inevitable, had stopped it as one might stop the ticking of a clock. Suddenly the absence of that background of noise was ominous.

Adam Munn glanced out the window quickly, at the rows of mill hands moving slowly down the street. All the street was filled with voices, now that the mill had closed.

Adam Munn hurried through the office toward the spinning rooms, already gray and ghostly in the dusk.

"Where's the watchman?" he shouted. "Where's Joe Lynch?"

And then Joe Lynch came toward him in dripping oilskins, with a lantern in his hand. Joe Lynch's face was shining wet from the rain. Joe was a steady man, as hard as nails, standing six feet two.

"Did you hear 'em?" Joe Lynch said. "The boys are getting ugly."

"Joe," said Adam Munn, "go out and find a dozen men. There're plenty out of work. And lock the gates. Lock 'em right away."

Mr. Lynch grinned. "Don't you worry, Mr. Munn," he said. "I've got two dozen men already and they're all fixed. Mr. Swale sent down word. Two dozen boys, all sworn in by the sheriff. Swale's a hard man, Mr. Munn."

"Yes," said Adam. The spinning room was growing

darker; the machinery stood before the windows, heavy and grotesque against the squares of fading light.

Adam Munn had never been inside of the Swale house, for until that day no one had ever asked him in, and any one could tell it was no place to go without asking. Already it was part of the past, as frigid in its gentility as Dennis Swale, inhospitable, aloof. Its brick walls, its white cornices and cupola, its lawn with the white, festooned fence before it, made it something for the village boys to look at, even when Adam Munn was a boy. He could remember the feeling that the Swale house was different from the rest of Haven's End, sheltering different people from those he knew. He could remember, even when he was a boy, a feeling of pride and distaste when he looked at it, distaste for the aloofness of the Swales and of pride that there should be such people in the town.

Back in the nineties it was already a place to show to strangers. "It's the Swale house," one would say. "Old Captain Daniel built it one hundred years ago, out of privateering money. They say it's elegant inside." And now that the rain was falling, as Adam Munn walked up the street, wrapped in his oilskin coat, it seemed to him that the Swale house was larger than it had ever been before. It was an enormous shadow among the elm trees on its lawn; the shutters were drawn already, so that only a few cracks of light showed through, and its very darkness made it larger. It was larger than the tavern, it was larger than the Whistle house and larger than the lighted stores farther down the street. It gave Adam Munn the feeling that he was going to a strange place, not to a haunted house, but to something which gave an impression as intangible as that, as he stood beneath the porch and raised the eagle knocker on the Swale front door.

He had been in a hurry, until he raised the knocker, but as it came down with a hollow sound beneath his hand, that sound was almost like a voice admonishing and stern. "Mind your manners!" it seemed to say. "There are only gentlemen here." As he stood upon the porch in the dripping rain, the sound seemed all around him still; it seemed to have roused other sounds, restive and half discernible. The rain was spattering against the bricks, the wind was moving through the trees, but there were other sounds.

A white-haired, old Irish woman in a white apron opened the front door. It was Bridget O'Rourke, and though he had seen her often on her way to church, she was different, standing in the doorway.

"What do you want?" she said.

Before he answered, Adam found himself staring curiously at the hall. A lamp was standing on the table with a long gold mirror behind it but, even in the lamplight, the hall was dim. A broad white staircase curved upwards into the shadows, and there were pictures on the wall of men and women in peculiar, old-fashioned dress. And there was a musty smell, a strange odor of age, such as one encountered always in old houses.

"What do you want?" said Bridget.

"I want to see Mr. Swale," Adam answered.

"You can't see him now," said Bridget. "Mr. Swale is at his dinner."

The Swales had dinner in the evening, when all the rest had supper at Haven's End.

Adam Munn looked at the hall again, and the faces in the pictures were staring at him, blankly, coldly, following him with their eyes.

"I got to see him," said Adam Munn. "Tell him it's about the mill."

Then he was standing alone in the hall, with the door closed behind him, dripping wet, with his hat on his head dripping on the carpet.

It was a queer place, the Swale hall, once the front door was closed. He seemed to be away from everything he knew, once the front door was closed. There were all sorts of sounds which he knew came from the wind and rain outside, but the sounds were different in the house. There were creaking noises like footsteps, and down the hall on the left he could hear the rattling of dishes. Then Bridget O'Rourke was back; she seemed like one of the pictures as she came hurrying toward him, dim in the faint lamplight.

"Mr. Swale will see you," she said. "Take off your coat and wipe your feet upon the mat. He's in the dining room, this way."

The dining room was very large and square, with wallpaper upon it of ships and mountains, all in colors. There was a sideboard along the wall, with silver upon it that shone in the light of two high candlesticks. In the center of the room was a round table, covered with a great white cloth, all white and silver, and there Mr. Dennis and Mrs. Swale were sitting, turning toward him as he walked through the door.

Mrs. Swale was all billows and ruffles, like something very fine and delicate. Mrs. Swale was very rich, the story went. She was one of the Prydes from Philadelphia, and Munn had seen her often in her carriage, but she was different seated at the table. She was as beautiful as the silver, as delicate as the china plates. You might touch her, Adam thought, and you would break her. But she was looking at him kindly, not the way that Mr. Dennis looked.

"You're early, Munn," said Mr. Dennis. "I said half-past seven, didn't I?"

"Yes, sir," Adam answered, "but I've come about the mill."

Mr. Dennis reached for a decanter of claret and filled his glass. "Go into the library and wait. Bridget, show him to the library."

Then Mrs. Swale spoke and she was different and her voice was kind.

"Bridget," said Mrs. Swale, "set a place for Mr. Munn; he's hungry. Sit down, Mr. Munn."

"Thank you, Ma'am," said Adam. His face was growing hot. "I can get along all right."

"Nonsense," said Mrs. Swale. "Dennis, pass the claret to Mr. Munn."

Mr. Dennis did not answer; he passed the claret over and he and the lady looked at each other across the table. And Mr. Dennis frowned and the lady smiled.

"What's the matter with the mill?" she asked.

"The men are angry, Ma'am," said Adam, "because the mill is closing down. They're sending up a deputation here to-night."

Mr. Dennis set his napkin on the table. "I thought they would," he said. "Let 'em come. I'll fix 'em. Thank you, Munn. Excuse me if I'm rude. I'm feeling very tired."

"It's the stock market," said Mrs. Swale; and she laughed. "Never have anything to do with the stock market, Mr. Munn. Dennis, do you know, just the other day Alfred Deene was telling me——"

"Suppose," said Mr. Dennis, "we don't speak of Alfred Deene."

"Why, Dennis?" said Mrs. Swale, and she laughed again. "Why shouldn't Alfred tell me? I suppose he can come here, if I want him."

That was all she said, but there was something more. And Adam Munn had sense enough to know it. He saw their glances meet again, and suddenly Mr. Dennis' face grew red, and suddenly he knew they had both forgotten him.

"So he comes here behind my back, does he?" said Mr. Dennis. "I thought he did."

"Dennis," said Mrs. Swale, "please not now." And she glanced at Adam Munn.

Dennis Swale rose, though his dinner was half finished, and his face looked grey and wooden, like a very bad painting. And Adam Munn felt an embarrassment which had nothing to do with his threadbare coat or the way in which he held his silver fork. "Munn," said Mr. Dennis, "come into the library. Bridget, bring the brandy and cigars into the library." And he walked out to the hall with Adam Munn behind him.

There was something physical and distinct about it; it seemed as though a crack had appeared in a blank, smooth wall, involuntarily showing something that was secret. For a sharp and quivering instant, Adam Munn had seen behind the façade of the Swales that night, and the Swales would never be the same to him again. He had seen behind the shuttered windows and behind the great front door; he had seen behind the glitter of the silver and the gestures and the modulated voice. The hardness of Mr. Dennis had not hidden it, nor the careless beauty of Mrs. Dennis, with her lace and her pearls and her fan.

The staid silence of the house was breaking, and Dennis Swale was a man just like himself, a plain man with a restless wife.

Once they were in the library, Mr. Dennis closed the door. Great shelves of dark-backed books made his face seem very white. Everything was dark in there, in spite of two lights and the dying embers of an open fire; there was dark mahogany furniture and wine-red, damask curtains and dark pictures on the wall and dark, faded prints. It was all as dark as something in Dennis Swale. He was thinking of John Scarlet still.

"Scarlet put 'em up to it," he said. "All right. Let 'em come."

Mr. Dennis drank down his cup of coffee and lighted his cigar. Once his cigar was between his teeth, one could imagine it was a bit in the mouth of a stubborn horse. Mr. Dennis bowed his head and walked toward the fireplace with his quick, springy step.

"Munn," he said, "I'm asking you a favor. Will you please keep quiet about what you heard? My tongue slipped, Munn."

"About what, sir?" asked Adam Munn, but, even when he asked, he knew it did no good to lie.

Dennis Swale glanced at him and as their glances met, he could see right behind Dennis' eyes, right into Dennis Swale. "Don't be an ass," said Mr. Dennis.

"You're clever, Munn. And any fool can put two and two together. I mean," he lowered his voice, "about Mr. Alfred Deene."

"No, sir," said Adam Munn. "I'm not the talking kind."

Mr. Dennis drew in his breath and flipped his cigar ash in the fire. "There are some things one doesn't talk about, you see," he said. "I believe in good high fences, Munn. There's something in a name."

It must have been hard for Mr. Dennis to say as much as that, because Mr. Dennis was a proud man. He was proud, but after all he was a man like everybody else.

"And now," said Mr. Dennis, "what's this about the mill? You say some hands are coming up to see me? Well, Scarlet put 'em up to it."

"It's a deputation, sir," said Adam Munn. "They want to ask you not to close the mill and throw them out of work. I — well, I can't hardly blame them."

Mr. Dennis smiled and leaned against the corner of the mantlepiece.

"And what good do they think it will do to ask me? Do you think I'll give Scarlet satisfaction? Well, I won't. I'm losing money running it. Do they think they own the place? I suppose they think I'm made of money. Do they think I'll throw it in the street?"

"Just the same," said Adam Munn, "I'd treat them square, if I were you. It isn't as though you couldn't afford it. It wouldn't hurt you with anybody to treat them right. Maybe you don't know, sir, what everybody's saying."

Mr. Dennis threw his cigar in the fire; there was a splutter of sparks from the embers where it fell.

"Why, confound you! Do you think I care what people think?"

Some barrier had broken down between them. Adam Munn was not afraid of Dennis then.

"Yes," he said, "I used to think you didn't. You're biting off your nose to spite Scarlet's face — that's all."

"Why, Munn," said Mr. Swale. "Why, Munn, I didn't know you were a preacher."

"Listen," said Adam Munn. "Here they're coming now."

"Why, damn their insolence!" said Dennis Swale.

Outside there was a sound of voices and there was a knocking on the door. And he looked toward the hallway with a sharp-lined face. There was a noise of voices outside, loud and foreign — such as the Swale house had never heard. The mountain had moved to Mohammed. The whole Swale mill had moved from the river up the street, and forces were moving with it which no one like Mr. Swale could understand. Something was stirring in those voices that was clear and strong, though one could not catch the meaning.

Yet, waiting in the library, Adam Munn could grasp it vaguely. Mass was moving against privilege, in its endless, restless way, and there was a justce about it as clearly defined as the laws of gravity and time and space. Two old forces were in conflict and the plebeians were moving against the Swales.

"Munn," said Mr. Dennis, "light another of those lamps. I'll see the men in here."

Adam's fingers trembled as he lit the lamp, because

there was something ominous hovering over all that place, and the injustice and the hardness of the Swales and their cruelty were coming home to roost. It was the end of something which had started long ago.

Yet the room was different in the added light. Suddenly there was something in it untouchable, like the sublimation of some thought. Mr. Dennis himself, with his long nose and his sideboards and his long, thin hands, was suddenly good to look at.

"All right," said Mr. Dennis, "show them in."

Though there were only five of them, they seemed to fill the room, as they stood dripping with rain. First there was Michael Towhig, staring curiously at the books, and then there was a Frenchman named Bill Trudeau, and behind them an Italian and two swarthy Portuguese. There was something in the room which stilled their voices. Michael Towhig reached out a hand and touched the back of one of the chairs and others shuffled their feet softly on the carpet.

"What do you want?" said Dennis Swale. He stepped away from the fireplace to look at them incuriously. "Stop wiping your feet on my carpet and tell me what you want. What's the matter? Have you lost your tongues?"

Michael Towhig cleared his throat and rubbed the back of his hand across his nose.

"Mr. Swale," he said, "are you going to close the mill?"

"You saw the sign," said Dennis Swale.

"Mr. Swale," said Michael Towhig, "what right have you got to keep the poor out of work? That's what I want to know."

"Towhig," said Mr. Dennis, "ask Mr. Scarlet that. He'll be more interested than I am. I'm not under any obligation to you. I'll give you work when there is work, and now put on your hats. Good night."

"Ah!" It was Trudeau speaking. "You get nothing out of him. Ah, shut up and come away."

"You give us work," said Michael Towhig, "or you watch your mills. That's all."

"So that's it, is it?" Mr. Dennis lighted another of his cigars. "So that's Scarlet's idea too? Now listen to me and keep your voices down. I know how to deal with you. I'm ready for you. Who asked you to come here? I didn't. You've got money in the savings bank. Why don't you live on that? Now go out quietly. There won't be trouble here."

"Won't there?" Mr. Towhig's voice became a shout. "Be gob, we'll burn your damned old mill."

"Try it," said Mr. Dennis. "But let me tell you this, for your own good. I've been expecting this . . . remember, I'm no friend of yours. I've got men and shotguns waiting for you to try it, and I have a dozen men in the kitchen waiting to put you out of this house. Do you want me to call them? Or will you go without it?"

Michael Towhig rubbed his hand across his face in a slow, bewildered way. "Mr. Swale," he said, "haven't you any heart? Mr. Scarlet ain't laying off his men."

"No," said Mr. Dennis, "but I'm not Scarlet — nor do I do what Scarlet wants. Suppose you remember that."

There was a bewilderment on those men that was amusing, almost, as they gazed at Dennis Swale.

Obviously, it had never occurred to them that he might meet force with force. They stood with their mouths half gaping and their heavy red hands half open at their sides, pathetic in their amazement and simplicity. And Dennis Swale looked at them with the same grim triumph with which he had looked at John Scarlet. They all were Scarlets to him then.

"So now you're whistling down the wind?" he said. "First you come to bully me, and when you can't do that, you beg. What's the matter with you men?" And for the moment Dennis himself looked puzzled. "I've treated you fairly and it never helped me. Get out and go home quietly."

"What I tell you?" It was Trudeau speaking again excitedly. "I say it does no good. Come on, get out."

"Mr. Swale," said Michael Towhig, "haven't you any heart?"

"Munn," said Dennis Swale, "will you show these men out, please?"

Adam Munn could remember what happened next as clearly as if it were the night before. The library door was open to the hall. He could remember looking toward it when there was a gust of wind that set the lamps to flickering. Some one had opened the front door without knocking, and whoever it was had been running, for there was a sound of sharp-drawn breaths.

"Who's that?" shouted Dennis. "Shut the door."

"Mr. Swale," some one was calling. "Is that you, Mr. Swale?"

Then Adam Munn saw who it was. It was Mr. Alex Brill, the cashier of the Penny Bank. Mr. Brill was generally a thin, neat man, but now he was hatless and dishevelled by the wind. His breath was coming in sharp gasps, and he reached toward the wall to steady himself. The thing that Adam remembered best were the faces, for the whole room seemed filled with strange, staring faces.

"Brill," said Dennis Swale, "whatever is the matter?"

"It's the bank." Mr. Brill seemed to forget that they were not alone. "I've just been to the bank and now I've come up here." That was all that Mr. Brill said, but Mr. Dennis must have known already what was wrong, for all at once his face went white, but he kept his voice on an even key.

"Sit down," he said. "Suppose you have been to the bank. What makes you look like that?"

"I swear," said Mr. Brill, "I swear it wasn't my fault."

"What wasn't your fault?" said Dennis Swale. "Can't you pull yourself together?"

Mr. Brill was not built to stand great strain; he was a quiet, accurate, easy man and nothing more, and something had broken him, and it robbed him of his poise and of his judgment. It was startling to see him in his chair, wide-eyed and motionless, stunned by something in his mind.

"I knew he was speculating," said Mr. Brill. "Of course, I knew that much."

"Oh!" said Mr. Dennis. "Who was speculating?"

"Him," said Mr. Brill. "He told us to keep our mouths shut. Oh, my God! We can't open up to-morrow."

"How's that?" Michael Towhig had been listening

and already any one could guess what had happened. "Has the bank gone busted?"

"Mr. Swale," said Mr. Brill, "the assets have been twisted. There isn't — there isn't — "

"Where's Deene?" said Dennis Swale. "Has he killed himself?"

"No," said Mr. Brill, "he's took the train and gone."

"That's not so," said Dennis Swale. "I saw him myself this morning."

"He got a telegram," said Mr. Brill. "He's took the train and gone."

Dennis Swale stood up straighter, but he seemed cloaked in a most preposterous stupidity; he was going over something very slowly, step by step.

"But he told me this morning everything was all right," said Dennis Swale.

"Did he?" said Mr. Brill. "Well, that's one on you, isn't it? Ha, ha, ha!" And Mr. Brill began to laugh and laugh, doubling himself over like a knife.

"Stop it," said Dennis Swale. "Will you stop that noise?"

"Ha, ha!" shouted Mr. Brill. "That's one on you, all right."

"Will some one take this man out? Won't some one take him somewhere?"

Then he stopped; he was staring at something and everybody turned. Even Mr. Brill turned in his chair. Mrs. Swale was in the library and it was no place for Mrs. Swale. She was like a little china ornament, in her evening dress, and her pink and white face was as petulant as a child's.

"Dennis," she said, "do we have to have all this

shouting? I can't imagine what's got into you. What-ever are these men? Whatever is the matter?"

"My dear," said Mr. Dennis, "please go out and go upstairs."

"Dennis," said Mrs. Swale, "I won't be spoken to like that."

"Oh, damnation!" said Mr. Dennis. "Don't you see your being here only makes things worse?"

"Why, Dennis," cried Mrs. Swale, "why, Dennis, how dare you swear?"

Suddenly she was a silly little woman, as silly as a doll, and as incongruous as a doll, and strangely enough, Mr. Towhig was the man who grasped the situation and took the matter in his hands.

"Sure, Ma'am," said Mr. Towhig, "this ain't no place for a pretty lady now. The bank has busted and Mr. Deene has gone away."

"Gone away?" Her voice was tremulous and faint. "Mr. Deene has gone away?"

"He's run away," said Dennis Swale. "Run like a coward, if you want to know."

"And he didn't tell me?" Her voice was fainter still.

"Hush," said Dennis Swale. "Why should he tell you? — Call one of the maids. The lady's fainted."

Mr. Dennis had sprung forward and had caught her in his arms.

"Come on," said Michael Towhig. "Come on, boys. Seeing a lady's present, I won't say what I was going to say. Come on, boys. He's getting paid enough."

Dennis Swale did not answer and perhaps he never heard; he was gazing at his wife's white face and he never turned his head.

Adam's mother was the one who asked him, when Adam got back home. The Munns lived in one of those white frame houses facing the river, near the mill. Like old Mrs. Munn, it all was very neat. The mantle ornaments were dusted, standing exactly so. The lamp burned brightly behind its globe of painted flowers. There was a flowered tapestry carpet and chromos on the wall. Years afterwards, those chromos still hung there, fly-blown, yellow, but in the same straight, even line.

"Adam," said Mrs. Munn. She was like an old witch of a woman then, wraithlike, querulous, as Adam was to grow in time. "What's been keeping you? What's that they tell me down the street? Adam, has the bank gone busted?"

"Yes," said Adam Munn. He remembered he was very tired. It was after his supper hour and there would be no supper for him, since he was not on time.

Mrs. Munn set down her knitting and her false teeth gave a click, like the snapping of a metal box. "I want to know," she said. "He said the bank was sound."

"Yes," said Adam Munn, "yes, he said it."

Mrs. Munn's teeth went snap again. She had known adversity too long to let it stun her, and she was not the sort to start in weeping. "I might have known," she said. "More fool me, to trust them Swales. Sly, that's what he is. He did it for his own good, like as not. Go out to the well and fetch a pail of water; there won't be a new pump in the kitchen now."

"No," said Adam Munn, "he wouldn't have done that."

"You're simple, like your father," said Mrs. Munn. "Them Swales are always sly."

"I don't know," said Adam. "I don't know; there's something in them Swales."

She treated him still like a little boy. He was in his attic room beneath the eaves, listening to the rain, but for a long while he could not sleep, and when he slept it was not like sleeping. All night, he seemed to hear the rain like pattering, hurried feet, and now and then the bell from the old First Church was ringing through the rain with a steady, low, stern sound. And in his mind, as though he still were there, was the Swale hall and the library and the faces of the Swales, long-nosed, arrogant in their gilt frames — Swales in black coats, Swales in blue coats, Swales in ruffles, Swales in strange cravats.

Then, all at once, he was awake; the room was gray and cold, and his mother was knocking on the door.

"Wake up!" she said. "Get up. Swale's black man's calling for you."

Malachi Cuffy, the black Swale coachman, was standing in the sitting room, tall and grave in his black coat, holding his high silk hat.

"Mr. Adam," he said, "Master Dennis wants you. He wants you right away."

"Where?" said Adam. "At the mill?"

"At the big house," said Malachi. "He wants you right away."

It seemed to Adam Munn that there must have been a death, the Swale house was so still. The rain had stopped, but the morning was cold and gray, and from the ground and from the river a cold gray mist was rising. The Swale house was very still; so that he could hear the drops of moisture falling from the elms, splash on the sodden lawn. The hall was very silent, so that one spoke in whispers.

Mr. Dennis was in the dining room, but he had not touched his breakfast. He was like a man who had stared death in the face and who had watched death take its course. Yet his voice was as sharp and harsh as ever. His collar was white and stiff. His cravat was carefully tied with a moonstone pin stuck in it.

"Munn," he said, "I'm going to the bank. Would you mind coming too?"

"No," said Adam, "I'll come if you want me."

"Thanks," said Mr. Dennis. "There's no one else to ask now. Thank you, Munn. I'll get my hat and stick."

He did not speak for a long time as they walked down the street. Though Adam tried, he could not tell what Dennis Swale was thinking. His cane went snap upon the brick walk and he held his head up straight. Adam Munn did not speak, because he felt a curious sort of awe. Dennis Swale seemed far away, different from everything in Haven's End, very lonely and set apart and thinking, always thinking.

Only once did he look at Adam Munn with a quick, sharp look. "You're right," he said. "Deene fooled me."

"It isn't your fault," said Adam. "You're not anyways to blame."

"I said the bank was sound," said Dennis Swale.

The street outside the bank was full of people standing silent, staring at the brownstone walls. There were men in overalls and women with shawls about their heads. Their faces all were stamped with the same bewildered look. There was no work, there was no money left in Haven's End.

"Look at them," said Mr. Dennis. "I said the bank was sound."

"Lookit," some one was calling. "Lookit; here comes Swale."

Then he could imagine every one was looking as Dennis Swale walked down the street. There was a whispering and the shuffling of a hundred feet, but every one was looking, and it seemed to Adam Munn that there was nothing strange in that, for Haven's End had always watched the Swales. Staring straight before him, Mr. Dennis moved along and every one stepped back. They must have also had that feeling that Dennis Swale was different from the rest.

Mr. Dennis did not seem to be aware that they were looking; he walked up the brownstone steps and brought his cane down on the bank's closed door.

"Lookit," some one was saying, "Swale is going in. Lookit, there goes Swale."

Mr. Brill was the one who opened the door, noiselessly, like an undertaker, Adam thought. The shades of the banking room were drawn; there were no clerks behind the desks.

There was a different sort of silence in that bank from any that Adam had ever known. The lack of sound was heavy as a load upon one's shoulders; the marble squares of the floor before the counter, still unmopped from the day before, showed a muddy blur of footsteps, with bits of crumpled paper lying all about.

On the bars of the teller's cage a notice had been pasted. Mr. Dennis thrust his head forward to read it through the shadows.

"As a director of the Penny Bank, I have examined the figures, and to the best of my belief the Bank is sound." And underneath it he could see the harsh angles of his signature.

"Take that thing down," said Dennis. "There's no further use for that." Then he turned to the directors' room, with Adam Munn walking by his elbow.

There were half a dozen men standing talking in low voices. The examiner from Boston had come already and was calling for the books. The other directors of the bank were there, most of them small tradesmen. The merchants had changed to small tradesmen with the decline of Haven's End.

"Good morning!" said some one, and then some one else spoke up. "Good morning, Mr. Swale."

Mr. Dennis nodded and stepped to the round table with its thick green baize and sat down on one of the ornate armchairs. Then he looked around the room very slowly, aware, perhaps, that every one was waiting for him to speak, but he did not say a word.

"It's a black morning," said Mr. Brill, "for all of us, Mr. Swale."

Mr. Dennis turned to Adam Munn.

"Get me a piece of paper and a pen," he said. And then he sat stiffly with his eyes on nothing.

"Mr. Swale," said some one, "do you want to see the balance?"

"No," said Mr. Dennis, "I don't want to see it now."

He picked up the pen and dipped it in the ink.

"This is a damned bad pen," he said.

"Do you want another one?" asked Adam.

"No," said Mr. Dennis, "this will do, but it's a damned bad pen."

He must have known exactly what he was to write, for his pen moved without a pause, once he started writing. When he had finished, he tossed the pen on the table and pushed back his chair.

"You can read that if you like," he said. "Brill, get a pot of glue and paste that on the door."

Then every one leaned forward. Years later, Adam Munn could close his eyes and still see how the paper looked. It was a piece of heavy ruled foolscap, he remembered; it lay askew upon the green baize table, among cigar ashes and memorandum slips, with Dennis' writing sprawled across it like a row of spears.

"Having said this bank is sound," it read, and the writing was as uncompromising as Mr. Dennis' voice, "I guarantee to the full extent of my resources that every depositor will be paid."

"You see it," said Mr. Dennis. "You can witness that I wrote it. All right, put it on the door."

He had written it as though it were a simple letter, and everything had been so simple that what he had done seemed to dawn on everybody slowly.

"But, see here!" It was Mr. Savory, the bank's attorney, who broke the silence. "There's no need for you to do a thing like that. You're no wise liable, Mr. Swale. A bank director serving without pay is no wise liable."

Mr. Dennis turned and nodded and he even smiled.

"Thanks," he said, "but I know when I'm liable without going to the law."

"But look here," said Mr. Brill. "You don't know what you're doing. You don't know what the assets and liabilities are."

Mr. Dennis raised his eyebrows. "What's that got to do with it?" he inquired. "This is my affair and I'm not asking what you think. I said this bank was sound. Well, it will stay sound if I can make it, and I want every one to know it. Get that notice on the door."

He looked around the room again sharply, almost arrogantly. "I wanted witnesses. I don't care a continental what you think."

Then some one was speaking in a hushed, awe-stricken voice. "I didn't know," some one was saying, "there was any one like that in town."

Dennis Swale reached for his hat and gloves. "Don't be a fool," he said. "Come on, Munn. There's nothing else to do."

It was curious to remember that all at once Mr. Dennis seemed majestic; all the obstinacy of the Swales seemed altered into something fine. All at once, everybody knew that there was no one like the Swales left in Haven's End.

"What's that noise?" said Dennis Swale.

There was a shouting in the street.

"They're cheering," said Adam Munn. "Ain't they got a right to cheer?"

"Who?" said Dennis Swale. "For me?"

"Yes," said Adam Munn, "for you."

Then he was out on the steps in the gray, harsh light,

but everything seemed different; an invisible wave seemed to rise to meet him, so that he paused for a moment before he walked down the steps.

"There's Swale," some one was shouting. "Hooray for Mr. Swale!"

Then they all were cheering; people were running from the shops; the street was full of noise. The thing that Adam Munn remembered best was the look in Mr. Dennis' face. He did not seem to be surprised or even pleased that every one was cheering; he seemed to take it quite for granted that every one should cheer a Swale in the streets of Haven's End.

It was surprising, even then, that no one tried to touch him, that no one tried to shake his hand. He was still apart from every one as he walked down the steps, unique, beyond the common thought.

"God bless you, Mr. Swale," some one was shouting. And Dennis nodded once and stepped out on the street, waving his cane before him. His manner no longer seemed preposterous and everything seemed in its place, all orderly and fitting.

They were down the steps and on the street when there was another sound; the bell from the First Church was ringing, tolling out the hour, and the bell was like a voice above the other voices. "Swale," it was saying slowly, "Swale, Swale, Swale."

And then a strange thing happened, just as Dennis Swale was turning up the street. Every one was moving back as Dennis Swale walked on, except one man, who stood before him until Dennis finally stopped. He and Mr. Scarlet were standing face to face, there in the street. Dennis Swale looked up at Mr. Scarlet and tucked his cane beneath his arm. Mr. Scarlet raised his hat; he was holding it in his hand.

"Mr. Swale," he was calling, "wait a minute, Mr. Swale."

Dennis Swale looked up. In the sound of all the voices, the lines of his face seemed gone; he seemed young and almost kindly as he glanced at Mr. Scarlet.

"Mr. Swale," said Mr. Scarlet, "I didn't know there was a man alive who would do a thing like that!"

"Don't be a fool," said Dennis Swale. "It was the only thing to do."

Noblesse oblige. John Scarlet had never heard of that, but he must have seen the sense of it, and some glimmering of the meaning. He must have seen it as every one saw it, rising bright above the dullness of the town.

It always seemed to Adam Munn that the thing that Dennis Swale did next was inevitable, beyond his own volition.

Mr. Dennis drew a paper from his pocket.

"Now this," he said; "there's this . . ."

Mr. Scarlet looked quickly at the paper and back at Dennis Swale. It was like Dennis Swale to remember even at a time like that. He was holding the notes of John Scarlet in his fingers. They had been in his pocket all the while.

"Now these," said Mr. Dennis. "I was just coming down to ask you——"

"I'm not begging," John Scarlet said. "You've got me, Mr. Swale."

"Yes," said Dennis, and he nodded very slowly, "and I don't want it. It's . . . Listen to them, Scarlet."

Was it all that Dennis had ever wished — to have them shouting for a Swale?

"Scarlet," said Mr. Dennis, "take this and pay it up next year. There's no reason for this now."

"Here," said Mr. Scarlet, "wait a minute. I don't understand."

Dennis Swale was smiling in a way which would have been insufferable half an hour before. John Scarlet was standing before him, with his hat grasped in his hand.

"Don't you?" said Mr. Swale. "There's no reason that you should. Have I ever asked you or any one to understand?"

10

Tom Swale

≈10≈

Tom Swale

EVERY ONE IN OUR TOWN KNEW TOM Swale. There is something in the echo of the name in our town still, though it is lost among all the other echoes whispering on the wind. Suppose you walked down Middle Street, past the old distillery to the river, where the waves are slapping against the soft swirl of the tide. Let it be the time toward sundown, when all sounds linger in the air, moving slowly seaward like the river, in a mellow golden light, and suppose you stood on the piling of the wharves and shouted out the name — Tom Swale — the sound would not be strange. It would fall in peaceful order upon all the other sounds that have stirred the air of Haven's End.

"Tom! Tom Swale!" You can remember how old Dennis Swale used to call him in his harsh, flat voice. It was not so long ago. It was down by the old yard where the Swales built the wooden chasers in Nineteen Seventeen, the last of the wooden ships that came out of Haven's End. You can see the last unfinished hull still standing in the blocks, already gray and weathered, just as they left it when the war was over.

"Tom! Tom Swale!" Perhaps you can remember the old man's voice above the hammering, for Haven's End in those days was stirring from its sleep. "Get down off that scaffolding! Do you want to break your neck, Tom Swale?"

"Tom," some one would say, "your old man's calling."

Then Tom would look up quickly. His face was as sharp as his father's face. He had the same long nose, high cheeks and narrow mouth of all the Swales, but his eyes were different. They seemed always to be looking toward the distance at things one did not see. "Yes," he said, "I hear him. He's afraid I'm going to die and then there wouldn't be a Swale."

Then Tom Swale would laugh. His narrow lips would draw apart and his whole face would change until any one could feel his amusement at absurdity. He was laughing at a vanity that must have been in him too, laughing at the town and the Swale house on the ridge above the river. And he was laughing at an old man's fear, secure in that illusion of immortality which is never lost to youth.

There used to be a garish recentness in that shipyard, even when the wood was rotting, which would bring the whole thing back. It was like a ruined building when you saw it in the dusk, poignant, lonely, like all the vanished hopes which the river bank had seen since the shipping had died out, and Haven's End had grown small and narrow. It lay like the last effort of the Swales, their last fling, like our town's last fling against a changing time. The sight of it would bring back that glimmer of excitement just before the war, when Dennis Swale was making money out of wooden ships, and when the tide of money turned back to Haven's End. And Dennis was the one who turned the tide. Any one could tell you that. He was already old in that restive time, when values toppled and wages rose, but he thought of wooden ships. . . . The yard was like a great house falling to decay, and right beside the rusted, barbed-iron fence the Scarlet shoe shop stood, freshly painted like something which had survived the wreck, a solid, heavy building, like the Scarlets in our town. A sign was reared in front of it in clear black letters, so that you could see it across that lonely yard, and that sign was like the ending of a story, as patently New England as the white houses and the elms.

"John Scarlet," it said. "Shoes and Findings."

Old Dennis Swale used to stare at it when the hammers and the saws were going. That sign represented the new commercialism, since everything was going into signs.

"Findings?" Dennis Swale once said. "What are findings, I'd like to know?" And then he smiled and gave his head a shake. "A trade word," he said.

That was the strange part about it. He never seemed to think that he was in trade himself; and that was like the Swales. The shipyard was always something more than that.

"Findings!" said Dennis Swale and then he laughed. "What the devil do you suppose they find?"

There was nothing strange about his laughing, because the Swales had laughed at Scarlets since our town began. The Scarlets were rich in those days, and they were solid people, but when Dennis spoke, you had a picture of old John Scarlet and young John Scarlet with bended backs, grubbing for their findings, the last of grubbing generations. And there you had the story standing straight before you, like all the stories of our town, with all the hopes of Dennis Swale rotting in the dark and the name of Scarlet black and clear, and you could almost hear the echo of Dennis' voice.

"Tom!" he was calling. "Can't you hear, Tom Swale?"

Sue Swale was the one to tell you, if you knew her. Susan was Tom's sister, and in a way to blame. She had been in the Swale House as long as she could remember, and she could see it through her father's eyes.

When you saw her in the wide front hall, which was always cool and dusky when one stepped in out of the summer sun, you could imagine her stepping from some shadowy chaos of all the other Swales who had walked that hall, and she alone seemed real.

"The house is awfully old," she said. "You understand it when you live here."

You could understand it when she told you. It was not like one of those museum houses, because the Swales were there. She could show you the rusty cut-and-thrust sword which Colonel Richard Swale had worn when he led a company in King Philip's War. She could show you the silver in the dining room which Swale privateers had taken. She could show you the paintings of the Swale ships, heavy Federalist vessels, with every rope and spar in accurate proportion; but, when she showed them, all those things seemed to come together into an austere, vague shape.

There was something in it which made her sad, as though she knew her own inadequacy. Yet she could put it all together, even so; she could break away from the silence of the house and shrug her shoulders at it, — pretty, awkward shoulders.

"You see," Sue said, "that I don't matter. There had to be a man to keep it all together. Now, let's go out. I'll tell you all about it out of doors."

She could sometimes think that they were never grown, she and her brother Tom. Whenever she began to think back, there would be Sue Swale and Tom, walking down the street in the hot summer sun. Her dress would be white and starched, with lace upon it. Tom would be in an Eton collar, and the wind would be always blowing the straight part from his hair. Then there would be the voices, half hushed and half derisive.

"Lookit, there's the Swale kids!"

They were always different from the rest of Haven's End. Dennis Swale could never see that he was standing for a worn-out custom, but Sue Swale must have been in revolt against it from the very first. She could see how the Victorian world was cracking before the war sent it galley-west.

"Are you laughing?" Sue Swale said. "I don't blame you laughing. We're preposterous. The whole thing was preposterous, — little, small-town people living in a house out of repair and acting as if we were important. And we weren't nice. We were nasty. . . . But Father believed in it. It's queer how things grow real, if some one just believes enough."

Yes, Susan could piece it all together, perhaps because she hated pompous make-believe. She was not the heir to the make-believe. She was not the one her father watched, but his voice was always chiming with her thoughts.

"Tom, keep the safety lock on that duck gun. . . . If it's blowing in the harbor, don't you take that boat outside. Do you think I want you drowned?"

On a long walk beside the marshes she could remember best; it would seem as though the wind brought it all back, when it blew at her short tweed skirt and set the strands of hair blowing across her forehead. As she looked across the marshes toward the sand dunes, her lips would twist upward, not exactly in a smile.

"Yes," she said, "do you believe in premonition? I do, sometimes. Father always was afraid. There were the things he stood for. There had to be a Swale."

Then all the rest would come back to her — the voices and the faces that once had stirred her thoughts. . . .

"Father," she was saying, "what's the matter?" And there would be old Dennis Swale, standing in the library in his woolen dressing gown, looking out the window toward the black and quiet street.

"Nothing," he was saying, "but I can't sleep. You'll find out when you're old."

And Susan knew that all the things he stood for were

moving in the dark, and leaving him alone with nothing but old voices.

Then there would be candlelight. John Scarlet told her that much. A candle would be burning on a damp board among the smells of moldy earth. Tom Swale would be standing, muddy but somehow clean in that dim yellow light, looking at John Scarlet's red, perspiring face.

"What time do you make it?" John Scarlet was saying. "How long before zero?"

Then Tom Swale was looking at him. She could imagine just how he looked.

"Five minutes," Tom Swale was saying. "You better set your watch. See you later, John."

"Where?" John Scarlet said.

"Good Lord!" Tom Swale was saying. "How should I know where?"—

Sue could not have been sixteen in those days before the war disturbed the peace of Haven's End, but she could remember exactly how it was, because it always seemed like yesterday. It was June; Sue Swale could remember June, Nineteen Sixteen, because the century was always just her age. The sun was coming through the curtains of her bedroom window, bringing the shadows of leaves which danced upon the curtains of her little four-posted bed. The sunlight glanced from the mirror on her dressing table and back to her dark, brown hair, making it almost golden as she combed it.

She remembered looking at the mirror with a sudden, sharp surprise at the brightness of her eyes and the straightness of her lips. It was as though she had never seen her face all those other mornings.

"Why, Sue," she said, "you're beautiful!"

It was not strange that she remembered, since it was the first time that she knew.

It was the first time she understood why John Scarlet had stared at her as though she had been a stranger, when he met her on the street, and perhaps one should begin with that.

She had been walking down the street when John Scarlet came around the corner just by the old First Church. Of course she knew, because the Swales knew everyone in Haven's End, that he was the son of old John Scarlet who owned the shoe factory by the river —a solid, red-faced boy with heavy hands.

"Hello," he said, "I didn't know you, Sue."

"Hello," she said, "you ought to."

Then something made her smile and pause. Why was it that she smiled? John Scarlet was in a blue serge suit such as the town boys wore, but she did not smile at that.

"Yes, I ought to," John Scarlet said. His voice had a singsong drawl, very slow and quiet, "but I never thought—"

"What about?" she said. The sun was moving on the old brick walk. She remembered exactly how the leaves made patterns on it that never stayed the same because the wind was blowing.

"I never thought," John Scarlet said, "you looked like you do now."

"Didn't you?" she asked him.

"No," he said. "I've got my boat out. I'll take you out to-morrow, if you'd like to go."

"Yes," she said, "I'd like it."

And that was all — his voice and her voice speaking words. She could say them over, one by one. There was a sort of peace in remembering exactly how they went, a gentleness and a kindness which she had never known, without a touch of pretense, without a flash of fire, and she knew why he asked her, now that she saw her face.

That was all, but everything seemed new. There was a simplicity about it which she could never quite forget. He had nearly said that she was beautiful, and it did not seem strange. Wide, patient eyes which looked at her and quietly looked away, steady shoulders, fresh color in his cheeks. . . .

"I don't care," she said. "He's nice. . . . I wonder if I'll love him."

"Sue," she heard her brother's voice outside the door. "Sue, are you up yet?"

Tom Swale was in his bathrobe with a wet towel around his head.

"Why, Sue," he said, "you're damn good-looking. I never thought of that."

"Didn't you?" said Sue. "Do you want me to get you something?"

"Yes, give me a glass of water. I came in to say good morning. What are you dressed up for? What are you doing to your hair?"

"Nothing," said Sue. "Where were you last night?"

Tom waved his arm vaguely. "Here and there," he said.

"Tom." Sue felt her voice grow hushed; she always felt an awe at the things Tom had seen and done. "Tom, were you—"

"Yes. Haven't you got eyes? And don't you tell the old man, either."

"You needn't say that," said Sue. "You know I don't tell."

"That's right," said Tom. He sat down on the edge of her bed and swung his feet slowly back and forth. "I'll tell you something else. There's hell to pay in Mexico. There's going to be a war."

"Tom!" She started from her dressing table. "You're not going, are you?"

She remembered how Tom swung his legs back and forth and crossed his hands behind his head.

"Why not?" he said.

"But, Tom," she said. "Tom, you mustn't go."

"Think I'll get killed, don't you? Well, who's going to stop me going?"

"Father is," said Sue.

For a moment Tom Swale did not answer. His eyes opened wider and he unwound the towel from his head. Some water from it trickled down his forehead and ran down his long, thin nose.

"Sue," said Tom, "my head is aching fit to bust. We've got to stick together, Sue."

Then they were down in the dining room. The coffee urn was boiling; the windows were open so that there was a smell of fresh grass and coffee. Dennis Swale was seated by the coffee urn, reading his morning mail.

Everything in that room seemed curiously his own. It was always so in the whole house, when Dennis Swale was there. The carpet, unchanged for twenty years, was worn into little paths, the block-print wallpaper of ships and lighthouses was dingy, half the brasses had fallen from the sideboard, two Chippendale chairs had broken backs, but when Dennis Swale was in the room, everything was complete.

"Well," said Dennis, "well." He never said good morning; she always remembered that. "Pour out the coffee, Sue," he said. "Tom, where were you last night?"

"Out, sir," said Tom.

"And drunk," said Dennis Swale.

"Yes, sir," said Tom. There was no good to lie.

"That's right," said Dennis Swale, "don't lie." His face was the same as always, but somehow he was different; "Tom," he said, "I've bought the old shipyard. What do you think of that?"

"Sir," said Tom, "what did you do that for?"

"The old shipyard?" said Sue. "Why, there's nothing there."

"Be quiet, Sue," said Dennis Swale. "I'm talking to your brother. I've bought the yard and I'm going to build a ship. Tom, you're going there this morning."

"A ship?" said Tom. He was staring across the table. "What kind of a ship?"

"A wooden ship, a schooner," answered Dennis Swale.

"Yes," said Tom; "but why?"

Dennis Swale leaned back in his chair, as though he had said nothing strange.

"To make money," said Dennis Swale. "Now I know what I'm talking about. There's enough tonnage being sunk to make a market for wooden ships. Your great-grandfather built them, and you're going to build them. Hurry with your breakfast; we're going to go there now."

"But, look," said Tom, "I don't know how."

"No," said Dennis, "but you're going to learn. I didn't think it would ever happen. There'll be ships on the river again."

The coffee was boiling with little puffs of steam and, all at once, everything seemed changing when he spoke, and Susan could tell that he had been thinking of the idea for weeks and months, turning it in his mind until it seemed already done. Dennis looked across the table straight at Tom and smiled.

"Yes," said Dennis Swale, "we're going to lay one down. They can laugh if they want to, but they'll see there's money in it. And shipping's an essential industry. Hurry with your breakfast, Tom."

She remembered, when Tom sat looking, that his eyes were dark and puzzled.

"All right," said Tom. "But if there's a war, I'm going to it just the same."

Dennis Swale set down his coffee cup.

"Well, you're not," he said. He did not raise his voice. "You're the only son I've got. That's why I'm going into shipping, one of the reasons why. They won't call shipyard workers out. I've looked into that."

"Look here," said Tom. "I knew there was something funny about this. You can't fix everything—"

Dennis Swale drew in his breath. There was something in his face which made Tom look away, something inexorable and hard as rock. "Don't shout at me. You're staying here," he said. "Some one has to live here after I am gone."

There was no trace of emotion in the way he said it, but Sue could understand. There were so many things her father could never say; all his thoughts were on Tom Swale.

"But I might go to war and live," said Tom. "Did you ever think of that?"

"No," said Dennis Swale.

"But why?" said Tom. "Won't you tell me why?"

"Because I'm afraid," said Dennis Swale. "God help me, I'm afraid."

In the silence which followed, they could hear the click of cart wheels or the sound of a motor horn on the street, and then the bell of the First Church was ringing, tolling out the hour of nine. Tom's face had grown red and so had her father's face, and they both sat looking at their plates, as though something had happened of which they were both ashamed. It was an amazing thing, but like him. It never seemed strange to her that her father started shipbuilding to keep his son from war.

"Give me some coffee, Sue," said Dennis Swale. And then the doorbell rang, and Sue tried not to start.

"Who's that?" said Dennis Swale.

"A young man, sir," the maid said. "He wants to see Miss Susan."

Susan felt her face grow hot because her father's eyes were on her.

"A young man?" her father said. "What young man?"

"It's Mr. Scarlet, sir. Young Mr. Scarlet, whose father owns the shoe shop."

Dennis Swale pushed back his chair. His forehead was broken in little furrows.

"What does he want?" her father said. Susan looked up at him and looked away, now that her turn had come.

"He wants to take me sailing," she answered. "He's got his catboat out."

"Sailing?" said Tom.

Dennis Swale sat looking at her; his forehead still in lines.

"You weren't going to go?" he asked.

"Yes," she said, "I said I'd go."

"What's that?" said Tom. "You said you'd go?"

"Be quiet," her father said.

There was a footstep in the hall and then John Scarlet was standing near the window in the sun. His hat was in his hand and his face was very red, and Dennis Swale was looking at him, rubbing his hands softly one against the other. As John Scarlet stood there in the dining room, Susan felt as though an iron door had slammed; she had never thought of John Scarlet standing in their house.

John Scarlet had looked well enough in his blue suit by the church, but in the Swale house he was different, suddenly ill at ease; his hands looked large, his shoulders slouched as he was standing by the window. She had never felt so sorry for any one as she did for him. He was not like them and he must have known it, for his voice sounded husky when he spoke.

"Good morning, Sue," he said. "Good morning, Mr. Swale. Good morning, Tom."

"Morning, John," said Tom. "Where did you get that tie?"

John Scarlet put his hand up to his collar; his tie was a flaming red, exactly like his face, and suddenly it seemed to Sue that Tom and Dennis Swale were just alike; their faces had the same look, half-surprised and half-amused, hard, sharp, watchful masks, staring at John Scarlet with cool, unblinking eyes.

"Well," said Dennis Swale, "I understand you've asked my daughter to go sailing."

"Yes, sir," said John Scarlet. "Yes, leastways I thought she might like to go. I've got the catboat out. There's a nice light wind."

Dennis Swale glanced out the window and shook his head. "The wind's too high," he said. "Thank you for asking her. I'm sorry she can't go."

John Scarlet must have known what Dennis meant, because the Scarlets were not fools.

"I can handle a boat," he said.

"Certainly," said Dennis Swale, "but — we're obliged to you for asking."

"John," said Sue, "I'm sorry."

"Oh, that's all right," said John. "I'd — better be going now."

"I'll see you out," said Tom.

As Tom closed the door behind them, Sue felt her heart beat faster and her breath was coming fast. It was as though something terrible had happened, though Tom had only closed the door.

Her father was looking at her sharply.

"Sue," he said, "will you listen to me, Sue? John Scarlet's quite all right; I have nothing against him, but we're different from the Scarlets. Do you under-stand?"

"Yes," she said, "I understand."

"Not that the Scarlets aren't all right," said Dennis Swale, "not that his father isn't admirable. He's richer than I am, if you want to put it that way. The Scarlets are an old family. They've been here as long as we have, if you want to look at records, and we've always known the Scarlets. It isn't exactly that. It's background."

He made a gesture with his hand, a single, sweeping gesture, but Susan could always remember it because it made a picture. It was the silver on the sideboard and the steaming coffee urn and the mahogany of the side chairs and the tallness of the room, against simple, homely chairs and tables. It was the smoothness of their father's hand and the precision of his voice against heavier hands and louder voices. It was austere, steely beauty standing against plenty.

"It's the way we're made," he said. "You'll see it sometime."

"Yes," said Susan Swale.

"Yes," said Dennis, "you saw him in this room. You saw him beside Tom. I am glad you saw him here."

"Yes," said Susan Swale.

The door had opened and Tom was back. "Tom," said Dennis, "did you see him out?"

"Yes," said Tom. "He's gone."

"That's right," said Dennis Swale. "What is it, Sue?"

For Susan was standing up and suddenly her voice had broken, and she forgot to be afraid.

"You're both unkind," she said. "That's what you are — unkind. You didn't need — "

"That will do," said Dennis Swale. "Susan, go upstairs; your mother's calling."

As she was walking down the hall, she heard her father's voice again. "What's getting into everybody? Has the girl gone crazy too?"

Her mother was sitting up in bed, wrapped in blue brocade and lace, with her breakfast tray across her knees. Susan wondered sometime if she would grow to look like her mother, if her hair and her eyes would also take on the dullness of unpolished glass, if her cheeks and her lips would droop into the same thin lines.

"Sue," said her mother, "you're too young to knot your hair like that. Don't forget you're not grown up."

But Susan knew it was not true; her mother was gazing at her in a cool, unfriendly way, as she might at another, better-looking woman, and Sue was better-looking; something told her that.

"Has your father had his breakfast?"

"Yes, Mamma."

Her mother sighed and looked down at her hands, white and soft with little tapering fingers. "Sometimes," her mother said, "I think your father is a little mad. Did he tell you? He's taking all the money he has left to build a ship."

"Yes, Mamma."

"Sue," her mother said, "please close that window and carry down my tray. Sue, when you get married, mind you find a man who doesn't stand for something. Do you know what I mean?"

"Yes, Mamma."

"I think," her mother said, "I think that every one who stands for something is a little mad. Take your father, Sue. He plays his life just as I play solitaire. He makes his rules and follows them. It has nothing to do with life. It isn't living; it's playing."

"Yes, Mamma," said Sue.

Sue always remembered what her mother said because everything that happened afterward was exactly like a game which had started in the house that very morning, in which they all must play, whether they wished or not, according to unwritten rule.

The Swales were in it and the Scarlets were in it too, and the Scarlets had their own pride. They were not the forgetting kind.

She and Tom were walking down a rutted road that afternoon, leading from the pastures toward the marshes in back of the Parlin Farm. Tom's two English setters were quartering before them through the grass, and she could turn her head and see the town, standing by the river. The wind was blowing fresh from the open water, making the air as clear and bright as though there had been a rain, and she could see the Swale house on the high ground, with all the other houses rising toward it. Though it was a long way off, the line of it was clear, and the distance made it seem perfect and unobtainable, not like their house at all.

Tom was walking with his quick, nervous step, kicking at the tufts of grass.

"What's the matter with you?" said Tom. "There's no use snapping at the old man like that."

"I don't care," cried Sue. "You were nasty. Both of you. You hadn't any right — "

"No right?" said Tom. "Are you crazy? You can't go out with Scarlet, and he should have had the sense to know it. It isn't — don't you see?"

"Hush!" said Sue, and she caught her breath. "Here's John Scarlet now."

He was coming toward them, walking down the lane with a heavy step, but when he saw them he stopped, though he was a long way off. He stopped and waited while they came walking toward him.

"I've been waiting for you," John Scarlet said. "Tell your sister to go home."

"I won't," said Sue. "John, what are you going to do?"

She had never seen violence but instinctively she knew. It was written on John Scarlet's heavy face.

"I'm going to lick your brother, if you want to know," John Scarlet said. "You go back, Sue, if you don't want to see it. So, I'm not good enough to take your sister out? Take off your coat, Tom Swale."

Beside John Scarlet, Tom looked very slim as he took off his coat. "Sue, hold the dogs," he said. "You might have picked some other time."

"I watched you in the hall," John Scarlet said. "I'll show you, Tom."

And then Tom Swale began to laugh, with his coat still dangling on his arm, and Sue remembered that she could hear the waves across the marshes beating on the outer beach.

"John," Tom Swale began, "won't you listen to me first?"

It must have been the laughter which made John Scarlet blind, for he struck Tom even before he raised his hands, flush upon the jaw. He struck Tom so that his body crumpled forward, and Tom lay on the grass flat upon his face; and then John was standing, looking at Tom stupidly, wide-eyed and open-mouthed. It all had happened so quickly that Sue could not believe it. First Tom Swale was laughing, and then he was on his face, clutching at the grass.

Next a strange thing happened. Before she could move a step, John Scarlet was on his knees, lifting up Tom Swale.

"Tom," he was saying, "I didn't mean to hit you then. You laughed; it made me mad."

John Scarlet placed his arm behind Tom's back and pulled him up, while Sue stood staring at them without the power to move. There was something immense about the scene which held her in a spell, for somehow the whole town was in it and hundreds of unspoken matters. She could always remember their two faces close together, John Scarlet's heavy with pain he could not express—a broad, coarse, kindly face—and Tom's was like a marble mask. In that moment the blood and life was out of it, leaving only a delicacy and peace.

"Sue," John Scarlet said, "so help me, I didn't mean to hit him then. The way he laughed, the way he laughed."

Then Sue heard herself speaking in a hushed, strange voice.

"He always laughs like that."

"Yes," John Scarlet said, "he's always laughed like that at me. Tom, I didn't mean to hit you. Tom, are you all right?"

The fixed, staring look had left Tom's eyes. He shook his head and blinked and struggled to his feet.

"I never had a chance," said Tom. "Aren't you ready to go on?"

"No," John Scarlet said, "I can't fight now."

Tom stepped toward him unsteadily and then he stopped. "You mean you won't?" he said.

"Yes," said John Scarlet, "I mean I won't. Tom, I wish that I was dead."

Tom brushed the dirt from his shirt and Sue could see his hands were trembling.

"All right," he said. "Later will be better. I'll see you later. But, no matter what happens, it won't make any difference."

"Yes," said John Scarlet. "Yes, I see."

He was looking at them both in a puzzled way, as though he had never known them.

"John," Sue Swale spoke suddenly because the spell had left her. "You mustn't fight again."

"No," said John, "I won't. It won't do any good."

"Oh, yes, you will," Tom Swale said. "We've got to finish this."

But John Scarlet must have seen that there was something hopeless, because he shook his head.

"No," he said, "it won't finish, ever."

Tom put on his coat and nodded. It was the strangest thing, Sue could remember, that she was sorry for John Scarlet. His strength had broken on something hard, where strength could be no help. The hardness of her father was in Tom Swale, though he had not struck a blow.

"Come," he said, "let's be going, Sue. I'll see you later, John."

As they walked on up the road, Sue looked back once and there was John Scarlet standing in the grass, with drooping shoulders and listless hands, staring at their backs. But Tom Swale did not look. She glanced at him timidly, afraid to speak. All his thoughts were struggling, narrowing his eyes, twitching at the corners of his mouth.

"We can't leave off like this," he said. "Sue, don't tell the old man, will you? I'd hate to have him know."

"Of course I won't," said Sue.

But her father guessed it, because her father's eyes were sharp and Tom's face was red and swollen. He was sitting in the library looking at his paper when he heard them in the hall.

"Come in here. Is that you, Tom?" he asked.

There always seemed to be a dusk in the library, even when the lamp was lit; the rows of old leather books were sinking backward into shadows which the lamp-light never reached. The portraits on the wall were all in shadow, and her father, Sue remembered, seemed half shadow, as he sat in his leather armchair, staring at them both.

"Tom, what's the matter with your face?"

"Nothing," said Tom.

"You've been fighting Scarlet. That's the matter," answered Dennis Swale.

Sue remembered that she felt no surprise; it was as

though the shadows in the room had told him. And then the bell of the First Church was ringing; the sound was coming through the open window in slow, strong waves. Sue loved to hear the sound; it always brought her back to lonely nights when she was very little.

"Swale," the church bell seemed to say, "Swale, Swale, Swale."

"Yes," said Tom, "we started fighting but I haven't finished yet."

"And don't you finish." There was a loud rattling sound; her father had crushed the evening paper in his hands. "He's too big for you. Do you understand? Do you think I want you killed?"

Tom walked to the table and lighted a cigarette; the flame of the match struck him exactly as the lamplight struck his father's face, and once again they were just alike, long-nosed, thin-lipped, staring at each other from the shadows.

"Mind you," said Dennis Swale. "I'll tell you when you have to fight."

"What's the news?" said Tom.

Sue saw her father look away, straight into the dark; then she saw his shoulders stiffen, as though he saw something coming toward him from the corner of the room.

"It looks like war," he said.

"Of course it does," said Tom. "We'll get in it some-time."

Then Dennis Swale was staring at the carpet. "But you won't go," he said. "Mind you — I can stop you. Tom, the carpet's old. I want you to get a new one when

I'm gone. And I want you to paint the stairs and have the elm cut down."

"Yes, sir," said Tom Swale.

That was nearly a year before the war, but the thought was with him always that Tom Swale was going to die.

Any one can tell you about war time at Haven's End; it was a fine time in a way, because the town was all awake. There seemed to be echoes from all sorts of other wars. Since the French and Indian troubles, Haven's End had grown rich when there was fighting. It had always been a matter of shipping and, though the open sea seemed very far away, the ships were coming back. Any one can tell you how it was, once the yards were going; men were coming from the back country; the stores were lighted long after dark each night.

Sue could remember walking with her father down the street in Nineteen Seventeen while every one stood watching.

"That's him," she heard them say. "That's Swale; he's the one who owns the yard."

The windows of the house in those days were always full of light. There were strange men coming from the city; the telephone was always ringing. She remembered what her father said one night, because it showed what he had been thinking all the time.

"They thought I was crazy," he said. "And now you can sell anything that floats. It's always that way in a war. Look how old Daniel Swale raked the money in, when he built this house. There'll be money for you, Tom, before this thing's through."

He was doing it all for Tom, but he must have known that something was moving nearer, the faster the yards were growing. She could tell by the way he looked at Tom, half startled, as though he had been afraid that Tom would not be there.

The thing that Sue remembered was that hammering and the shrieking sound of saws, rising harshly like the sea-birds' cries, and the smell of fresh wood by the river. The smell of wood and all the sounds blended curiously together, making thoughts rise in a sudden, great, formless shape. There would be the yard by the river, surrounded by old warehouses with blank, broken windows, gray with their rotting shingles and clapboards, staring at the open water where the wharves once stood. But the shipyard was all new; the wood was so fresh that it was hardly seasoned.

Back on the ridge, above the river, the Swale house stood, and then there were the elm trees budding in the spring, and the tower of the old First Church above the roofs, with the weathercock upon it almost golden in the sun. Out on the river the waves were dancing, glittering, like diamonds shaken on a deep, blue cloth. It was all like something that had happened long ago, Sue Swale always said, though it was only April, Nineteen Seventeen.

Tom Swale was just beside her, looking at the river, and Dennis Swale was standing by himself, listening to the shrieking of the saws, when a voice made Susan turn. It was old Mr. Scarlet, who owned the shoe shop.

He was walking toward them with a hurried step. He must have seen them from his office window.

"Mr. Swale!" he was calling. "Mr. Swale!"

As Dennis Swale turned around, it always seemed to Susan that he had a startled look; she sometimes thought that Dennis had known what was coming, and that he was bracing himself to meet it.

Mr. Scarlet took off his brown felt hat.

"Good afternoon, Miss Swale," he said, and Susan felt her face grow hot under Mr. Scarlet's look. He seemed to be saying just as clearly as though he spoke, "So my son isn't good enough for you?"

"Hullo," her father said. "What is it, Scarlet?"

"Have you seen the paper?" Mr. Scarlet said.

"No," said Dennis. "What?"

Mr. Scarlet mopped his forehead; he looked tired before he spoke.

"We've gone into the war," he said. "I thought I'd come to tell you." Mr. Scarlet had pitched his voice almost to a shout to make it heard above the noise of sawing, but somehow, as he spoke, the noise seemed blotted out. They both must have known what the other thought, — old John Scarlet and Dennis Swale.

"Well," he said. "Any one can tell we'd have to fight."

"All right," said Mr. Scarlet, and he looked inquiringly at Dennis. "There's no harm in my telling you, is there? I just came to ask what we were going to do."

Sue saw her father's forehead gather into little lines, and then his lips moved upward. "Is there any reason," he asked, "why we should do the same?"

"Well," said Mr. Scarlet. "Now there's you and me, and we stand for something in this town. We've got to set an example; we've got to do what's right."

Her father's scowl made his whole face sharp and narrow, and black as thunder.

"Do I understand," said Dennis Swale, "you've come here to tell me the right thing to do?"

"Now, Mr. Swale," said Mr. Scarlet, "there's no need to get so hot. We've only got to do what's right. That's all. Now we've got sons."

"Yes," said Dennis Swale, "and my son is staying here. This is an essential industry. He'll have his orders to stay on."

Mr. Scarlet mopped his forehead again. "I know," he said. "I don't blame you, but I ask you, is it right? Shouldn't we be examples, Mr. Swale?"

"Damnation!" shouted Dennis Swale, and the blackness in his face leaped into his speech. "What are you here to preach at me for? I've only got one son."

Mr. Scarlet thrust out his jaw and stepped towards Dennis Swale. "I guess my son's as good as yours," he said. "You may not think so, but he means as much to me."

"Scarlet," said Dennis Swale, and his voice was shaking, "if you want to kill him, go ahead. It's no affair of mine."

Then they were all looking at Tom Swale, as though the same thought had impelled them. Tom did not appear to have heard the talk. He was looking at the river where the gulls were circling by the harbor buoys, and, somehow, he seemed light and unsubstantial. Something in his slimness, something in the way he looked, made Susan Swale afraid.

"You mean," John Scarlet's voice grew louder, "you mean you'll make a slacker of him? Is that right, Mr. Swale?"

There was a buzzing from the saw, like a sound of tearing cloth; it seemed to be tearing at Dennis Swale, for his lips moved with the sound.

"Damn your impertinence!" he shouted. "What right have you got to libel me? Now wait a minute. Don't you speak. I'm not afraid of what you think or of what anybody thinks. My son's more useful here than dying in a ditch. And he'll stay here. Do you understand?"

Mr. Scarlet looked at Tom Swale and mopped his forehead again.

"My boy's as good as he is," he said. "John's worth three of him."

Then Sue felt a hand upon her arm; it was Tom and he had heard.

"Let's get out of here," he said. "Did you see the look on the old man's face? Sue, the old man's afraid."

"But, Tom," said Sue, "where are you going? What are you going to do?"

"Be quiet," said Tom. "I know what. You've buried me already, but I'm not dead yet."

Then Tom walked on in silence, until they were at the foot of the main street, which ended in the cobbled square, where the town well and the whipping post once stood.

"I'll go alone," said Tom. "I'll see you later, Sue."

Old brick rows of storehouses built in the early

nineteenth century, stood all around that square. Though they had been converted into shops with new plate-glass windows, you could always feel that the present and the past were clashing, and the present seemed unstable, not the past. In front of the Shoe-Shine Parlor a group of men were gathered, and Tom Swale was walking toward them, straight across the street. As Sue stood watching, her heart gave a sudden leap. John Scarlet was standing by the Shoe-Shine Parlor in that group of men, and they were already speaking, and Tom must have seen him first.

"Hi, Tom!" some one said. And then an older man was saying, "Good evening, Mr. Swale."

Tom nodded and walked toward them with his quick, nervous step.

"Who's got a drum?" he said. "John Scarlet, can you beat a drum?"

"What do you want a drum for?" Sue heard John Scarlet asking, in his deep, singsong voice.

"Because there's always been a drum."

"Are you crazy, Tom?" she heard John Scarlet's voice. "What do you want a drum for?"

"Because we're going," she heard her brother saying. "Come on. Who isn't going to wait until he's drafted? Who's going to this war?"

11

Many Mansions

≈ 11 ≈

Many Mansions

GOSSIP STILL KEEPS RUNNING SOFTLY
in our town, like the tide about the pilings of
the old wharves on a misty summer night, and
it has that importance of trivial affairs in a lonely place,
where continuity stretches back and back into matters
which should have been forgotten.

Now, just a little while ago, every one knew Johnny
Scarlet was sweet on Susan Swale, when he got back
from France, except old Dennis Swale. Every one knew
Sue and Johnny Scarlet met by the river's edge at dusk,
but no one dared tell old Dennis that. Johnny Scarlet
was a good boy, and the Swale house was growing
slovenly and its drive was full of weeds, but any one
could tell you that it wasn't right for a Scarlet to be
going with a Swale. They could tell you that it wasn't
right, if they couldn't tell you why.

"Lookit," some one used to whisper. "Here they
come!"

There they would come walking down the street,

John Scarlet's broad shoulders moving easily with his shortened stride, his red face heavy and serious and plebeian, like all the Scarlets' faces; and Sue Swale would be beside him with slender waist and slender hands. Beside John Scarlet any one could see the delicacy and breeding of three hundred years of Swales. Her face seemed molded by adroit, painstaking hands into a still perfection. No Scarlet ever had that half smile on his lips; no Scarlet's eyes would ever have her level, careless glance as she looked straight before her and spoke in a low, clear voice. Somehow one could tell that he had never touched her, that he always looked at her as he did then. In the narrowness of Haven's End, there would seem to be a whispering in the elms, from unseen things, gentle, but forbidding.

"You mustn't touch," the whispers said. "A Scarlet mustn't touch a Swale."

You could see half the story once you saw those two together. All the pretense of Dennis Swale walked beside them, and all his cold dislike of novelty and change. All the grimness of the Swales seemed to stride beside them in the gentle evening light.

"Say," some one used to whisper, "what would the old man say?"

Jeff Pingree was the one who could tell you about it best, if you cared to hear, because Jeff Pingree was the Swale's counselor at law. He could go back to the beginning, if you cared to give him time; to the Swale and Scarlet grants on the first plantation.

"Yes, sir," Jeff Pingree said, and his lanky hands would twitch in odd, eccentric gestures. "It wasn't right, you understand. The Swales and the Scarlets have been here since the first plantation. But the Scarlets have been plain, and the Swales were never like that. I hope you understand."

And Jeff would look out his office window to the main street and put his feet upon his desk. Jeff had seen the Scarlets coming up through the heat of the postwar boom; he had seen the Scarlets buy the corners on the main street and throw the common pasture into house lots; he had seen the Scarlets change the tavern to catch the motor trade.

"Mark my words," Jeff Pingree used to say. "It wasn't right, that's all. There's order and there's precedent, just as there is in law. The Swales aren't what they used to be, because the times have changed. He was the sort who lives in the past. There's some who don't keep in step with things as they get older, and all Dennis had to think of was the Swales. He was getting queer — but it made you sort of sorry. I hope you understand."

And we could understand it, because the queerness of old Dennis was like the eccentricity of our town, withdrawn into its past, now that it was small. There was an illusion of old greatness and a spurious importance in half-forgotten things. Once you heard old Dennis turning over reminiscences about this and that, in those days when he grew garrulous, you could believe the Swales were great, if only from the certainty of the old man's belief. There was a contagion in it, like the wind from the marshes; and, curiously, the obsession of Dennis Swale struck to the root of living matters and all the little struggles of our town became immense, though the Scarlets were real and the Swales were make-believe.

Leaning back with the tips of his fingers together, as though he were dealing with a matter of great importance, Jeff could trace the controversy of the Scarlets and the Swales. There was the trolley line upon the main street, and who said this and who said that, and the permit for a filling station on the corner, and the routing of the motor traffic through the street along the ridge, and the cutting of the big elm, down on India Lane. Yet all those little details would rise and take a shape, and make a cloudy picture of two contending wills, until those details made a world, like a greater world outside, and Haven's End became an amazing place, exactly like a world.

"Yes, sir," Jeff Pingree used to say, "it would have been different, if it wasn't Dennis Swale. His mind was set about the Scarlets — set, you understand; and what with Dennis thinking . . . Some one had to tell him. I was the one who told."

It happened in Jeff's office up one flight of stairs to the south of Water Square. Dennis Swale, with his close-cropped white hair, stout about the waist but thin in the face, with a sinking look to his cheeks and a thinness to his hands, was seated stiffly, holding his gold-headed cane between his knees. His mouth was set like plaster with all sorts of little lines around it — the thin, tight mouth of all the Swales. It was after five in the afternoon and the sun was coming through the dusty windows of Jeff Pingree's office. On the shelves by the wall above the Acts of the General Court were six record boxes marked D. Swale Estate, and through the dirty window the whole length of the street was visible, beginning with the Shoe-Shine Parlor and the stores, up to the brick walks to the Penny Bank, and thence to the head of the street where the Swale house stood.

"I tell you they won't get it," Dennis Swale was saying. "They want the motor traffic past my house so it'll pass their inn. They don't care about anything as long as they make money. That's what it always is with them, but they won't get it — do you hear?"

"Now, Dennis," Jeff Pingree said, "you can't stand in the way of progress. If the Scarlets want it — "

"Confound 'em!" shouted Dennis Swale. "They want the automobiles past my house — do you understand? Past my house. It's the young one. He's worse than all the rest, but the whole tribe's just the same. Have you ever seen them do a decent thing? Cheap as dirt — everything here's cheap now. I tell you they want a roaring motor highway through the center of this town so they can make money. They want it past my house. And — do you think I'll stand for that?"

"Wait a minute," Jeff Pingree said, "have you spoken to Johnny Scarlet? Maybe if you spoke to him, perhaps he'd change his mind."

"Have you lost your head?" said Dennis Swale. "Do you think I'll ask favors of the Scarlets?"

"Wait a minute," Jeff Pingree said. Dennis turned toward him quickly, and his long nose was as sharp as a knife, and his eyes were suddenly narrow. "There's something I want to tell you. It's worse than any road — and everybody knows it, Dennis, or else I wouldn't say — "

Dennis Swale was leaning forward, listening. Jeff could hear the old repeater watch ticking in his waistcoat, and it seemed as though all of Haven's End were changing.

"Dennis," Jeff Pingree said, "Sue's sweet on Johnny Scarlet. Being your only child, I think you ought to know."

Dennis did not move; his very immobility was startling, because it spoke of all the things which he might do.

"Pingree," said Dennis Swale, "How do you know that?"

"Look out the window," Jeff Pingree said. "They're walking down the street."

Dennis Swale rose slowly and leaned on Jeff Pingree's desk as he stared through the dusky glass, and sure enough, they were walking down the street. There was nothing strange in that; the strange thing was that you could imagine all the other Swales and Scarlets walking down the street behind Johnny Scarlet and Susan Swale; and Dennis must have seen them too.

"Open that window," he said.

Jeff Pingree turned and stared at him. Dennis had not raised his voice, but it was not like Dennis' voice that spoke.

"Open up that window," said Dennis Swale. "I want to speak to Sue."

Jeff Pingree gave the sash a jerk. And then it went creaking upward and a gust of wind blew at the papers on the desk and sent them rattling on the floor.

"Sue," called Dennis Swale, "come up here for a minute."

"Say," said Jeff Pingree quickly, "that's no way to do. Don't talk to her like that."

"Sue," called Dennis Swale, "come up here for a minute."

Sue Swale must have known what was coming, because her lips were shut tight exactly like her father's. She had on a silk dress with flowers on it. The wind from the open window blew it softly so that it seemed like the drapery on a statue. It blew against her brown silk stockings and blew against her hair.

"Sit down," said Dennis Swale. "You might as well have nothing on as that confounded dress."

"Might I?" said Sue Swale. "Did you want to tell me that?"

"Now here," said Jeff Pingree, "it's just the way things are. It isn't Sue's fault she's good to look at."

Sue turned toward him and smiled, and there was no doubt that she was good to look at then. She was above all coldness, warm and gay with a secret knowledge, once she smiled.

Dennis leaned forward. He had never taken his eyes from her once the office door had closed. All his days were hard upon him, little, narrow days. All his face spoke of a small man's triumphs, but there was more than that. There was a strength in the very smallness of his thoughts, as though his will had been tempered by undeviating years, until it was a blind and arrogant faith. The fire of a belief was burning in him, hot beneath the coldness of his cheeks.

"You're too good-looking," said Dennis. "You get that from your mother's side. I saw you out the window."

Then there was a faint pink in her cheeks, exactly like the pink in Dennis' face.

"Say," said Jeff Pingree, "maybe I'd better be going."

"No," said Dennis, "no, you don't. Sue, I saw you with John Scarlet. Is there anything between him and you?"

Jeff was used to faces changing when questions were asked sharply. The light from a flame seemed to flicker across her face, but she did not turn her head away.

Dennis Swale hitched forward in his chair. "You haven't answered me. Speak up. What is there between you and Scarlet, Sue?"

"Nothing," she said. "Why should there be? What's the matter, Father?"

Her voice made Jeff turn quickly. Dennis' cheeks had grown brick-red and his eyes were glazed and staring.

"Father," cried Sue Swale. "What's the matter, Father? Don't you"—suddenly her voice had broken —"don't you know I love you? I wouldn't hurt you, dear."

"Pingree," said Dennis Swale—his voice was hoarse and thick—"get me a glass of water. You lied then, Sue. I saw it in your face."

"Don't!" cried Sue. "Father, please don't look like that!"

"Give me that water," said Dennis Swale.

Then Jeff Pingree remembered that his own glance met Susan Swale's. Though they did not speak, they might as well have spoken, because her eyes were deep with fear and crying out a thought.

"It would kill him!" she was saying, just as plainly as though she had spoken, and they both had seen it, Jeff and Sue. It had been there for a moment in that room; for a moment among the voices and sounds from the street outside, the shadow of Death had been beside them, touching Dennis Swale. And again her eyes were speaking, deep and dark against the stillness of her face.

"It would kill him," they were saying. "It would kill him, if he knew!"

Dennis leaned his head against the wall, and the ugly red was draining from his cheeks, leaving them sickly. It was the first time that Jeff Pingree had seen him look so old.

"Father," Sue was saying, "why do you hate him so?"

And when old Dennis answered, everything he said was true.

At first his words came slowly. "Are you listening to me, Sue? When you get as old as I am, ideas take a shape. They are not cloudy to me the way they are to you. They get etched out in your mind. They wake you up at night when you get old. They touch you with their hands. It's an idea — do you understand me? — not a person that I dislike. Don't think I haven't eyes. This town is changing. Is that any reason I should change? We've stood for something here that's sinking down. Once we were Haven's End, and it's the Scarlets now. They are changing it to suit themselves. I've seen them put their hands on everything. Do you think I want a Scarlet walking in my hall and looking at my portraits?"

"Father!" cried Sue. "Don't get so excited! Father, please — there's nothing —"

"Yes," old Dennis said, "you think that it is nothing. Is it nothing to try to be what we used to be — gentlemen and ladies? Is it nothing to see the name of Swale turning into Scarlet?"

"Here now," Jeff Pingree said. "Dennis, it don't do any good —"

"Don't you stop me, Pingree," old Dennis said. "I've got a right to speak, if it's the last thing I ever say, and I wish it was the last, with a Scarlet reaching for my house. Are you listening, Sue? You say it's nothing. Your mother says it's nothing. 'Dennis,' she said this morning, 'you're living on illusion. Who are you, Dennis Swale?' Well, an old fool can't change. Are you listening to me?"

"Yes," said Sue, "I'm listening. Father — please —"

Dennis pulled himself out of his chair, and leaned on his gold-headed cane.

"Then listen to this," he said. "I want your promise. You're through with Scarlet, if you don't want to see me dead. I won't have it, do you hear me? I've got other plans."

She must have seen death on him, just as Jeff Pingree saw. There was a silence broken by Dennis' heavy breathing.

"Don't look like that!" cried Sue.

"Did you hear me? Do you promise?" shouted Dennis Swale.

"Yes," said Sue, "I promise. Please don't look like that."

Dennis squared his shoulders and sat down.

"Good," he said. "You won't break your word. I thought you'd understand."

Jeff Pingree remembered that he was frightened. Once the thing was over, he could see it all more clearly. He had bent her to his will as though he had laid his hands upon her. He had played upon her sympathy and her habit of obedience without a thought.

"Sue," said Dennis, "they say I'm hard, and I suppose I am, when I've set my mind. I want a Swale in the Swale house after I am gone."

Dennis cleared his throat and tapped his cane upon the floor. He had no idea that his wish was fantastic, because it was too much a part of all his eccentricity.

"I've been thinking," said Dennis. "There isn't much left for me now but thought. There's a connection of ours, an Arthur Swale living in New York. I've taken the liberty of writing him —"

"Do you know him?" asked Sue Swale.

"I've taken the liberty of writing him," said Dennis, "asking his son to visit us. He may be here any time."

"Any time?" asked Sue with a strange note in her voice.

"Yes, any time," answered old Dennis.

"There's one thing," said Sue Swale. "When I promised, I didn't say —"

And then her face turned red. A heavy step was on the stairs, regular and plodding, and then John Scarlet was standing in the doorway, holding his new straw hat. He looked at Dennis Swale and smiled, though he must have known what Dennis thought. Beneath the eyes of Dennis Swale his ease was falling from him, as it always did. His heavy fingers moved nervously on his hat brim, and he shifted his weight from one foot to the other.

"Don't look at me like that," he seemed to say. "Why should you look at me like that?"

But Dennis Swale kept looking, incurious and cool, reading the plainness of Johnny Scarlet as he might have read a printed sign.

"Did you want to see me, John?" he asked.

"No, sir," John Scarlet answered. You could tell he knew what was going on, Jeff Pingree always said, but the Scarlets were always obstinate.

"No, sir. I — I was taking a walk with Sue."

"Were you?" said Dennis. "Don't let me keep you, John. Show her the house lots on the common pasture. That used to be a pretty walk before you ripped it up."

"You don't like 'em, do you, sir?" John Scarlet said.

"No," said Dennis Swale. "I don't like anything you do."

"Well," said John Scarlet, "there're two ways of looking at everything. We're bringin' business into town."

"John," said Sue, "please be quiet."

"Yes," said Dennis Swale, "gasoline pumps and the motor trade."

"Well, you don't want everything to be dead, do you?" John Scarlet said. "We have to hustle these days to make a living, Mr. Swale."

"John," said Susan Swale.

"All right," said Dennis, "hustle, then." And he smiled and nodded as they walked out down the stairs.

"That finishes him," he said; "Sue won't break her word."

Though Jeff Pingree had never liked the Scarlets,

he felt sorry for John Scarlet then. "Godfrey!" Jeff Pingree said. "But you're a narrow man."

Dennis put on his old felt hat and flicked at the papers with his cane. "Pingree," he said, "you're one personality, and I'm another. It's the name, and things may be better some day. I've been in the house a long time — there has to be a Swale in it. You wouldn't understand."

Even when Dennis was gone, Jeff Pingree said that he could feel him in the office still, and nothing was the same as it had been half an hour before.

He stooped and picked up the papers from the floor; arranging them in little piles upon his desk. Then he looked out the window, over the roofs of the house toward the river. It was already growing dusk and the mist was beginning to rise from the marshes where the coolness of the evening struck the water.

"I've got to be on his side," Jeff Pingree said. "I'm his lawyer, but it isn't right."

It was time for him to be going home, but something told him that it was not finished yet.

When he heard voices in the hall he was not surprised. First he heard Sue and then he heard John Scarlet's voice, ominous and angry.

"Won't it?" John Scarlet said. "I'll see him just the same."

And next, Sue Swale and John Scarlet were in the office. The light was growing dim, but Jeff could see the flush upon John Scarlet's face. He was scowling and Susan Swale was standing just behind him, calm, aloof. She had told him everything — Jeff Pingree could see that — and now she stood there, watching.

"Well, go ahead," said Sue. "It won't do any good."

John turned upon her as though they were alone. "You love me, don't you?" he said. "You said you did."

John Scarlet sat down clumsily and mopped his forehead, and Jeff knew the way he felt, bewildered and utterly alone.

"Mr. Pingree"—John Scarlet mopped his forehead again—"she won't let me see the old man. You're his lawyer. You've got to see him for me."

"Well," Jeff Pingree said, and he put his thumbs in the armholes of his vest, "what do you want to say?"

"I want to ask him what he's got against me." There was something hopeless in John Scarlet's voice. "I can look after Sue."

Jeff Pingree cleared his throat. "Now, John," he said, "there's no use getting hot about it. You're all right, but you're different from the Swales."

"Why am I different?" John Scarlet said. "We've always lived in town."

"Yes," Jeff Pingree said. "But you and I, John, we're different from the Swales."

"Why?" said John Scarlet. "I tell you I don't see."

"John," said Sue, "there isn't any use. Didn't I say I promised?"

"And it doesn't mean a thing," John Scarlet said. "Can't you see that? Your father's got ideas. Sue— haven't you laughed about 'em?"

"Yes," said Sue, "but I'm not laughing now. I said I loved you, and now you'd better go."

It might have been Dennis speaking, because Sue had her pride, like all the Swales.

"All right," said John Scarlet. "That's enough. I'm through with you."

"Good-by, John," said Sue.

For a moment she stood listening to his footsteps on the stairs and then the door slammed, making the floor shake. Then Jeff Pingree felt her eyes were on him and he turned to look. Her lips were trembling and her dress was crumpled like a faded flower.

"Well," said Sue, "that's that."

"I wish it was," said Jeff, "but it isn't anything at all."

It was horrible to see her crying, because something had snapped inside her, and her whole body shook with sobbing.

"Jeff," Sue Swale was saying, "you've got to take me home."

They did not speak a single word as they walked up the street; it was dusk by then and the street lights were on and the moths were flying about them, white against the darkness of the trees. Jeff Pingree had the feeling that every one was watching and that everybody knew.

Sue Swale turned toward him as they reached the great front door. It stood framed in its carved wood arch with its tarnished eagle knocker, and the leaves of the ivy on the bricks were whispering in the wind.

"Don't tell about it, will you please?" she said.

Then they were in the hall where the lamp on the table was already lighted, and the shadows of the hall seemed to close about them eagerly.

Sue's mother was standing in the hall. She was in a black silk dress with ugly, dowdy lines. She had given up trying to be beautiful years ago. Her face was harshly wrinkled, almost bitter, but her eyes were brightly suspicious and there was acid in her voice, though it was hardly more than a whisper.

"Sue," she said, "what's your father been up to now?"

"Nothing, Mamma," said Sue.

"Sue," said Mrs. Swale, "what's the matter?"

"There's nothing," said Sue. "Nothing."

"Oh!" she said. "It's John Scarlet, is it?"

"No, Mamma," said Sue.

"Then go upstairs," said Mrs. Swale, "and wash your face. I want to speak to Mr. Pingree. Pingree, you come here."

Then they were in the parlor, standing in the dusk, and Mrs. Swale had closed the door. The parlor was musty and very still. There were mirrors behind gilded chandeliers which seemed to be shining from the light of vanished candles. In the dusk there was a great teakwood cabinet which some Swale had brought back from the China trade, and figures of little men and animals, carved upon it, seemed to be walking in the dusk.

"Pingree," said Mrs. Swale, "what's Dennis been up to now?"

"Nothing, Ma'am," Jeff Pingree said. "Nothing that I can say."

"He's shut in the library," said Mrs. Swale. "Sue's been crying. Do you think I am a fool?"

"No," said Jeff. "I won't say that. You're a smart woman, Mrs. Swale."

Her eyes kept darting back at him from the wrinkles

of her face. "Pingree," she said, "I'm too smart for you. What's Dennis been up to? Is it about John Scarlet?"

"Ma'am," said Jeff Pingree, "everything is confidential. There's nothing I can say."

Then Mrs. Swale laughed harshly. It was shocking to hear her laugh. "Don't I know about the Swales? Don't I know he's going mad?" she said.

"Now, Ma'am," said Jeff, "he isn't going mad. He just keeps thinking of the Swales."

"Yes," said Mrs. Swale. "You can't forget 'em in this place. After all, who are they?"

"Really, Ma'am," Jeff Pingree said, "I should think you ought to know."

And still her eyes were on him, and she laughed again, and it wasn't right to hear her laughing.

"Yes," she said, "I know. One of them was a Puritan and one of them was a pirate. And the rest of them were tradesmen. But what have they ever done?"

"Done?" said Jeff Pingree. "Why, Ma'am, they've been here three hundred years, or mighty close to that."

Suddenly she seized his arm and Jeff Pingree started, because her touch seemed cold as ice. "He's ruined my life," she said, "but he sha'n't ruin hers."

Jeff Pingree walked down the hall and opened the great front door. The hinges creaked and the evening breeze came in fresh upon his face. A feeling came over him, as it often had before, when he stood upon the doorsill looking across the lawn, that he was glad to go. There was a sensation of something just behind his back. The tall clock was ticking on the landing where the stairs went upward in a graceful curve, and everywhere there was a sense of waiting. Old loves, old hates were pulsing through the air, like the whisperings of a hundred secrets. With the slamming of the door, the whisperings seemed to rise into a shout, and the whole shape of the house was distorted in the dusk into unreality.

He could remember when he was a little boy, barefoot in overalls, peering through the bars of the high white fence before the Swales' front lawn. An old man, his grandfather, was with him, leaning on a cane. His grandfather had started as a cabin boy and ended as a mate back in the China trade.

"It's the Swale mansion," his grandfather was saying. "There ain't no house like it in the county. Look at the garden hedge; it came from England. Look at the carvings; shipwrights made them. Captain Daniel Swale built it out of privateering money and I've seen him. Yes, sir, I've seen him; a little man with a face like a stone. They're harsh gentlemen, the Swales."

The shadow of the elm trees was like a black veil upon the roof, and all the old stories Jeff had heard seemed to gather in those shadows. There were stories of men playing cards for gold, of coaches with silver-studded harness.

Then the thin-toned bell of the First Church was striking out the hour of seven o'clock as Jeff Pingree walked down the path toward the street. The street lights were glowing through the elm trees, and now and then a motor car would pass, throwing rivulets of light upon the lawn, and, as he walked, the bell was striking in time with his slow steps.

"Swale," the bell was saying, "Swale, Swale, Swale."

Jeff Pingree's mind was in a narrow channel as he approached the street. He was not aware that any one was near him until he opened the front gate.

"Here!" said Jeff Pingree. "What are you doing here?"

It was John Scarlet. He was a bulky shape in the half light, and the light upon his face gave it a curious lividness.

"I've come to see Swale," John Scarlet said.

"The more fool you!" said Jeff Pingree. "You can't see Swale."

"You watch me," John Scarlet said. "I'm going up to slam that knocker and have a talk with Swale."

"Now, John," Jeff Pingree said.

"You're afraid of him, aren't you?" John Scarlet said. "Listen, Mr. Pingree. Why is every one in town afraid of this place? Do you think it's full of ghosts?"

"Yes," said Jeff Pingree, "that's what. It's full of ghosts."

"It's full of rubbish," John Scarlet said. "I'll tell Swale what I think of it to-night."

It wasn't right, John Pingree always said, and John Scarlet wasn't himself that night, and Dennis was too old for a scene like that.

"No, you don't," Jeff Pingree said. "John Scarlet, you go home."

"You're an old man," John Scarlet said. "You step aside. This is my business, not yours, Mr. Pingree. I've got to do something, I tell you. Don't you see I love her?" And all the loves and hates of Haven's End and all the vain desire and all the pain came into John Scarlet's voice.

"No, you don't," Jeff Pingree said. "Don't you lay a hand on me or I'll summon you for assault! Don't you lay a hand on me——"

Then they were wrestling on the lawn. That was the only way Jeff Pingree could describe it.

"You damned old fool!" John Scarlet said. "Won't you go away?"

And suddenly Jeff Pingree felt as dry as dust and all his thoughts seemed old and wrinkled.

"You can't go there," Jeff Pingree said. "You take your hands off me."

He could not see plainly as they wrestled on the lawn, because his mind was filled with the indignity of it. John Scarlet was gripping him by the shoulders when, suddenly, his hands fell away as if the whole thing had been imagination.

"Hey!" John Scarlet said. "Who's that?"

Neither of them had noticed what had happened. Jeff Pingree always remembered that everything was so sudden, that there was no beginning.

He turned toward the gate, following John Scarlet's glance, and then he stood like John Scarlet. A motor had drawn up to the sidewalk and a man was standing before it. It was one of those long runabouts, covered with nickel trimmings. Jeff Pingree remembered that there was a bag and golf clubs tied to the trunk rack, but he was looking at the man.

He was tall, Jeff Pingree remembered, and thin. In the dusk there was an opulence and cool authority such as our town once had a hundred years ago. There was an air of insolence and faint amusement, as that stranger spoke, but somehow the voice was familiar.

"Excuse me," he was saying, "do you hear me now?"

"Hey?" said Jeff Pingree. "What's that?" The stranger's face was in the shadow, but Jeff knew he was amused.

"This is an eccentric place," the stranger said.

"Hey?" said Jeff Pingree. He was feeling a trifle dizzy; his dignity had left him on the lawn, but there was something he resented in the voice.

"I said eccentric," the stranger said. "It seemed perfectly natural to see you sporting on the lawn. Just as I came off the main road, I felt a strange miasma."

"Say," said John Scarlet, "what do you want?"

"Now you ask me," the stranger said; "could you tell me where a place is, called the Swale mansion? That's the word, mansion, and I don't see any mansion here."

"Don't you?" John Scarlet said. "Well, this is Swale's house."

The stranger walked a little closer, peering through the dusk, and then Jeff Pingree saw his face. The nose was long, the eyes were steady, the lips were set and narrow.

"Where?" the stranger asked.

"There," Jeff Pingree pointed. "Don't you see it, Mister, right there in the trees?"

"Really?" said the stranger. "Is that shack all it is?"

"How do you mean, a shack?" John Scarlet said.

"Excuse me," said the stranger. And then his tone became conversational. "I thought it was a mansion, do you see? And look at that, I ask you. I came to see the cradle of the race and will you look at that?"

"Say," said Jeff Pingree, "who are you, Mister?"

"Swale," the stranger said. "I'm Sinclair Swale." And then he began to laugh. And he was like all the Swales; his laughter was short and harsh, without humor in it.

"And there's the Swale mansion," he said. "Does any one live there named Dennis Swale?" It wasn't right, Jeff Pingree always said, to hear a Swale laughing at the Swale house.

Jeff Pingree could not speak. The shock of it was physical, like a blow which struck to the very heart of things. He could see why Sinclair was laughing, and that was the worst of all. Suddenly all of Haven's End seemed as any one might see it, forgotten and gone to seed, and crumbling to decay. Then Jeff Pingree heard John Scarlet speaking.

"Now here, you ought to know what's decent — stop that noise."

Though the light was very dim, it was plain that Sinclair Swale was smiling. Somehow he was like all the Swales. He was jesting with the Scarlets as the Swales had always jested. You might have thought he was a ghost, Jeff always said, rising from the dark to smile.

"Is this a lecture on etiquette?" inquired Sinclair Swale.

"Maybe it is," John Scarlet said, "and maybe it isn't. I live in this town, and no outsider laughs at it — like that — while I'm around. If you don't like it, keep it to yourself — and wait. I'm not as smart as you are, but I can shut your mouth."

"Please," begged Sinclair Swale, "don't stop on my account."

"I suppose," John Scarlet said, "there ought to be some one else here to tell you, but as there isn't, I'll do just as well. If my people built this house I wouldn't laugh at it. It's a good house, a fine house, and we've got fine houses in this town. No one could build a house like it now, and you ought to see that much. And I've traveled about some. I've seen other buildings, but none of them were better than this. I remember thinking of it often when I was away. And in case you want to know it, fine people have lived in this house and died here — ladies and gentlemen such as don't live now, perhaps. I never thought to be standing up for this house. I've never been inside of it except once, but I know this. It's too good for you — and now get out of here!"

Sinclair Swale had been listening, as though in polite absorption. "Are you through?" he asked.

"Yes, I'm through," John Scarlet said; "I'm waiting for you to move."

Sinclair Swale drew his hands from the side pockets of his coat.

"I've got another suggestion," Sinclair said. "Now we're on the subject — suppose you get out of here yourself."

And then another voice broke in, so suddenly that all of them were startled.

"Just a minute." Dennis Swale was speaking. He was not ten feet away, bareheaded, leaning on his cane. "I'm here now, John."

Jeff Pingree always said that you could only guess. You could not tell how long Dennis had been there, or what he might have heard, because he gave no sign. He simply stood stiffly formal, looking at Sinclair Swale, a stout, small shadow of a man, but for some reason no one spoke. Dennis moved two paces forward and peered intently through the dusk.

"You've got our nose," he said. "You're Sinclair Swale. Don't apologize. I said I'd expect you any time."

All the Swales had manners. If that young man was ill at ease, he did not show it.

"I thought I'd be here early in the afternoon," he explained. "I thought I should put up at some inn until morning, you see, but when I found I was right in front of your house . . . Hadn't I better wait till morning?"

"Don't apologize," old Dennis said. "A Swale is welcome any time. Shall we come in? Pingree, I want you too. John Scarlet, where are you going? I want you to come in. It isn't every night we see a Swale."

"Thank you," said John Scarlet. "It's getting late."

"No, you don't," said Dennis Swale. Suddenly he seemed childishly garrulous. "No, you don't. You found him, John. You've got to show him in. Come in where there's light. I want to see you better, Sinclair Swale."

There was no way of telling what Dennis Swale had heard, but there was no need of asking John Scarlet into the house, except to gratify a sinister dislike, and to see John Scarlet suffer. There was something unholy in Dennis' triumph, once they stood inside the hall.

"Here we are," said Dennis Swale. "Pingree, close the door."

Dennis' lips were twisted in a thin, impervious smile, and his eyes were very clear. He rubbed his hands softly on the gold head of his cane and gazed at his relative. All the world seemed shut out once Jeff had closed the door. In the shadows on the landing where the white stairs curved, the tall clock was ticking in its slow, even way, and that noise was time itself, moving evenly in a great, unbroken stream. The hall and everything in it seemed a part of that level cadence, once Jeff had closed the door, and a new vividness came over everything with that dull, steady sound, and everything seemed centered around that stranger.

He was standing with his back to the row of portraits. He was looking up the stairs and frowning slightly, as though some thought had disturbed him, but it was natural to see him standing there. There was life in him, like the life of all that house. Jeff Pingree could never describe it. He always said that you might think once you saw him that all the talk about the Swales was true. White buckskin shoes, white broadcloth trousers, lean hands half hidden in the pockets of his double-breasted coat, the lean, watchful face, the sharp eyes, the thin lips — they all contrived to make a timeless memory of something else, and he seemed to be all the Swales.

Dennis was the first who spoke, almost as though he did not know that he was speaking. "It's the blood. I'm glad to see a gentleman again."

Before Sinclair Swale could answer, John Scarlet

stepped heavily toward the door. "Mr. Swale," he said, "I've got to be going now."

"No, you don't," said Dennis quickly, "no, you don't. This is Mr. Scarlet, Mr. Swale. The Scarlets have always been in town — yes, always. Sue" — he raised his voice — "where are you, Sue? Here's your cousin, Sinclair Swale!"

"Mr. Swale," John Scarlet said, "I guess I don't belong here — "

And then he stopped. He seemed to have forgotten what he was saying. Sue Swale was coming down the stairs, but John Scarlet's eyes were fixed on Sinclair Swale. He must have seen him change, because any one with half an eye could see. His faint amusement and aloofness left him, and a surprised intentness took their place. For a moment one could read his thoughts as easily as John Scarlet's, though Sinclair did not speak.

"You're beautiful," he was saying.

Although he did not speak, Sue must have understood him, for she smiled at him, unembarrassed by his stare.

"Yes," she seemed to say, "I know I am. Tell me — didn't you ever think of that?" And any one could tell he had not thought of that, but only for a moment, and then his face was still, and his smile was faultless, formal and polite.

"Hello," said Sue.

"Why — hello," said Sinclair Swale.

Then their hands met and their glances met, and then Sue Swale was laughing. "Why are you so surprised?" she asked.

"Sue!" It was John Scarlet speaking in a hoarse, choked voice, and Dennis Swale turned toward him.

"Don't interrupt them, John," he said. "Don't they make a pretty couple standing by the stairs?"

"Look here," John Scarlet answered, "if you think I'm going to stay—"

"Yes," said Dennis Swale, "I think you're going to stay. Look at them. Do you think she likes him, John?"

There was a ring of modulated voices. Over everything was a suavity and ease, bright like burnished metal, and politeness in a shimmering veil seemed to cover John Scarlet's anger. There was a perfection which John Scarlet must have felt, which made him dull and clumsy, impotent of thought and speech — and all the while Dennis Swale was watching.

"He's got manners—don't you think?" murmured Dennis Swale. Words, polite and musical, were drifting through the hall, as Sinclair and Sue Swale stood talking.

"You know," Sinclair was saying, "this reminds me of an English house. It has the same *patine.*"

Through the curtain of those words Sue Swale looked up and caught John Scarlet's glance, and then she looked away, back at Sinclair Swale.

"You're beautiful"—any one could see his thoughts running through his words—"oh, Lord, you're beautiful."

"Manners," murmured Dennis softly, "yes, we have 'em still." Then he raised his voice. "Sue," he said, "bring the lamp. There are some things I want to show him. Come along, John, I want to show you too.

There're the portraits and the silver. Have you ever seen them, John?"

Dennis Swale was off. Nothing gave him greater pleasure than to show the treasures of the Swales. He stood pompously erect, stirred to pedantic eloquence.

"Father——" began Sue.

"I know," said Dennis, "you always try to stop me. I want Sinclair to see." And he pointed to the even line of the pictures on the wall. And then, Jeff Pingree always, said, they seemed to be surrounded by blurred, smoky faces of the Swales. "That old one"—Dennis' voice kept running through one's thoughts, and surely no one listened carefully, but he was used to that. "There's Colonel Richard Swale, who came from Norwich with the first plantation. He was the town's first magistrate. He had a Scarlet whipped once. Did you ever know that, John? And there's his son. The paint is cracking badly. And there's his grandson, Micah Swale, at the age of ten. He ran away to sea."

"Now I know where I got my nose," murmured Sinclair Swale.

"And there's Pierre Levesser, a collateral branch. He was married to a Swale. Distinguished, don't you think? And there's his wife—a trifle hard, but beautiful; yes, beautiful. They were married in the old First Church. Every hour you can hear their wedding bell. And there's Captain Daniel Swale, the privateersman, and his wife. I'll show you his ships in the library. Copley did them both."

His voice was all about them, as they walked along, and Jeff Pingree wished that he would stop. Sinclair Swale was walking beside him—glancing at the pictures, but always back to Sue, and any one could tell he was not listening.

"And here's the silver," Dennis was saying. "Those tankards were the second Richard's — English made."

"He must have been a heavy drinker," Sinclair said. "We're always too intense. Don't you think so, Cousin Sue?"

"Those bowls," said Dennis Swale, "were taken off a British man-of-war. Those jars came from the China trade."

"Beautiful," said Sinclair, and he looked at Susan Swale.

"And here" — old Dennis was holding a bottle in his hand — "this is Madeira. It traveled in a ship's hold to Charleston and then back. It's the last bottle. Shall we take it in the library? Get the glasses, Sue."

"I'll help," said Sinclair Swale. "I'm always fond of glass."

Dennis touched John Scarlet's arm. He had seen him move toward Sue. "Let him help her, John," he said. "Will you please come with me?"

As they were walking down the hall, Jeff Pingree heard a voice.

"The old school," Sinclair Swale was saying, "and very nicely done."

Then they were in the library, Jeff and John Scarlet and Dennis Swale. The light from a lamp on the center table could not drive the shadows from the rows of books, and the air was musty with cigar smoke and old leather. Dennis glanced slowly about the room and smiled, and moved slowly toward the fireplace and stood upon the hearth.

"John," said Dennis, "how do you like the house?"

John Scarlet turned and faced him. "I stood and took my whipping, Mr. Swale," he said.

"Out on the lawn" — Dennis did not appear to hear him — "you stood up for this place. I heard you. Why did you do that?"

"Mr. Swale," John Scarlet answered, "I know why you brought me in — you wanted her to see me beside — him. Well, I stood and took my whipping."

"That's enough," said Dennis quickly. "Be quiet. Here they come."

Sue came first with a silver tray and glasses, and Sinclair Swale, who was just behind her, had an enigmatic look. Sue's face was flushed and her chin was high. Any one could tell what had happened. Sinclair Swale had not been afraid to touch.

"Fill the glasses, Sue," said Dennis, and he stepped forward from the hearth.

Then Jeff Pingree became aware of something. Dennis was standing beside the mantel, short and stout, holding his wineglass in his fingers. Suddenly he was urbane and cool.

"I hope you've liked my house," said Dennis, and all the wrinkles deepened about his eyes and the corners of his mouth.

Then that young man was looking at him as though he had just seen Dennis Swale, and he must have caught some hidden shade of meaning. "I wouldn't have missed this for the world," he said.

"Neither would I," said Dennis. "Here's to you, Sinclair Swale."

Their glasses touched, and Dennis set his glass upon the table.

"I hope," he said, "you've nothing to complain of. I've tried—please believe me—I've tried to give you a pleasant memory."

Sinclair Swale raised his eyebrows. There was something about it that was out of his experience, something out of tune.

"Complain?" laughed Sinclair Swale. "I've never had a better time."

Dennis sighed and nodded. "I'm glad," he said. "I'm sorry you must be going. We don't have much good company."

"But I'm not going," cried Sinclair Swale. "Don't worry about that!"

Dennis' voice became harsh and flat. "Yes," he said, "you're going. Yes, you're going now."

"But why?" cried Sinclair Swale, and then he stopped.

"Because I heard you laughing," Dennis said. "Thank God I heard you laughing. I asked you here. You've been here. Now you're going."

"But look here," cried Sinclair Swale, "I didn't mean—"

"I don't care what you meant," said Dennis Swale. "You've been amused, and so have I. Pingree, Mr. Swale is going out. Will you show him down the hall?"

"Mr. Swale," Jeff Pingree said when he came back, "he wanted me to tell you something."

Dennis Swale was standing by the fireplace, his hands behind his back, and Susan and John Scarlet were by the window, side by side. It was curious to look at John Scarlet; something strange had happened, but Susan was smiling at him, and she reached and touched his hand.

"Well," said Dennis, "what did he want to say?"

"He wanted me to tell you" — Jeff Pingree paused, because the whole place seemed unreal, and everything that had happened seemed impossible, until he looked at Dennis — "he wanted me to tell you that he was ashamed. Those were his words — ashamed."

"Good," said Dennis mildly. "He was a gentleman. Pingree, I want you to draw a contract. There's paper on the desk. In the event of John Scarlet marrying my daughter — do you hear me, Pingree? I'm not dead yet — in the event of John Scarlet marrying my daughter, John Scarlet agrees to use his influence to divert the motor traffic as I may direct. Scarlet understands. And they both agree — do you hear me, Pingree, — that their first male child shall take the name of Swale. There will be a Swale in this house — after I am gone."

12

Going – – Gone

≈ 12 ≈

Going – – Gone

THE SUN HAD COME OUT HOT through a still, murky sky, pouring its heat like a tangible, breathless liquid over the crowd on the Swale front lawn. Heat was shimmering in waves from the roof by then; the leaves of the elms were drooping with it, until only the windows and the front door of the Swale house seemed shadowy and cool. But the crowd was standing in the sun without noticing the heat. They were watching the Swale house, which seemed larger than it had been, and the perspiring, stringy figure of Sam Whistle on the steps.

The bidding was moving fast by then, and, like the Whistles who had gone before him, he was transfigured by the bidding. The sonorous sound of money made him agile, bright and scintillating, not as much from desire of gain as from the drama. His head on his scrawny neck moved like a bird's as he sought like a professional for gestures in the crowd, since none of the bidding was done by voice. Sam Whistle's glance was the only indication of where the bidding came from, making the transaction mysterious, but any one could catch the sense of motion.

There was something going, something which would not return, once his mallet fell. Without his being conscious of it, he was holding illusion in his hand, which would dissipate momentarily in the sultry air.

"Eight thousand!" Sam Whistle was calling. "Thank you . . . but that's not near enough. Now who's going to make it nine? Now look at the hall back of me — cool in all this heat. That building's as tight as when she was new. Come the hottest day in summer, that building's cool. . . ."

Now and then some one stirred uneasily beneath the hard, constant patter of his voice. A hot breeze from inland stirred the leaves above the lawn; and muttered questions and answers sounded like the breeze.

"God — eight? That's not nothing."

"Why don't Sue Swale keep it?"

"Johnny Scarlet, he won't live there."

"There's been too many Swales in it. . . . He said he couldn't live here — couldn't, when he tried . . . Yes, he tried."

"Nine!" Sam Whistle was calling. "Ninety-five hundred. . . . Ten. . . . I want to tell you something. It's more than a house you're buying."

And a bell sounded out the quarter hour.

"Do I hear any more? Is the bidding closing here? It's what I said. You couldn't duplicate it for under a hundred thousand and here it's up for ten. Gentlemen, it isn't right, but I can't keep this open. Ten thousand. . . . Ten five hundred . . . going . . ."

The sound of the bell and then his voice started time again on an endless, remorseless flow.

"Ten five hundred . . . going . . ."

Time was flowing, but the Swale house had not moved. It stood aloof and beyond time, untouched by Sam Whistle's call. By a single, nameless instinct, every one was staring at the house, waiting for something to happen, as though it held the breath of life, but its serenity was not broken. The auctioneer's voice rose to a rhythmic chant.

"Ten five hundred for this land and buildings . . . going . . ."

The shadows from the elm branches were dancing across the bricks. Something was going, but the Swale house was not. Sam Whistle mopped his forehead.

"For the last time," he shouted. "Going . . . going . . . *gone!*"

But the Swale house had not changed.